THE MARK

Also By Heather Burnside

The Working Girls Series

1. *The Mark*
2. *Ruby*
3. *Crystal*
4. *Amber*
5. *Sapphire*

The Manchester Trilogy

1. *Born Bad*
2. *Blood Ties*
3. *Vendetta*

The Riverhill Trilogy

1. *Slur*
2. *A Gangster's Grip*
3. *Danger by Association*

THE MARK

Heather Burnside

HEAD of ZEUS

An Aries Book

First published in the UK in 2019 by Head of Zeus Ltd
This paperback edition first published in the UK in 2022 by Head of Zeus Ltd,
a part of Bloomsbury Publishing Plc

9 7 5 3 1 2 4 6 8

A CIP catalogue record for this book is available
from the British Library.

ISBN (PB): 9781803282909
ISBN (E): 9781789542073

Printed and bound in Great Britain by
CPI Group (UK) Ltd, Croydon CR0 4YY

Head of Zeus
First Floor East
5–8 Hardwick Street
London EC1R 4RG

www.headofzeus.com

For Pascoe and Kerry

I

2004

The two women sitting side by side in the run-down Manchester pub couldn't have been more different, so they made for unlikely friends. Maddy was an attractive middle-class woman in her late thirties, outwardly confident and self-assured. Her background showed in her clothing, which screamed of quality. She was wearing a neat top, pristine leather jacket and expensive fitted jeans that flattered her trim yet shapely figure.

Her blonde hair was shoulder-length, lustrous and wavy but today Maddy had it in a loose chignon. The style emphasised her perfectly formed face with high cheekbones, smooth complexion and large cat's eyes. She wore a light dusting of premium-brand make-up, carefully applied to enhance her striking features.

Crystal, on the other hand, although only in her early twenties, already had a careworn complexion, which was overemphasised by cheap, garish make-up. Her messy bright red lipstick was paired with a darker shade of lip-liner, which extended beyond the natural outline of her lips and made her look clown-like.

Likewise, Crystal's eye make-up was heavy and there were thick clumps on some of her eyelashes where the mascara had clogged. Her eyebrows had been plucked to death then pencilled back on in a shade of brown that looked out of place against her intense, dark eyes. Even her hair let her down; it was overdyed in a lurid shade of red and was dry and coarse.

Although it was growing cold outside, Crystal wore a short skirt displaying her bare, skinny legs, which were covered in sores, and the backs of her feet were red and inflamed from wearing plastic, high-heeled shoes. Her top clung tightly, exposing the mounds of her huge breasts, which were at odds with her skinny frame. She had obviously had a boob job, under the guidance of her pimp rather than her plastic surgeon.

The Rose and Crown was tucked away in the back streets of Manchester where it had managed to avoid the redevelopment that had taken place in other parts of the city centre. Its dated, shabby décor and worn furniture were reminiscent of a previous era. Although close to the thriving main streets, the pub seemed a world away from the twenty-something revellers, hen and stag parties, and excitable young students who thronged nearby. This was the sort of place frequented only by those in the know and who were up to no good.

Inside The Rose and Crown customers chatted, joked and struck illicit deals while a grubby-looking dog lay sprawled lethargically beneath one of the battered tables. The sound of Girls Aloud played quietly through outdated speakers; it was the pub's only nod to the early twenty-first century.

Maddy was sitting amongst a group of women who were dressed similarly to Crystal, their clothes selected for maximum exposure rather than as a defence against the chilly night air. Although Maddy's clothing and make-up weren't as bright as the other women's, she stood out from the crowd, for Maddy had class as well as charisma, and a way of dealing with people that immediately put them at ease.

Her ability to mix with people from all walks of life enabled her to gather information that others were barred from. This was part of the reason she was such a successful freelance journalist, who could command top rates of pay for her in-depth, thought-provoking articles and skilfully crafted features. Maddy was currently working on an exposé about the life of a prostitute. She had been in the pub for less than fifteen minutes but already the working girls were eagerly gathering round her to share information.

Maddy knew how to build up their trust, starting with innocuous questions then ramping up the pressure till the questions became increasingly probing. Having already covered the reasons the girls had gone into prostitution, she moved on to other questions involving the life of a prostitute.

'Have you ever experienced any strange fetishes from customers?' she asked Crystal.

'Depends what you call strange,' said Crystal. 'Some things are par for the course, like slapping, pulling our fuckin' hair and coming in our faces.'

Maddy tried not to let her repugnance show as she jotted down a few notes.

'I've got a few customers who do that every time,' said Ruby, a tall black girl with deep red lips, cornrows and tormented eyes.

'What, you mean…?' began Maddy.

'Yeah, come in my face,' said Ruby, casually.

'And how does that make you feel?' asked Maddy.

Ruby shrugged. 'I suppose you get used to it,' she said.

'There's some real fuckin' weirdos out there though,' chipped in Crystal.

'Really?' asked Maddy.

'Oh yeah,' said Crystal, looking over at one of the girls and laughing. 'Remember that one you had, Amber?'

Amber, a short blonde girl wearing a bralette and a black denim miniskirt with a zip running all the way up the front, giggled. 'Oh, yeah. He wanted me to pretend he was my pet dog. I had to keep stroking him for ages. He got that fuckin' excited that he came before we even had sex.'

'OK,' said Maddy, stifling a grin and taking more notes. 'What about drink and drugs? Do you take them to help you do your work?'

'Yeah, most of us,' Crystal replied. 'It helps, y'know.'

'What about when you're sober?' asked Maddy. 'How does it feel then?'

'Shit!' said one of the girls at the back of the group.

'Yeah, that's why we all take,' said Ruby.

'It helps to block it out,' Crystal added.

Maddy worked her way down to the next question on her list. 'Have you ever caught any STIs?'

'Not a fuckin' chance!' said Crystal. 'I always use condoms. It's just not worth the risk. Some customers will pay more for sex without one but I always turn it down.'

The other girls muttered in agreement except for Amber, who kept quiet. Maddy suspected that the draw of the money had tempted her to go without, but she didn't probe any further.

Maddy was just about to ask the girls about violent customers when she noticed Crystal looking across at the bar. There were several men standing there with their backs to them so Maddy found it impossible to tell who Crystal was looking at, but she noticed the change in her body language.

Where Crystal had been cooperative and willing to answer questions, she now looked uncomfortable. Maddy could see the way her limbs tensed and she guessed that whoever was standing at the bar spelt trouble for the girls. She chanced one last question.

'How much of your earnings does your pimp take?' she asked.

'Too fuckin' much!' said Ruby but she was soon silenced by a shush from Crystal, whose eyes flashed across to the bar area again.

Not wanting to find either herself or the girls in danger, Maddy quickly rounded up the interview.

'That's all for now, girls,' she said. 'Thanks very much; you've been really helpful. Do you mind if I pop in again another evening?'

As soon as she'd fixed up a suitable time with the girls, Maddy stood up to leave, packed her notepad and pen away, then headed to the door, clutching her shoulder bag and jacket.

Gilly was standing at the bar of The Rose and Crown, sporting a black eye, which he'd recently acquired following a disagreement with a rival pimp. He was deep in conversation with Finn the Fence, a guy who could get hold of anything, from knocked-off cigs to expensive artwork.

'What the fuck's happened to you anyway?' asked Finn, once he had exhausted all conversation relating to the stolen items he had for sale.

'What?' asked Gilly, suddenly becoming aware of his black eye and subconsciously pulling the peak of his baseball cap down further in a vain attempt to cover it.

'Did someone give you a good beating?' asked Finn.

'Like fuck!' snapped Gilly. 'You wanna see the fuckin' state of his ugly mug.'

'Trouble brewing?' asked Finn.

'Nah, it was all over in a few punches,' said Gilly. 'I doubt the bastard will try it on again.'

Finn sniffed. Momentarily silenced by Gilly's hostile words, he glanced round the pub, his eyes reluctant to settle on Gilly's swollen and discoloured face. 'What's going on with them lot?' he asked.

Gilly followed his gaze till he spotted a bunch of working girls gathered round a corner table. He recognised one or two of them straight away, even from this distance. They were his girls and, like Finn, he wondered what the hell was going on.

'Dunno,' he said. 'But there's only one way to fuckin' find out.'

Gilly finished the last dregs of his beer and slammed the glass down on the bar, then made his way over to the corner table. He was just in time to spot a classy-looking piece walking away from his girls and muttering something about seeing them again soon, before she made her way to the exit. God, what a looker! he thought to himself. She spoke well too, more Cheshire set than the mean backstreets of Manchester. *Just what the bloody hell was she doing in this dive.*

He was soon standing next to his girls. 'What the fuck's going on?' he demanded of Crystal as the other girls quickly dispersed.

Although Crystal was of average height, the tall skinny frame of Gilly towered above her and she visibly flinched as he got up close. 'Nothing,' she said, pulling away as she tried to create some distance between them. 'She was just asking us a few questions, that's all.'

'What kind of fuckin' questions?'

'Just about what we do, y'know.'

'What is she, a fuckin' copper or summat?' demanded Gilly.

'No, she's a journalist. She's doing an exposé about us,' said Crystal, emphasising the word exposé, hoping it made her sound sophisticated.

'Are you fuckin' stupid?' roared Gilly. 'You don't tell the press fuck all!'

'It's all anonymous,' pleaded Crystal.

'I don't give a toss! I don't fuckin' pay you to waste time chatting with no fuckin' journalist. Now get back to work!'

As he hollered the last words, he slapped Crystal on the back of the head. Then he watched with wry amusement as she legged it out of the pub, trying to run as quickly as possible on her tottering high heels. That was the thing he liked about Crystal: she knew who was boss. He only had to say the word and she'd do anything to please him, anything at all.

Crystal was the first girl he'd recruited, several years previously when he'd started out in his present line of business. She was all right as working girls went, and attractive in her own way even if she was a bit rough around the edges. Crystal had always remained loyal to him too; she knew better than to cross him. But she could be fuckin' clingy at times.

As he stared into the space that had been left by the group of women, he couldn't help but wonder about the journalist. She was a stunning-looking woman, that was for sure, and streets ahead of any of his girls. She also had a certain way about her.

He had noticed that, although she had obviously left the pub on his account, she didn't seem frightened or timid. Instead she held her head high as though she was sure of herself. She was different in every way from the women he was used to dealing with, and he was intrigued.

2

Maddy was behind the wheel of her Audi. Sapphire blue and polished until it was gleaming, the vehicle was just as easy on the eye as its driver. She turned into the tree-lined road in Flixton where she lived. She owned a three-bedroomed detached house, which she shared with her eight-year-old daughter, Rebecca.

As Maddy sped into the drive, she glanced again at the clock on the dashboard. 19:58. She'd just made it. Maddy was surprised that her first interview with the prostitutes had taken so long but at least she'd gleaned some good information from them and had managed to arrange another meeting, before the girls had all become nervous of someone at the bar.

Maddy's ex-husband, Andy, was bringing Rebecca back at eight o'clock and, although he was fairly easy-going, Maddy always liked to be on time. Thank God his working hours were flexible. It meant he could pick Rebecca up from school whenever Maddy had to work late. As she parked the car, Maddy put thoughts of her working day out of her mind. It was time to concentrate on family now and, in her line of business, it wasn't always a good idea to mix the two.

As soon as Maddy stepped inside her hallway she had that familiar comforting feeling she always got when she returned home. Like everything else surrounding Maddy, her home was immaculate and tastefully furnished. But it was more than that; it was a cosy home that felt lived in. She quickly switched on the hall lamp, which bathed the interior with a subtle amber glow, highlighting the polished wooden flooring, expensive rug, and stunning artwork that hung on the walls.

Maddy walked through the house, switching on the lights in the main rooms and plumping up cushions before flicking the switch on the kettle. She had no sooner pulled a mug from the cupboard than she heard the doorbell ring. Maddy dashed to answer the door, delighted to find her daughter Rebecca standing there with Andy by her side.

Rebecca gave her mother an affectionate hug. 'I scored a goal, Mum,' she gushed before rushing indoors.

'Everything OK?' Maddy asked once Rebecca was inside.

'Yeah, she's fine,' said Andy. 'She's been to netball club after school. They had a practice match and apparently she was the hero of the hour.'

Maddy smiled. 'Great,' she said. 'I must go and congratulate her.'

'OK. See you next weekend,' he said.

'Yeah, see you then,' said Maddy.

Then she shut the front door straight away and went through to the lounge to find Rebecca. That was how it was with Andy now. After being divorced for four years, emotion didn't come into it as far as she was concerned. They were just two adults sharing joint responsibility for their daughter.

Maddy was well over those early days when their separation had torn at her heart. It had been difficult to walk away but Andy's infidelity had left her with no choice. She was too proud to carry on with the marriage after that and knew that she'd never be able to trust him again.

Nowadays they maintained a united front when it came to anything involving Rebecca whilst getting on with their own lives. Maddy preferred it that way and she knew that it was the best way to deal with the situation.

Rebecca had already switched on the TV and Maddy sat down beside her, stroking Rebecca's hair as she held her close.

'So, you scored a goal, did you?'

'Yes, and all the girls were cheering. And Jade Coulson said after the match that I'd saved our side from getting beat. Jade Coulson doesn't normally bother with me much. She's, like, so-o-o cool. I can't believe she likes me now.'

Maddy congratulated her daughter. 'Well done, love.' Then she smiled as Rebecca gushed about her day, listening patiently and offering her input whenever it was required.

Maddy agreed to let her daughter watch TV for half an hour before she got ready for bed. Then she went through to the kitchen to grab herself a quick bite to eat. While she was buttering a sandwich she heard the phone ring and went to answer it.

'Hi, Clare. How are you?' asked Maddy on hearing her best friend's voice at the other end of the phone.

'I'm good, thanks. How are you?' asked Clare.

'Good. You'll never guess what I've been doing today.'

'Go on,' said Clare.

'Interviewing prostitutes in a run-down pub for an exposé I'm writing.'

'Wow! I bet that was interesting.'

'Oh, it was, and definitely a bit of an eye-opener.'

'And how are you apart from that?' asked Clare.

'Not too bad, getting on with things at last.'

'So, you've finally got him out of your system, have you?' asked Clare, referring to Maddy's ex-boyfriend.

'What? Rob? Oh, yeah. You can't keep a good woman down for long.' Maddy laughed, but even to her own ears it sounded a bit forced.

Maddy's relationship with Rob had ended two months previously. She had only seen him for eight months but, nevertheless, he had made his mark. She had given him her all, secretly hoping that she had finally met 'the one' but, unfortunately, as time had gone on his jealousy and possessiveness had been more than Maddy could handle.

To the people around her it seemed that Maddy had it all: good looks and intellect, a beautiful home, great career and a lovely daughter. But, despite her outwardly confident nature and great life, Maddy had one weakness: men, and usually younger ones.

If she were to analyse the situation she would probably come to the conclusion that her ex-husband's infidelity had left her more vulnerable than she was willing to admit. The upshot of that was a penchant for younger men, attempting to prove to herself that she was still young and attractive enough to bag one.

But Maddy chose not to acknowledge her true feelings. Instead she put on a brave face while her love life lurched from one brief and disastrous relationship to another. And, in between, she feigned female liberation through a series of meaningless one-night stands, which left her feeling hollow when the stark difference between sex and love hit her over and over again.

Clare probably knew Maddy better than anyone, having been her friend since university, but even she hadn't fully penetrated the protective armour that Maddy wore so well. Clare was also single but, unlike Maddy, she didn't hide the fact that she was longing to meet her Mr Right.

'Well, I'm glad you're getting over Rob,' she said, 'because I've got an idea that will cheer you up.'

'What's that?' asked Maddy.

'A wild night on the town.'

'Sounds great!' said Maddy, giggling. 'We've not been into Manchester for ages.'

'Well, it's about time we did.' Clare laughed. 'We deserve a bit of fun. And, you never know, one of us might just meet someone special.'

'That'll be the day,' said Maddy. 'When is it, anyway?'

When Clare named the date Maddy said, 'Go on, then. I'm sure Andy will be able to have Becky. If not, I'll ask my mum.'

When the call ended and Maddy put down the phone, she had a smile on her face. Even though she suspected it would be a let-down, she found herself looking forward to it already. Maybe it would be just the tonic she needed after her ill-fated relationship with Rob.

3

It was lunchtime and Gilly was sitting in a corner of The

It was lunchtime and Gilly was sitting in a corner of The Rose and Crown waiting for Crystal to arrive. He had a pint of lager in front of him and was surreptitiously smoking a roll-up, hoping the landlord wouldn't notice it was cannabis, but the sweet, pungent smell gave him away.

'Turn it in, Gilly,' said the landlord as he passed by, collecting empty glasses. 'Last thing I need is to lose my fuckin' licence.'

'All right, keep your hair on,' said Gilly, extinguishing the roll-up and putting it back in his pocket.

He kicked out his legs and relaxed back in his seat, smiling at the women on the next table.

'You being a naughty boy, Gilly?' laughed one of the women, a peroxide blonde with a plunging cleavage.

'Not, me.' Gilly laughed back. 'I'm one of the good guys.'

'Like hell you are!' said the woman.

They shared a few minutes of friendly banter until Crystal arrived. She looked harassed, her red hair messy and her top lopsided as though she had thrown it on in a hurry.

'You took your fuckin' time!' said Gilly, deliberately speaking loudly for the benefit of the people sitting close by. He liked to keep up his reputation as someone who shouldn't be messed with.

'Sorry, I overslept. It was late when I got to bed cos of my last punter,' said Crystal, pulling up a seat next to him. 'I couldn't get rid of the bastard.'

'Well, I hope you charged him fuckin' extra for taking up so much of your time.'

Crystal's forehead puckered and stress lines appeared round her mouth, displaying her discomfort. She spoke hesitantly. 'Not really. It took me all my time to get the money out of him as it was. He was a nasty piece of work.'

'Really? Well, if you ever see the bastard around, make sure you point him out to me and I'll sort him. No one fuckin' takes the piss with my girls!'

He could see Crystal preen at his reference to ownership. Silly cow! Some of these women made it all too easy.

Gilly stuck his hand out, palm upwards. 'How much have you got anyway?' he asked.

Crystal withdrew a bunch of notes and passed them to him. He counted them out.

'Bit fuckin' short, aren't you?' he asked.

'Sorry, it was a bad night,' she said, looking down at the floor.

Gilly's hand shot out and grabbed hold of Crystal's chin, squeezing it tightly and turning her face up till her eyes met his.

'You'd better not be fuckin' pocketing any of it!'

'No, course I'm not,' she said, her eyes wide with fear.

On the next table the women kept their eyes averted and pretended to be deep in conversation even though they had seen his aggressive treatment of Crystal. So had the landlord. But none of them were willing to get involved. There was an understanding in The Rose and Crown: what went on between a pimp and his girls was his business and no one else's. As long as his pub stayed open and the customers continued to spend large amounts of money, the landlord wasn't interested.

'You must be losing your fuckin' touch, then,' said Gilly, letting go of Crystal's face before giving it a sharp slap. 'All of the girls earnt more than you last night and they weren't fuckin' late either. It wasn't so long ago that you were a top earner but now you're a waste of fuckin' space. Just look at the state of you! You need to smarten yourself up a bit. Try taking a fuckin' iron to your clothes before you put them on in future.'

Crystal covered her smarting cheek with her hand and her eyes wandered to the crumpled top that Gilly was referring to. 'Sorry,' she said. 'I was in a bit of a rush today with getting up late.'

Gilly took five pounds from the wad of notes in his hand and flung it at Crystal, who quickly grabbed hold of it. 'I suppose you'd better get yourself a fuckin' drink now you're here,' he said.

Crystal stood up. 'I'll have to give it a miss,' she said. 'I can't stay.'

'Why not?' he asked, holding out his hand for her to pass him the money back.

Crystal reluctantly placed the five-pound note back in Gilly's outstretched hand. 'I've got to pick Candice up from my mam's,' she said, referring to her three-year-old daughter.

'Go on, then. Fuck off! I'll see you here tomorrow, but you'd better not be fuckin' short again.'

Crystal hesitated before walking out of the pub. 'Can you spare us a tenner, Gilly?' she asked.

'You've got a fuckin' nerve, haven't you? After what you took last night! And I only just gave you a load yesterday. What the fuck happened to that?'

'It's gone. I had to pay the leccy. I got a red reminder.'

Gilly tutted and leaned back even further in his seat, giving her a cold, hard stare.

'Please, Gilly. I need to get some food in for Candice coming home.'

'All right, shut yer fuckin' whinging,' he snapped, chucking a ten-pound note towards her and watching with satisfaction as it floated down to the floor. As Crystal bent to retrieve it, he slapped her hard on her backside. 'Go on, fuck off,' he repeated. 'And don't forget what I said.'

She was about to walk away when he stopped her. 'By the way,' he said, 'when are you seeing that fuckin' journalist again?'

'One night this week but it's all right, Gilly, I'll cancel it if you want,' she said, and he could tell she was worried about how he would react.

Gilly grinned, thinking about the stunning, self-assured woman from the previous evening. 'No, it's OK,' he said. 'Let the meeting go ahead. But let me know if she steps out of fuckin' line.'

He was still interested in Maddy, despite his suspicion that she might be a police officer. The woman was a looker, the sort of woman he rarely came across in his everyday life. There was also something about her that fascinated him. Her mere presence was so out of place inside the drab interior of The Rose and Crown. It gave him a weird kind of kick knowing that her work had led her to a place like this where she was forced to sit amongst all the low-life scum.

But at the moment he didn't know what he wanted to do about the classy blonde. All he knew was he looking forward to seeing her again.

4

Crystal was completely in awe of the woman called Maddy who was once again sitting next to her in The Rose and Crown. Not only was Maddy beautiful, but she wore nice clothes and had a lovely, friendly way about her. But, although Crystal was envious of Maddy, she didn't aspire to have what Maddy had, readily accepting that it was well out of her reach. Crystal's life experiences had brainwashed her to the extent that she almost saw Maddy as belonging to another world; a distant world that wasn't attainable to people like her.

'OK,' said Maddy, 'I'd like us to go back to where we were at our last meeting. I was asking you and the girls about your earnings and how much your pimp takes.'

Crystal shuffled uncomfortably, conscious of Gilly standing at the bar. Maddy followed her eyes to the back of the tall man in a baseball cap. 'Are you OK to talk?' she asked.

Crystal recalled how Gilly had condoned her meeting with Maddy and tried to relax. 'Yeah, but can we be a bit quieter?' she asked, lowering her voice.

'OK,' said Maddy, with an amiable smile on her face. Then she asked quietly, 'What percentage does he take?'

'I dunno about percentages,' whispered Crystal. 'I dunno how he works it out but I know he has most of it.' Then, noticing the concerned expression on Maddy's face, she quickly added, 'Oh, but it's worth it. I mean, he looks after us. There's some right weirdos about and if it wasn't for him they'd well take advantage.'

'I see,' said Maddy, scribbling down some notes. 'What about unwanted pregnancies? Does that happen often or do the girls protect themselves from that?'

Crystal's jaw dropped as she thought about her daughter, Candice. Although Crystal hadn't planned to have her, she didn't like to think of her as unwanted because she wasn't, at least, not as far as she was concerned anyway. It was a different matter when it came to Candice's father though. Crystal had always known that it was Gilly, but he refused to acknowledge her.

When Crystal had first become pregnant and told him he was the father, he had gone berserk, calling her a lying bitch and telling her the baby could belong to any one out of hundreds of men. But Crystal knew she was his. He was the only man Crystal allowed near her without using protection so he had to be the father. Every time she mentioned it to Gilly though he turned nasty, yelling at her and slapping her around, so she learnt to keep quiet and join in his pretence that Candice was nothing to do with him.

There was no way she was going to explain all that to a journalist, especially with Gilly watching, so Crystal decided instead not to mention Candice at all, saying, 'A few of the girls have been pregnant, those that don't use protection.'

'And what happens to them?'

'They either get rid or they have to find a way of bringing the kid up.'

'I suppose that must mean they're unable to work as well?' asked Maddy.

'What, you mean, cos they're pregnant?'

'Yes.'

'Depends. Most punters don't mind. In fact, some of the kinky bastards prefer it.'

She thought back to that period when she was carrying Candice, and how difficult life had been, even more so after she had given birth. Gilly had made sure that she went back to work as soon as possible.

Crystal became aware that she was letting her thoughts run away with her when she heard the journalist ask, 'Are you OK?'

'What? Yeah, course I am,' said Crystal. 'I'm just thinking about the time, that's all. I need to get back to work soon.'

Gilly was standing at the bar watching Crystal and Maddy through the mirror on the back wall. The difference in the appearance of the two women was striking and Gilly noticed again how refined the journalist appeared. Her clothing was obviously quality and her hairstyle and make-up had probably cost plenty too. Alongside her Crystal looked just what she was: cheap.

As Gilly watched he wondered again whether the woman might be an undercover police officer but, somehow, he didn't think so. Nevertheless, he was curious and wanted to find out more. He was attracted to her, for sure, but he knew he didn't have a chance with someone of her class. Would it be worth his while wasting time on someone who would only knock him back? He wasn't sure; especially as he knew he could have as many women as he wanted. Sex was on tap in his line of work.

Gilly also knew that a woman like Maddy could present him with all kinds of opportunities – from blackmail to extortion and even kidnap. There must be numerous ways of making money from her.

At the moment he wasn't sure what he wanted to do about her. Nevertheless, when she rounded up the meeting and left the pub, Gilly felt compelled to follow.

'Where you going, Gilly?' asked Crystal as he dashed towards the door.

'What's it to you?' he replied, gruffly.

'I just wondered if you might want to come back to mine later, that's all,' she said, winking saucily.

'Nah, not tonight,' he muttered. 'Maybe tomorrow.' He answered without stopping to look at her as he sped through the door.

Gilly walked onto the street just in time to see Maddy rounding the bend at the end of the narrow side street where The Rose and Crown was situated. As he followed her round the corner he saw her getting inside a flash blue

Audi. He dashed back into the side street where his own car was parked, then quickly got in and started the engine.

As he zoomed out of the side street he saw Maddy's car driving up the road with three other cars between them. He quickly overtook two of the cars and edged into the space behind the car nearest to Maddy's Audi. He was near enough not to lose her but not so close as to arouse suspicion. As he tailed the blue Audi he felt a buzz of excitement he hadn't felt in a long time...

5

It was late evening and, because the roads were quiet, it took less than thirty minutes for Maddy to arrive home, with Gilly following close behind. As he parked a few doors down from the three-bedroomed detached home where Maddy's car was parked, Gilly eyed the tree-lined road. It was around ten miles from the city centre, but it felt as if it were a million miles away from the dingy interior of The Rose and Crown, where Gilly had just spent the best part of his evening watching her.

Flixton. He was familiar with the area, and, although it wasn't the best district in Manchester, it was still seen as desirable. Flixton was the sort of area occupied by the middle classes. As well as teachers, civil servants and bank employees, the area housed a lot of medical professionals due to its close proximity to Trafford General. Although the consultants were more likely to live in nearby upper-class areas such as Hale and Altrincham, many of the lesser qualified medical staff opted for Flixton and the surrounding areas.

Gilly watched Maddy step out of her car and walk up the drive of the nearest house. Her confident air was still apparent but she also had a sexuality about her. It wasn't blatant like Crystal and the other girls'; instead it was subtle, which he found more alluring. As he watched her firmly rounded hips smoothly swaying in her tight-fitting jeans he could feel himself becoming aroused.

He switched his attention to the house, which was presumably hers. It was an immaculate, 1930s-style home with large bay windows and an archway over the wooden front door, and it was obvious to Gilly that the house had been well maintained. The leaded windows had frames that appeared to be natural wood, but which Gilly suspected was the more modern wood-effect uPVC.

Large wrought-iron gates opened onto a sizeable, weed-free block-paved drive. At the head of the drive was a garage attached to the house, which had an up-and-over door painted a gleaming white. Glazed planters stood to either side of the front door, each housing a small conifer. There was a low brick wall at the front topped by a neatly trimmed hedge.

Gilly guessed that while Maddy wasn't exactly loaded, just what her circle would describe as 'comfortable', nevertheless, her world was far removed from the one he inhabited. She had the type of life he might have had if things had panned out differently for him.

He was tempted to get out of the car and take a closer look at the house, maybe catch a glimpse of the inside, but he decided against it. Instead Gilly started his engine. He'd seen enough for one evening. Besides, he wanted to get back home. But at least he knew where she lived now, and he had all the time in the world to decide what he was going to do about it.

It was late when Gilly arrived home at his flat on the main road in Levenshulme. It was situated above a kebab shop, which was sandwiched between a discount off-licence and a charity shop. An ever-present aroma of cooking and grease from the kebab shop wafted up the stairway and into Gilly's home.

It was in a noisy area. Because of its location on the main road, the sound of passing cars never stopped. At night Gilly could hear people in high spirits, or some of them arguing, as they made their way home from the surrounding pubs, restaurants and takeaways. Then there were the youths who hung about outside the off-licence. They didn't worry him too much though. Most of them were aware of his reputation and he only had to open his window for the kids to move on even before he spoke.

Inside his flat was a small hallway with doors leading off to the living room, bedroom and bathroom. Gilly made his way into the living room, which had a doorway in the far corner through which was a small kitchenette. The living room had little in the way of comfort. Its only furniture was an old sofa, two mismatched armchairs and a 1970s teak coffee table with an oval glass insert. A huge widescreen television dominated one wall, its pristine presence mocking the spartan furniture in the rest of the room.

Despite the lack of luxury, Gilly did his best to keep the place clean and tidy. As soon as he arrived home, he walked into the bedroom and hung his coat on a peg behind the door. Then he went back to the kitchen and fished around in the cupboard where he kept his supplies.

He lit up a spliff and settled back onto his sofa to watch some TV. After a while he could feel himself becoming more relaxed and at ease with the world. Eventually he drifted off to sleep. For precious minutes the outdoor sounds and sparse environment were forgotten as his dreams transported him. In his mind he pictured the attractive blonde with her subtle sexuality, stylish motor and nice home, and a warm glow lit him up from within.

Despite his surroundings, Gilly wasn't willing to accept this lifestyle as his due. Unlike his sometime girlfriend, Crystal, Gilly aspired to greater things. The fact that he squandered his earnings from prostitution on drugs and booze was lost on him. To Gilly the difference between Maddy's home life and his own was startlingly apparent. He wanted what she had. And, somehow or other, he would find a way to get it.

6

It was the evening of Maddy and Clare's big night out. Maddy had mixed feelings about the evening ahead. She thought it might be a let-down, just like many of the other nights out she'd had since being single. Despite her doubts, however, she couldn't help but feel some enthusiasm. It would make a nice change from going out locally and there would perhaps be more men to choose from.

By the time they arrived at the first pub, the excitement of the evening ahead had taken hold and they were giggling like a couple of teenagers going to a school disco. They ordered drinks at the bar and went to sit down. It wasn't long before they were joined by a balding man with an overenthusiastic smile and stuffy dress sense.

'Do you come here often?' he asked, and Maddy steeled herself for a few minutes of boredom.

Thankfully he eventually picked up on their lack of interest and left them alone.

'Hurrah!' whispered Clare. 'I thought he was never going to go.'

'I know,' laughed Maddy. 'He was cramping our style a bit, wasn't he?'

She gazed round the room, her instinct to look for attractive men, but the only ones she noticed seemed to be in couples. 'Shall we go to the next pub?' she asked Clare, noticing that both their glasses were almost empty.

'Aw, I like it here,' said Clare. 'Let's just stay for one more and then move on.'

'OK,' said Maddy before heading to the bar.

Maddy had worked her way to the front of the queue when she felt a presence beside her. She glanced to her left and spotted a really good-looking guy. Tall and blond, he returned her gaze and smiled. 'I bet you thought you'd never get to the front,' he said.

'Yeah, it is a bit busy tonight,' said Maddy, smiling back.

For the next few minutes they made small talk until Maddy was served. She collected her drinks and smiled at him again before heading back to Clare.

'Hang on a minute,' he said.

'What?' asked Maddy, feeling a bit awkward standing there with her hands full while other customers waited for her to pass so they could get nearer to the bar.

'It's OK, I can see you've got your hands full,' he said. 'I'll come over later.'

Maddy felt a tingle down her spine as she took in his handsome features and dazzling smile. 'All right,' she said, before making her way back to Clare.

'I saw you, chatting to that hunk at the bar,' Clare teased.

'I know, he's gorgeous,' said Maddy. 'A bit young though.'

'So what?' said Clare. 'That doesn't usually bother you. Go for it. You only live once.'

'Oh, I dunno,' said Maddy. 'Maybe he's like that with all the women. Anyway, he said he'll come over so we'll wait and see.'

For the next half-hour Maddy and Clare remained at their table until their glasses were empty. Maddy was secretly hoping the hunk from the bar would come over but, although she could see him watching her, he didn't make a move.

'Are we moving on?' asked Clare.

'Erm, maybe just one more,' said Maddy.

'You're incorrigible,' said Clare, tutting jokingly. 'Go on, then, just one more and if he hasn't made a move by then, we're going.'

Maddy was thrilled when the man came straight over as soon as Clare went to the bar. He introduced himself as Aaron and continued to chat to her until Clare returned. Then he asked for her phone number. Maddy knew she really shouldn't. After all, she'd only just met him and hadn't had chance to find out much about him. But she was tempted and, as Clare had said, you only live once. So, against her better judgement, she gave him her phone number.

It was late when they headed home, with Clare dropping Maddy in the taxi before continuing on her way. Thank God Becky is staying at her dad's tonight, thought Maddy, on noticing the time. She was in good spirits as she thought about the gorgeous man she had met, called Aaron. She couldn't resist checking her phone to see if he had texted her yet. He hadn't but, then again, it was a bit early. He had only left her a couple of hours ago.

She locked up and shut the front curtains, which she'd inadvertently left open before going out, forgetting that it would be dark outside by the time she got back. Maddy didn't notice the man sitting in a car opposite her house, watching her. And, even if she had done, she wouldn't have been able to describe him because he had a baseball hat pulled low over his forehead to hide his features.

The following day Maddy checked her phone for the umpteenth time. She had been trying to finish the exposé about prostitution but was finding it difficult to concentrate as her mind kept drifting back to the gorgeous man she had met. To her delight she had received a message from Aaron. Maddy quickly read the words that appeared on her phone screen.

Hi, I'm Aaron. I hope you remember me from the pub last night. I'd love to meet up with you and go for a drink if you fancy it. Please text me and let me know.

As she read the message a buzz of excitement shot through her. Aaron had been one of the best-looking men she'd seen last night. He was young, tall and slim and had blond hair in a trendy style, shaved in at the sides and longer on the top. He also had perfectly formed features, including lovely blue eyes and a nice smile. In fact, in Maddy's opinion he was a bit of a Matt Goss lookalike and she smiled at the thought.

Checking that Rebecca wasn't within hearing distance, she picked up her phone and rang Clare.

'Guess what?' she asked. Before Clare had chance to respond, she added, 'I've got a message from Aaron, that guy I met last night. He wants to take me out.'

'You lucky bugger,' said Clare. 'I wish I could have met someone like him. When are you seeing him?'

'Don't know. I've only just seen the text. I thought I'd tell you first before I message him.'

'Go on, then. What are you waiting for? Good luck and let me know how you get on.'

'Will do,' said Maddy, cutting the call then going to her contacts and adding Aaron's number.

Without waiting any longer she sent him a text.

Hi, I'm Maddy who you met last night. Thanks for your lovely message. I'd love to go for a drink and get to know you a bit better. I'm free Friday night if that suits.

Then she put down her phone and waited.

7

Crystal was standing at her usual spot on Minshull Street when a red Toyota pulled up and the driver wound down the window. She approached the car.

'Do you wanna do business?' she asked.

He was ugly, with a huge beer belly hanging over the top of his trousers, but in her profession that wasn't an unusual sight. 'Yeah, blow job,' he said. 'How much?'

'Twenty quid,' said Crystal.

'OK, get in.'

Crystal held out her hand and, once the man had given her the money, she pulled open the car door and plonked herself down in the passenger seat. As soon as she was inside, the driver locked all the doors. That was the first sign she was in trouble.

'What the fuck are you playing at?' she demanded.

The driver ignored her and kept his eyes on the road while Crystal continued to protest, demanding that he stop the car and let her out. It was only a few minutes before they arrived at an industrial area on the other side of Deansgate where Manchester met Salford. The driver turned into a desolate side street and parked the car.

Knowing that she wasn't going to escape before the customer had got what he came for, Crystal took a condom out of her handbag. She held it out towards the man while she waited for him to unzip his trousers.

'You won't be needing that,' he said, grinning lewdly at her.

It was then that Crystal noticed the smell of alcohol on his breath and a musty smell from his well-worn clothing. His teeth were rotten, his skin pockmarked, and there was something distinctly weird about him. As he grinned, his face didn't seem to fall naturally; instead the lines of his features were hard, like an overstated parody of a human being. Crystal had dealt with some strange people in her working life but this guy topped them all. He really gave her the creeps!

'I won't do it without,' she said, feeling a tremendous sense of trepidation. 'And you've only paid for a blow job.'

'You'll do as I fuckin' say!' he snarled as he reached his hand over to the switch at the side of her seat.

Crystal felt the seat tip back and, before she knew it, she was lying flat on her back. The beast of a man had slipped his hand under her miniskirt and was groping the tops of her legs with his grubby hands.

'Get your fuckin' hands off me!' she yelled, but it was no use.

She could feel her flimsy knickers being yanked from her and heard the material tear. Crystal carried on struggling and trying to push the man away from her but she was losing the fight. He was too big and strong. As she fought desperately to escape his clutches the man withdrew his hand and started raining punches on her head and torso.

Crystal lifted her hands in front of her face to try to protect herself. She was too late; her face and body were already beginning to swell and bruise. While she tried to recover from the shock assault, she felt the man heave his bulk roughly on top of her and she let out a scream.

Later that evening Gilly was standing at the bar in The Rose and Crown when he heard Crystal shouting his name.

'Gilly, Gilly!' she yelled, tugging sharply on his sleeve.

Gilly spun round and was about to admonish Crystal for her heavy-handedness when he caught sight of her face.

'What the fuck?' he demanded, taking in her black eye and bloody nose. 'Who the fuckin' hell did this to you?'

He could feel his temper rising. In Gilly's mind it was all right for him to knock his girls around; it was just his way of keeping them in line, as far as he was concerned. But if anyone else abused them he took it as a personal slight. They were his girls and anyone who got out of line with them was also taking the piss out of him.

'My last punter. I came straight back to tell you,' she said, pulling down the neck of her top to reveal heavy bruising to her shoulder.

'Who was he? What was his name?'

'I don't know. Clients don't usually give us their names, do they?'

'Didn't you suspect something was fuckin' wrong when you got in the car?'

'I… well, not at first, no. He seemed all right when I got in the car. But then he locked the doors. He'd paid for a blow job but he wanted full sex. I told him it would cost more but he wanted it for the same price. When I told him no he just fuckin' took it anyway and then started laying into me with his fists. Then he made me hand over all my cash.'

'Bastard! That's *my* cash he's nicked. I hope you used a fuckin' condom.'

'I wanted him to but he wouldn't. He said he wanted it bareback.'

'Shit! Right, well, you can get yourself down to the fuckin' clinic tomorrow and get checked out. I don't want anyone saying my girls aren't fuckin' clean.'

Gilly could see Crystal's bottom lip quiver but she knew better than to cry. Street girls didn't cry; they were hardened to it. And his girls especially didn't cry, not if they knew what was good for them. He couldn't be doing with all that emotional bullshit.

'What did this bastard look like anyway?' he asked. 'And where did he pick you up?'

'He was big and ugly, with dark hair and a beer belly. And there was something really creepy about him. He picked me up at my usual place on Minshull Street.'

'Where did he take you?'

'I dunno, somewhere near Salford where there's loads of cash and carries. Then he dropped me back at Minshull Street after.'

'What car was he driving?'

'A red one. Big. A Toyota, I think. It had one of them little badge things on the back with a funny T.'

'Right, I want you to keep your eye out and if you see his car again you get straight on the fuckin' phone to me. All right?'

As Gilly spoke to her he was furiously hitting the keys on his phone.

'What you doing?' asked Crystal.

'Putting the word out. What d'you think I'm fuckin' doing? I don't want that bastard getting his hands on any more of my girls. And as soon as anyone spots him I need to know, so I can fuckin' go after him.'

'Oh, all right,' said Crystal, who then hovered around the bar area waiting for Gilly's next move.

Once he had finished texting, Gilly put the phone back into his pocket and fixed his eyes on Crystal. She was staring up at him, as though pleading for his sympathy and, just for a moment, he actually felt sorry for her.

'I suppose you'd better have a drink,' he said, summoning the barmaid.

'What? You mean I don't have to go back to work tonight?' Crystal asked.

'No, knock it on the head for tonight,' he said.

'Aw, thanks, Gilly,' she said, reaching up to him and flinging her arms round his neck.

'All right,' he said, pulling her arms away then letting them drop as though breaking free of his chains.

It was another three hours before Gilly and Crystal left The Rose and Crown. During that time the only first aid Crystal received was when a barmaid fetched her a wet cloth to clean her face. Crystal then held the blood-stained cloth over her bruised eye to reduce the swelling.

Gilly plied her with brandy till she was feeling tipsy, and Crystal was making the most of it. She snuggled up to him while they stood at the bar and felt his arm around her shoulders. Crystal knew it was the closest she'd get to any sign of affection from Gilly. As the night drew to a close she realised that she didn't want to go back home alone. Although the brandy had helped to anaesthetise her, she was still shaken from her ordeal.

'Are you coming back, Gilly?' she asked.

Gilly grinned at her. 'All right, then.'

Crystal left The Rose and Crown feeling much more upbeat than when she had entered. She smiled as she looked forward to a night snuggled up in bed with Gilly, who she saw as her lover and protector.

8

It was late when they arrived at Crystal's home, a rented two-bedroomed 1970s terraced house in Longsight, a couple of miles from the city centre. Crystal giggled as she searched for her front door key and let them inside. She kicked off her shoes in the hall.

'Aren't you gonna put the fuckin' light on?' asked Gilly, searching for the switch on the wall.

'Shush,' said Crystal, holding her finger to her mouth then giggling again as she let out a hiccup. She pointed drunkenly up the stairs. 'Candice is asleep.'

Gilly felt a stab of guilt at the reminder of the daughter who he had denied. 'You mean you've left her on her own?' he asked, incensed.

'No choice,' whispered Crystal. 'My mam couldn't have her. Anyway, she'll sleep through most things, Candice.'

Gilly looked at her with contempt. He was already regretting coming back. Candice was an inconvenience that he preferred not to think about. While she was out of his mind, he could continue to live out his pretence that she wasn't his, but being in the same house as her brought back the realisation that she probably was.

Gilly knew the reason he'd come back, just as much as Crystal did. Like any other man, he had his needs and he knew that Crystal would be only too eager to satisfy them. But he also knew that he wanted something to help him along his way and deaden the pangs of guilt that had besieged him.

'You got any gear?' he asked.

'Yeah, some coke. Upstairs,' whispered Crystal.

They trundled up the stairs. 'I need a piss,' said Gilly, heading to the bathroom while Crystal went to check on Candice.

By the time Gilly had finished in the bathroom, Crystal was already in bed, naked and waiting for him. He tried not to look at her bruises as he took off his clothes and slipped into bed beside her.

'Where's the gear?' he asked.

Crystal pulled out a drawer in her bedside cabinet where she had the cocaine. They took turns snorting lines of the white powder through a rolled-up five-pound note.

'You got some condoms?' he asked, once the cocaine had kicked in, and he was feeling high.

'Yeah, but they're for clients. It's different with you. I thought you knew that.'

'You think I'm gonna go bareback after that bastard fucked you without?'

Crystal didn't say anything, just pouted sulkily. 'All right,' she said, 'but can we go without once I've been checked out?'

40

'Course we can but I wanna make sure you're clean first. I'm taking no fuckin' chances!'

'Good,' she said. 'Cos I want it to feel special with you, Gilly. You know, like it was before,' she said, stroking his flaccid penis till it began to swell.

'Yeah, I know. Come on, then,' he said, taking the condom she was handing him and tearing the wrapper.

For a few minutes Gilly went through the motions, indulging in a little obligatory foreplay while the sexual tension built up within him. It was while Crystal was riding him that he finally let go and felt the tremendous release. As his body shuddered to a climax he closed his eyes, focusing on the wonderful vision in his mind. But that vision wasn't of the woman he was with. It was of the attractive, classy blonde who was increasingly occupying his waking thoughts.

The following night, unaware of Gilly's growing obsession with her, Maddy was on a high. She couldn't help but feel a frisson of excitement as she thought about her forthcoming date with the delectable Aaron. She tried to recall what he looked like: blond hair, blue eyes and that lovely smile. It was the smile that dominated her thoughts whenever she shut her eyes and pictured him.

Then she chided herself. She was getting carried away as always! For all she knew the guy could be the biggest jerk on earth. She'd thought Rob was OK and look how that had ended. And it was so difficult to tell in just a few minutes. Well, at least tonight she'd get to know him a bit better, and then she could decide what she really thought of him.

They'd arranged to meet in a bar just off Deansgate. It was an older pub, which didn't get as crowded as some of the more popular new bars that were springing up all over the city centre. And she'd decided to drive. After all, she didn't know the guy yet so she didn't want to have one too many and make a fool of herself or, worse still, rush into something she might regret.

Maddy had selected her clothing carefully. She wanted to look neither too frumpy nor too tarty, so she'd selected a pair of fitted jeans that she knew showed off her shapely hips and thighs and she wore them with ankle boots that had a small heel. Her black silky blouse she had unbuttoned just enough to show a little cleavage but not too much.

So it was with confidence that she strode into the city-centre pub, noticing the admiring glances from men as she made her way through the lounge. Aaron had already arrived and she saw him sitting on a leather sofa and looking relaxed with his half-empty glass in front of him. He stood up as soon as she approached and gave her a tentative hug.

'What can I get you to drink?' he asked.

'Just lemonade for me, thanks. I'm driving,' said Maddy.

'Lemonade it is,' he said, making his way to the bar.

Maddy took a seat at the opposite end of the sofa. Manners, I like that, she thought. She had taken in his appearance in the few seconds before he went to the bar. Tonight he was wearing a smart pair of trousers with another nice shirt, a blue patterned one this time. She saw the same leather bomber jacket he'd worn before, on the back of the settee. It looked like quality leather. And he looked just as ravishing as the last time she had seen him with his dazzling smile and sparkling blue eyes.

She watched him walk back from the bar: he was gorgeous! Then she averted her eyes, trying to appear nonchalant as he placed the drinks on the table and sat down. There was a gap between them on the sofa and she was impressed that he hadn't tried to come on too strong by sitting too close to her. He carefully moved his jacket from the back of the sofa and placed it between them. Then he turned to face her and draped his arm casually in the space where his jacket had been.

'I must say, Maddy, I was really pleased when you messaged me back.'

She smiled. 'I was pleased when I received your message,' she said.

'So, tell me more,' he continued. 'Where are you from?'

'Flixton. What about you?'

He laughed. 'NFA at the moment.'

'NFA?' she asked, puzzled.

'No fixed abode. I'm joking. Actually I've just come back to Manchester and haven't found a suitable property yet, so I'm staying in a hotel for now. I've been tied up with business so I haven't really had the time.'

'Really?' asked Maddy. 'Where were you living before?'

'Yorkshire, although I'm from Manchester originally.'

Maddy had noticed the slight trace of a Mancunian accent but it wasn't guttural or pronounced; instead it was subtle and refined. He sounded educated and was perhaps from one of the better areas of Manchester.

'Aah, so what made you come back to Manchester?' she asked.

'Business. Well, I've still got a base in Yorkshire. That's where my electrical goods warehouse is,' he said, 'but I'd like to open up another one in Manchester seeing as how that one is doing so well. And, as I'm from Manchester originally, I thought I might settle back here.'

Maddy recalled that he'd touched a little on his business the first night she'd met him but the few minutes they'd spent chatting hadn't given her chance to find out much. She remembered they'd spent most of that time talking about favourite holiday destinations for some reason. Now, she decided to delve a little deeper.

'Have you sold your place in Yorkshire?' Maddy asked, presuming that he must have owned a house where he used to live.

'Yes. I preferred to sell that one before I bought a place here. Otherwise, it becomes a bit stressful trying to synchronise everything. So, I thought this way I'd be able to take my time and find the perfect place.'

'Sounds like a good idea. What areas are you looking at?'

'Bramhall, Cheadle, Poynton, although I haven't done many viewings yet.'

'Nice areas,' Maddy commented.

'Yes, it will be nice to live somewhere a bit out of the hustle and bustle but still near enough to the city centre if I need to come in for any reason.'

He smiled and his eyes lit up. The little hint about having a reason to visit the centre of Manchester wasn't lost on Maddy. Maybe he was referring to future dates. She smiled back as she felt a sparkle of joy.

'I must admit I've spent more time looking at warehouses than houses,' he said. 'I want to get the business up and running as soon as possible.' He reached for his drink and took a long swig before putting down his glass and continuing to speak. 'So, Maddy, I'd love to hear more about you. What do you do for a living?'

They continued in that vein for several hours. By the time they were ready to leave, Maddy had told Aaron all about her job, divorce and eight-year-old daughter. She had also found out that Aaron was born in Heaton Mersey in Manchester, but his family had moved to Yorkshire when he was ten years of age. He had attended private school in Yorkshire then gone on to university, where he had studied business. That would account for the refined accent with just a hint of Mancunian, she thought.

He had only been back in Manchester for a few weeks and his family still lived in Yorkshire, but he popped back to visit them whenever he could. At twenty-nine, he was nine years younger than Maddy but the age difference didn't seem to bother him. In fact, he'd made light of it and teased her by calling her a cougar.

Maddy had thoroughly enjoyed being in his company. He was very attentive and polite as well as interesting. They'd also shared some laughs together. Aaron was the sort of man who made her smile and she liked that. He'd even made a joke about the amount of male attention she'd received on the way back from the ladies. He's so unlike Rob, she thought. Rob would have become morose if another man so much as looked at her.

At the end of the night he insisted on seeing her safely to her car and wouldn't take no for an answer. 'You never know who's hanging about in the city centre,' he said as he led her out of the pub.

When they reached the car he gave her a polite hug then left her, promising to text her soon. Maddy's sparkle of joy had become intense pleasure. The man was a delight; such good company, so refined and so good-looking! And, what was more, he seemed to be just as enamoured with her. She drove home on a high, confident that she would soon receive a text from him asking to take her out again. And she couldn't wait.

As it was late at night, the drive home didn't take long. Maddy parked her car on the drive and quickly checked her phone in case she already had a message. There was nothing yet. She knew it was foolish of her to expect a message so soon and the lack of one didn't dampen her spirits. Maddy strode up to her front door as though walking on air. She noticed her curtains were still open and once inside went to shut them. Her thoughts were so full of the delectable Aaron that she failed to notice the vehicle that stopped on the other side of the road from her house.

From the driver's seat of his car Gilly keenly watched Maddy walk to her front door, then saw her silhouetted behind the living-room window. Later, the light was switched on in her bedroom and her silhouette appeared once more behind the curtains. This time Gilly could see her peeling off layers of clothing. The detail was missing but his imagination filled in the gaps. When there was no more to be seen, Gilly started the engine and his car zoomed off up the road.

9

The following night Gilly was hanging around on Minshull Street, near Crystal's usual spot. He had parked his car and was now on foot, hidden in the shadows of one of the sizeable red-brick buildings. As he felt the chill of the late night air, Gilly shivered and zipped up his fleece-lined hoody, not giving a moment's thought to the street girls who hung out there in all weathers wearing little clothing.

Gilly decided to keep moving so he would stay warm. While he meandered up and down the street he watched the street girls operating. Amongst them he spotted one or two of his own and was pleased to see they were keen at their work, constantly on the lookout for potential clients and sidling up to kerb-crawlers offering them business.

He then caught the eye of Ruby, one of his girls. She looked surprised at seeing him and was just about to speak, but Gilly shot her a look that told her not to bother. Tonight, he preferred it if nobody knew who he was. He passed her by and continued on his mission to find the big, ugly, dark-haired guy with a beer belly, driving a red Toyota.

After an hour Gilly was becoming bored. The warmth of The Rose and Crown was beckoning to him but he decided to wait around a bit longer and it was only ten minutes later that he was rewarded by the sight of a red Toyota Avensis stopping further up the road.

As Gilly raced towards the car he saw one of the prostitutes approach the driver's window, then, after exchanging a few words, go round to the passenger side. By the time Gilly reached the car she was sitting in the passenger seat and was just about to shut the door.

'Hang on!' he shouted, pushing the door fully open with the side of his fist.

The girl looked at him, alarmed, and continued to pull the door towards her. 'Fuck off!' she yelled. 'I'm taken. You'll have to find someone else.'

Gilly was too impatient for explanations. Instead he grabbed hold of the girl's hair and hauled her out of the car.

'What the fuck's going on?' he heard the driver shout.

Gilly plonked himself in the passenger seat and looked across at the driver. A scrawny, balding man in his fifties stared back at him. Gilly could see the fear in his eyes, which were like saucers.

'What do you want?' asked the timid, pathetic-looking driver, with a catch in his voice.

'Not you, dickhead!' said Gilly, his anger and disappointment showing as he gave the man a sharp slap with the back of his hand and got out of the car.

'Fuck!' he cursed. He had been so sure he'd had him.

He stormed off and headed towards The Rose and Crown. He'd had enough for one night. His vengeance would have to wait till another time.

A day later Maddy stepped inside an upmarket restaurant on Deansgate in the city centre and was led to her table by a polite waiter. As she walked through the restaurant, with its polished tables set out in neat rows and adorned with perfectly aligned glasses and cutlery, she spotted Aaron, his golden hair shining under the subtle lighting.

She reached the table and Aaron smiled across at her, his handsome features turning her insides to mush. He was just about to get out of his seat when the waiter motioned with his hand and then pulled out Maddy's chair.

'This is lovely,' said Maddy, gazing round the wonderful restaurant with its wooden parquet flooring, tiled pillars and plush leather seating, as the waiter handed her a wine list and menu then left them alone.

'Not as lovely as you,' said Aaron.

Coming from anyone else the line would have sounded cheesy but from Aaron it added to his charm.

'Thank you,' she said, opening the wine list then staring, wide-eyed, as she saw the prices. 'Oh, my! This is a bit expensive, isn't it?' she asked.

'Yes, but you're worth it,' said Aaron. 'Do you fancy wine?'

'You sure?' asked Maddy, thinking about the expense.

'Course I'm sure. Would you like to choose it, or should I?'

'I'll leave it to you,' she said, not wanting to select anything too pricey.

'OK. Red or white?' he asked.

'Red, please.'

They settled on an Australian Shiraz then turned their attention to the food menu.

'How have things been?' asked Maddy, once the waiter had gone. 'Have you seen any nice houses since the last time we met?'

'No, I've been too busy looking at warehouses,' he replied.

'Where?'

Aaron shuffled in his seat before replying. 'Oh, just in and around Manchester.' Then he seemed to stop and ponder before continuing. 'Actually, I wouldn't mind you coming with me to see what you think. I don't really know anyone in Manchester any more and I miss having someone to give me a second opinion.'

Maddy was flattered that he was already asking for her input. 'I'd love to,' she said. 'Have you found somewhere of interest, then?'

'No, not yet. I meant, when I do, perhaps you would come with me to look.'

'Yes, course I will,' she said, smiling.

They turned their attention to the menu and Maddy gulped again when she saw the prices, although the wine list should have given her an indication of how high they would be.

'Do you fancy a starter?' asked Aaron.

'No, I'd best not,' she said.

'Look, have what you want,' said Aaron, smiling. 'Don't worry about the cost. It's my treat.'

'Are you sure?' asked Maddy.

'There you go again,' said Aaron, sighing in mock exasperation.

He reached out and covered her hand with his own, then gazed intently into her eyes and smiled. 'Course I'm sure. I've told you: have whatever you want. It isn't a problem.'

Maddy noticed the way his lovely smile lit up his face and was alarmed to feel herself blush under his gaze. She felt like a schoolgirl with an unrequited crush, and lowered her head, focusing on the menu to hide her embarrassment.

Once they had finished placing their order she looked at him again. 'Which hotel are you staying at while you're looking for a house?' she asked.

'The Midland.'

'Oh, right,' she replied, thinking of how much it must be costing him to stay at such a luxury, landmark hotel, but taking care not to comment on the price this time. Instead she said, 'Really? I bet it's a bit of a pain living in a hotel, isn't it?'

'It's not too bad. The staff are really attentive and they see to it that I don't want for anything. It's really central as well so it's handy for getting out and about when I'm checking out premises.'

He then shuffled in his seat again before excusing himself to go to the gents. He was gone a while and Maddy was beginning to worry when she saw him returning to the table. She didn't say anything though. As soon as she saw the lovely smile on his face she relaxed again, glad to have him back in her company.

The rest of the evening passed by in a blur. The food was delicious and they got through two bottles of wine followed by cocktails, which Aaron insisted on. They spent so long in the restaurant that it was getting late by the time they finished. Although she was tempted by Aaron's suggestion of continuing the evening elsewhere Maddy insisted on going home as she had work the next day.

'OK,' said Aaron, 'I'll walk you to the taxi and make sure you get home safely.'

The nearest taxi rank Maddy could think of was Albert Square and, although she felt that the restaurant staff would have been happy to order a taxi for her, she fancied the walk outside with Aaron. As they stepped out of the restaurant Aaron took her hand and they chatted amiably while walking hand in hand.

'Well, this is it, then,' she said when they arrived in the square.

He let go of her hand and turned towards her. 'Thanks, Maddy. It's been perfect,' he said.

'Thank you!' said Maddy, smiling.

For a few moments they stood gazing at each other, and Maddy could feel an irresistible pull. They leaned in at the same time, their actions automatic and unforced. Then his mouth met hers and he held her close. His lips felt soft and moist, his embrace comforting as they melted into each other, and a frisson of pure delight rippled through her body.

It was a while before Maddy pulled away, knowing it would be too easy to get carried away, and suddenly conscious of putting on a show in front of the queue of taxi drivers. 'I've got to go,' she said. 'Work tomorrow.' Then she giggled coyly. 'I'll have a terrible headache as it is.'

She saw the look of disappointment on his face and quickly backtracked. 'Oh, but it'll have been worth it,' she added, smiling as she stepped away. 'Thanks again for such a wonderful evening.'

He reluctantly let her go, calling to her as she made her way to the taxi. 'I'll message you.'

'OK. See you soon.'

Maddy got inside the taxi and watched him walk away as she gave the driver her destination. She was thrilled when Aaron looked back and waved. Then she settled back in her seat and felt a warm glow inside her, which lasted until she fell asleep in her own bed at the end of the night.

10

Crystal was just about to walk out of The Rose and Crown when Gilly shouted to her.

'Hang on! I'm coming with you tonight.'

She turned back and smiled at him, the clown-like lipstick giving colour to her pale features. 'Ah, cheers, Gilly,' she said.

They walked out of the pub and turned down one of the dingy backstreets behind Piccadilly. Their surroundings were a depressing sepia image and a sharp contrast to the vibrant shops, bars and restaurants on the main streets, which were a neon, multicoloured billboard of delights for both locals and visitors.

Crystal led the way as they passed industrial-sized bins overflowing with refuse, and the steel back doors of shops, daubed in graffiti and decorated with torn fly posters. Gilly noticed how quickly Crystal made her way through the streets. Anyone would think she was looking forward to it, or was it a chemical high that was driving her? He assumed the latter. After all, it wasn't unusual for street girls to take something before they went to work. It helped give them the courage to get through the night.

Crystal was addicted to heroin and crack. Now in her early twenties, she'd had her first experience of drugs when she was just fourteen. Gilly often paid her in drugs rather than in cash as they were a bigger incentive for her to keep selling her body to the many clients who used her each night.

While he walked behind Crystal, Gilly took in her appearance from the rear. Her skinny, pale legs. The sores on the backs of her feet. The small tear in the back of her leather-look jacket. Her lurid, red hair, which stuck up haphazardly in all directions. And as he made his critical observation, Gilly realised that what he felt for Crystal wasn't just indifference replacing his previous attraction. It was more than that. In Crystal he saw a reflection of his own failure in life and it left him with a bitter resentment.

Gilly didn't try to keep pace with Crystal. He preferred to stay a few steps behind. It was rare to see them walking anywhere together at all, let alone side by side. Normally Gilly only dealt with Crystal in a work capacity or when he needed her to satisfy his own sexual needs. In the case of the latter, they'd usually get a taxi back to her place when they were both high from drink and drugs. It wasn't what Gilly would have termed a relationship, despite what Crystal seemed to think.

Eventually they emerged from the dim back streets and alleyways, and stepped onto the pavement bordering London Road, one of the main routes into the city, dominated by Piccadilly station. Here the crowds jostled for space as they rushed towards the popular bars and restaurants.

Crystal stepped onto the busy road, dodging the buses and cars, whose drivers tooted their horns. For the first time, Gilly rushed to catch up with her, and grabbed her by the arm.

'Steady. You'll get yourself fuckin' killed!' he said.

Crystal didn't say anything; she just looked at Gilly, her dull eyes full of love, and a slight smile of appreciation shaping her lips. He kept a tight hold of her until they had reached Aytoun Street, where the cars and trams competed for prominence. Once he had her safely across the road, Gilly let her go, saying a few words before he did so.

'Don't forget what I told you last time. Any cars that stop, you send them to another girl unless it's him. We're here for one reason and that's to get the bastard who did that to you,' he said, nodding at her face, which still showed some faded bruising round the eye sockets.

As soon as they arrived at Minshull Street, Gilly faded into the shadow of the buildings while Crystal hung about at the roadside along with the other working girls. He lit up a cigarette and prepared to watch till he got a sign from Crystal.

Almost an hour later Gilly was becoming impatient. Car after car had stopped and been urged on by Crystal. The only time that Gilly had almost stepped out of his hiding place was when one of the drivers had hurled abuse at Crystal for refusing to do business, his disappointment evident in the foul words that had streamed from his mouth. But he'd soon moved on when he'd realised he was wasting his time.

It was the third time Gilly had gone with Crystal to search for the man. As Crystal repeatedly turned customers away, and Gilly thought about how much money they were losing, he became annoyed. They weren't only losing out from Crystal's earnings, but he was also having to sub her from his own money to pay for her drugs and other things she needed.

Even before Crystal gave him the sign, Gilly spotted the red Toyota Avensis pulling over. He dashed across the pavement and, while Crystal stepped into the front passenger seat, Gilly jumped into the back. He half expected to see the bald, scrawny man behind the driving wheel again but instead he was rewarded by the sight of a big, dark man.

He couldn't see the man's face from behind but a quick nod from Crystal told him they'd got the right guy. Gilly quickly withdrew the hunting knife that he had secreted inside his hoody, and jabbed it into the back of the man's neck.

'What the fuck's going on?' asked the man, his voice filled with panic.

'Just get fuckin' driving or this knife will be across your throat!' Gilly ordered.

The man put the car clumsily into gear and stepped onto the accelerator. As the Toyota sped away from the pavement, Gilly checked round to make sure no one had seen him with the knife. To his relief, although there were plenty of people around, no one was looking at them. To be on the safe side, Gilly pulled the sleeve of his hoody down till the knife was obscured from view and he sidled up behind the driver so it looked as though he were just giving him directions.

'Where are we going?' asked the driver, his voice now trembling.

Gilly felt a buzz of adrenaline. 'Just keep fuckin' driving till we're out of the city,' he demanded. 'Then I'll tell you where.'

It was a few nights since Aaron had taken Maddy to the Hawksmoor restaurant, and she was on the phone to Clare. As she regaled her friend with details of her last date with Aaron, she was unable to contain her excitement.

'I've seen him twice already and I'm seeing him again on Saturday. I think we might be going back to the Midland.'

'The Midland? You mean the Midland hotel?'

'Yes, that's where he's staying.'

Maddy had also rung Clare after her first date with Aaron and had told her all about him being between homes, but it was the first time she'd mentioned where he was staying.

'Bloody hell! That's a bit expensive, isn't it?' asked Clare.

Maddy could hear the surprise in Clare's voice at the mention of the Midland, a luxury hotel in the heart of the city centre.

'I don't think he's short of money,' said Maddy. 'From what he told me, his business in Yorkshire is doing really well. That's why he's looking to set up another warehouse in Manchester.'

'It sounds like you've landed on your feet,' said Clare. 'But don't let him rush you into anything. He's bound to want you to sleep with him if he takes you back to the hotel.'

'What's wrong with that?' asked Maddy, giggling.

'You've only seen him twice, Maddy. Don't you think it's a bit soon?' asked her friend.

'No. I don't. He's bloody gorgeous, Clare. So why shouldn't I? We're both free agents when all's said and done!' Then her voice took on a dreamy note as she said, 'I think I'll make arrangements for Becky to stay at her dad's on Saturday so I don't have to rush home.'

Clare didn't reply straight away so Maddy filled in the silence. 'It feels right, Clare!'

'OK, well, as long as you know what you're doing. I'm pleased for you, Maddy. It's about time you found some happiness. I just don't want to see a repeat of what happened with Rob, that's all.'

'You won't,' said Maddy. 'He's completely different from him.'

When Maddy eventually finished the call she sat still for a few moments, deep in thought. Clare's comments niggled her a bit. Anyone would think she didn't want her to be happy.

But Clare's words had also sown a seed of doubt in her mind. What if he was too good to be true? Seeking reassurance, she went over their last two dates in her mind. The way he'd acted and the things he'd said brought her to the rapid conclusion that Clare was overreacting. After all, Clare wasn't the one who was seeing him. So how could she possibly be expected to know just how wonderful he was?

Gilly ordered the driver to head towards the Peak District once they were out of the city centre. Throughout the journey the only words they exchanged were when Gilly gave out directions. The driver stayed silent and Gilly could feel his heavy bulk quivering under the blade of the knife, which Gilly kept pointed at the back of his neck all the way there.

As they left the towns bordering the city centre, the area became more remote. After twenty minutes of driving up and down the hilly roads, Gilly spotted a narrow country lane leading off to the right, just as they passed it.

'Turn down there!' he shouted.

The driver slammed on his brakes then reversed before turning into the country lane. It was unlit in the dusk of evening, and lined by trees, which obscured it from the roadway. As they drove along it felt increasingly secluded and after a few minutes Gilly was satisfied that they had reached an ideal spot.

'Pull over in that lay-by up there,' he ordered the driver.

The driver did as instructed and Gilly could sense his trepidation as he took in his isolated surroundings. The man sucked in a deep, shuddering breath as the car drew to a halt, and Gilly knew he was preparing himself for what might follow.

Gilly jumped out of the car and quickly swung the driver's door open. 'Get out!' he demanded, stepping back to give the man space.

He kept the knife pointing at him all the time while the man stepped from the vehicle then straightened up just in front of him. Gilly also carried on watching the man till he felt Crystal's touch as she stood close by his side. In a swift movement Gilly leapt forward and shoved the man aside, throwing him off balance so he could get behind him. Before the man could react, Gilly had one arm round the top of his chest with his other hand holding the blade to his throat.

'Now let's see how *you* enjoy being slapped around,' said Gilly.

'I didn't do anything,' protested the man.

'Don't tell fuckin' lies!' yelled Gilly, pressing the knife down hard till he drew blood. 'How do you think she got those fuckin' marks on her face?' He paused a moment, gaining satisfaction as he felt the man shaking. 'And she was right,' he continued. 'You are a fuckin' ugly bastard. No wonder you have to buy it, mate!'

'I didn't mean any harm. It's just – she wouldn't give me what I wanted. I thought they were supposed to be up for it.'

'Well, you thought fuckin' wrong!' shouted Gilly. 'You get what you fuckin' pay for.'

Crystal aimed a sharp kick at the man's shin and he yelped in pain. 'Yes, you cheeky bastard!' she said. 'It's not a fuckin' free for all. And no girl deserves to be beaten up, no matter what they are.'

Gilly jabbed the knife again. 'I ought to slit your fuckin' throat now. It's what you deserve. But I wanna see you suffer a bit more first. Go on, Crystal, hit him again.'

'He deserves to suffer,' said Crystal, slapping the man across his face.

Gilly wanted to frighten the man and to let him know that he couldn't go round beating his girls up without repercussions. He also intended to take his money. It might go towards recouping some of his losses for what Crystal could have earned while they'd been looking for him.

'Go through his pockets,' he said to Crystal.

She stepped forward again and began to search the outer pockets of his jacket but her hands came out empty. Then Crystal grabbed his lapels, pulling his jacket towards her and trying to get to the inside pockets. Gilly loosened his hold on the man's chest so that Crystal could reach inside. It was then that the man made his move.

He lunged forward, gripping Crystal's throat tightly with both hands.

'Drop the fuckin' knife!' he shouted. 'Or I'll strangle the bitch.'

Gilly took in the alarmed expression on Crystal's face, but he hesitated a moment. Then he saw her eyes bulge as the man tightened his grip on her throat. Gilly knew he had no choice; he had to do something. He might no longer have many feelings for Crystal, but even he had a conscience, and Gilly knew he couldn't let the man strangle her to death.

'All right, all right!' he said, taking the knife away and stepping back.

But the man didn't wait for Gilly's next move. He took his hands from Crystal's throat and gave a mighty shove, launching her across the muddy ground. Then he swung round and charged Gilly with his head bent down. He had his fists held out in front, like the horns of a raging bull.

Gilly heard the man's loud roar, an indomitable war cry, and felt a huge blow as he crashed into him, throwing him off his feet. Then Gilly felt the wind being sucked from his lungs when he landed on his back with the weight of the man on top, crushing him. He instinctively put out his hands to break his fall and as he touched down, the knife flew from his fingers, landing a couple of metres away. Gilly heard the clinking of the metal blade as it hit a stone, then the man started pummelling his face. Gilly tried to fend him off but he was too powerful, and Gilly was still winded.

He couldn't see Crystal. Just a big ugly face and some iron fists hammering at him. The man let up and looked across to see where the knife had landed. Keeping Gilly pinned down, he stretched out his left arm towards the knife but he couldn't reach it.

Regaining some of his breath, Gilly yelled, 'Quick, Crystal. The knife. Get the fuckin' knife!'

Then Gilly saw her, racing towards the knife, but she came too close. The man grabbed her ankle and yanked, felling her once more. Gilly tried to push the man off but he retaliated, trading punches. Each of the man's punches fell harder till Gilly felt stunned. He was losing the fight.

While the man grappled with Gilly, Crystal seized her chance. Still sprawled on the ground, she reached out and grabbed the knife. Then she crawled towards Gilly and thrust it in his hand.

'Quick, get him!' she yelled.

Gilly was becoming dizzier with each painful blow of the man's fists. He knew it was his only chance. Summoning up his last vestiges of energy, he swung the knife back. Then he plunged it deep into the man's throat till the blood spurted out.

Gilly would never forget the look of that man in his dying moments with a myriad of thoughts expressed in his features. Anger. Realisation. Defeat. A brief melodrama played out as Gilly felt the man's blood dripping onto him, and his body slumped, pinning Gilly to the ground once more.

In a panic, Gilly pushed the man away. Then he shot up off the ground and dashed from him. For several seconds he stood staring in shock as the man's life blood seeped out of him. Next to him, Crystal was just as immobile. Then her delayed reaction kicked in and she got up off the ground.

'Oh, my God! I think he's dead. You've fuckin' killed him!' she yelled.

'Shut the fuck up!' shouted Gilly, looking furtively around him. 'Someone might hear you.' Then the tone of his voice changed as he started pleading with Crystal. 'I didn't mean to. I had no fuckin' choice. It was the only way I could get the fucker off me. He would have killed me if I hadn't done it. You know he would.'

Crystal began weeping. 'I can't believe you've killed him.'

'What the fuck did you expect?' said Gilly. 'I couldn't just let him beat me to death, could I? And then what would he have done to you?'

'Oh, my God!' Crystal repeated. 'What are we gonna do?'

Gilly felt on the verge of tears himself. The shock of what he had just done took a hold and he paced frantically round the narrow country lane. Searching for answers. For some way out of the terrifying mess that he'd got himself into.

He could hear the sound of traffic in the distance. 'Right. We need to get him off the road quickly,' he said. 'Before someone finds him. Come on.'

He stepped towards the body and waited for Crystal to join him. But she remained rooted to the spot, staring in terror as the tears tumbled from her eyes.

'Fuckin' move!' howled Gilly. 'I can't shift the big bastard on my own.'

Between them they managed to heave the man's body through a gap in the hedgerow that skirted the narrow lane. 'Over there,' said Gilly, pointing to a clump of bushes nearby.

They continued to drag the body. 'Right, push him in there,' said Gilly, indicating a small space beneath the bushes.

Once they had the body under cover of the bushes Gilly straightened up and got his breath back. Crystal stood facing him and he could tell she was waiting for further instructions. He began pacing again till he stopped at the fallen branch of a tree. He picked it up and dashed back over to where the body lay.

'People will still be able to see him from the road,' he said, plonking the tree branch on top of the man then searching for something else he could use.

He pulled at some shrubbery till it broke loose, then covered the body with that too. 'Come on, fuckin' help me,' he ordered. 'We need to make sure no one can see him.'

With Crystal helping him, they soon had the body camouflaged. Then Gilly picked up another tree branch, rushed out to the lane and used the leafy end of it to brush over the blood on the dusty ground till it was covered with dirt. He walked back to where the body lay and slung the branch on top of the others. Then he turned to Crystal, who had remained near to the body.

'Not a fuckin' word to anyone about this,' he warned. 'Don't forget, I did it for you!'

Crystal just stared back at him, her eyes still misty. But she didn't speak.

'We'll have to come back tonight and bury him properly,' said Gilly. 'We can't risk anyone finding him. And we need to take the knife as well so I can get rid of it. It'll be covered in fingerprints.'

Crystal nodded and they made their way back to the man's car, Gilly jumping in the driving seat. 'We'll dump the car before we get back to town,' he said. 'We'll go the rest of the way by taxi. Then we can pick my car up and come back here.'

He was just about to start the engine when a thought occurred to him. 'Have you got a handkerchief or anything with you?' he asked.

'No. Why?'

'We'll have to mark the spot so we can find it when we come back. It all looks the fuckin' same otherwise.'

Crystal rummaged through her handbag but the only thing she could find was a sweet wrapper. She stepped out of the car and hooked it onto a small branch sticking out of a tree trunk.

'It'll have to do,' said Gilly. 'But take a good look around before we set off. We need to make sure we can find it.'

Gilly didn't wait for her reply. Instead he started the engine and turned the car round before setting off back down the country lane.

12

They remained quiet for most of the journey back to Manchester until Crystal said, 'Gilly, why are we doing this? Couldn't we just report it to the police?'

'Are you fuckin' stupid?' he snapped. 'How will we explain what we were doing bringing him here? Not to mention the fact that I was carrying a fuckin' hunting knife. Besides, who's gonna believe us? We've both got a fuckin' criminal record, haven't we?'

'Sorry,' said Crystal. 'I didn't think.'

'You don't say!' he snapped sarcastically. 'This is the only way so let's just get it done with.'

It was dark by the time they returned to the country lane with two spades and other gardening tools in the boot of Gilly's car. Gilly had borrowed them from a friend who knew not to ask questions. At first they passed the place where Gilly had killed the man but when they'd doubled back more slowly Crystal recognised the spot. It wasn't the sweet wrapper that gave it away but the brush strokes in the dusty lane picked up by the car's headlights.

'Right, you can do a better job of covering that blood up while I start digging a hole,' said Gilly.

'How?'

Gilly handed her a rake from his car. 'Rake it over more evenly then stamp it down,' he said. He looked at her plastic, high-heeled shoes with distaste. 'You'll have to use a spade to flatten it down. And make sure no fuckin' blood shows through.'

He left Crystal working on the lane while he went in search of the body secreted under the bushes. When he'd found the gap and saw the shape of the body, covered over with tree branches and shrubbery, he began digging close by.

He felt a tug of repulsion at what he'd done but fought to control it, immersing himself in the arduous task of digging a hole long and deep enough to bury the man. While he dug he tried to take his mind off what had happened, but he couldn't hide from his thoughts.

With every thrust of the spade he was reliving what he had done. That earth-shattering act of plunging the knife deep into the man's neck. The look on his victim's face. And that sickening moment when he realised he'd killed him.

In the past few years Gilly had done a lot of bad things. Most of them he wasn't proud of. But he'd never killed a man before. Not until tonight. He would always have the man's death on his conscience. So would Crystal. Even though Gilly knew he hadn't done it intentionally, he still felt an overwhelming sense of guilt. And Crystal would always act as a reminder of that guilt.

By the time Gilly and Crystal reached The Rose and Crown Gilly was mentally and physically exhausted. The landlord had already called last orders but Gilly was a regular and he and his girls brought a lot of custom his way. An unspoken acknowledgement passed between Gilly and the landlord as he ordered his drinks, confident the landlord would serve him for as long as he wanted.

He and Crystal had nipped home on the way there to clean themselves up. They didn't want to arouse suspicion but Gilly still didn't feel clean. He probably never would again.

As he stood at the bar Gilly noticed a familiar face and nodded at him. After plonking the drinks on the table where Crystal was sitting, he went through to the gents knowing that the man would be there waiting for him.

It was his supplier. Tall and slim, he was similar in appearance to Gilly but much more smartly dressed and well groomed.

'You all right, Gilly?' he asked.

'Yeah, sure. Just a bit knackered, that's all.'

'Do you want the usual?'

'Yeah, but double up on it.'

'You sure?'

'Yeah, course.'

They made the exchange and returned to the bar. It didn't pay to hang around and risk getting caught out. Even pubs like The Rose and Crown didn't condone the dealing or use of class A drugs.

Gilly didn't stay in the pub long. He was keen to get back home and administer something stronger to himself than alcohol. Tonight he needed hard drugs. It was the only way he could think of to block out what had happened that evening.

'You not coming back to mine, Gilly?' Crystal asked.

'No, not tonight,' said Gilly. 'I need to be on my own.'

Although Crystal just shrugged in response, it was obvious she knew what he meant. Gilly had warned Crystal that they had to pretend the killing had never happened. It was the best way. But although Gilly tried to brush it aside, after that night things would never be the same again.

13

Maddy gazed at the grand red-brick baroque-style building. Above her, ornate gold lettering spelt out the words, Midland Hotel, which were back-lit, making the gold shimmer in the darkness of late evening. She climbed the granite steps, passing under one of the huge, impressive archways before going through the revolving doors and into the splendour of the hotel's interior.

She'd always liked the look of the Midland hotel but until tonight she had never stepped inside it. Although Maddy had occasionally visited luxury hotels on business with her ex-husband, the Midland still couldn't fail to impress. It was a prime example of early twentieth century grandeur.

Maddy tried to remain nonchalant as she took in the wonderful marble-tiled lobby with its magnificent pillars, subtle lighting and sumptuous fixtures. Upstairs, the bedroom didn't fail to impress either. Everything about it spelt quality from the artistic arrangement and plush furnishings to the tasteful colour scheme, but Maddy didn't spend too long scrutinising the bedroom. She had other things on her mind.

She looked at the man who had entered the room with her: another thing of beauty. Aaron, the six-foot, slim, handsome demigod who had swept her off her feet ever since she had met him. And her eyes were filled with desire.

After hanging the Do Not Disturb sign outside the door and turning the inside lock, Aaron crossed the room. 'Welcome to my temporary home,' he said, smiling warmly as he stepped up to the table where there were a bottle of champagne on ice and two champagne flutes, which he'd had sent up to the room.

He filled both the champagne flutes and handed one to Maddy. 'To us,' he said, clinking his glass against Maddy's then raising it to his lips and taking a long sip.

Aaron quickly downed his full glass and then waited for Maddy to finish too. Once she had emptied her glass and placed it on the table Aaron took her into his arms. They embraced passionately, their kiss deep and lingering, and Maddy could feel herself melting into him, the rest of the champagne suddenly forgotten.

Aaron broke away from their kiss, his hands gently resting on her waist as he spoke to her. 'Should we get our clothes off?' he asked.

His touch felt like electricity zipping through her body and firing her up till her nerve endings tingled. Maddy responded by undoing the buttons on her blouse then unzipping her jeans and dropping them to the floor. Within no time they had both undressed. Aaron held her at arm's length while he gazed longingly at her naked body.

'You're just as beautiful as I imagined,' he said, his voice cracking with emotion.

Maddy felt a delicate shiver as his eyes travelled up and down her body. Then he took her in his arms again and they kissed once more. She felt herself being led gently to the bed, her body responding in a dreamlike state. They lay down, their bodies folding naturally into each other, as though they were meant to fit.

Her heightened senses responded to his loving touch, and they kissed till she felt giddy. When his hands brushed her erect nipples Maddy felt an irresistible thrill. It shot through her body, tickling inside her stomach till it reached her genitals. She almost cried out for more till his fingers found her clitoris and Maddy thought she would explode with pure joy.

She climaxed even before he entered her, the intense pleasure sending huge spasms of delight right through her body, down to her toes and up to the top of her head. Then he skilfully guided his penis inside her and she let out an ecstatic squeal. But he was a skilled lover who kept her hovering on the brink of her second orgasm till she thought she could wait no more.

They carried on making love until they eventually fell asleep. After a few hours Maddy woke up to go to the bathroom and she was surprised to see Aaron sitting up in bed.

'What's wrong?' she asked, gently stroking his arm.

His body seemed to tense under her touch, and she gazed at him quizzically.

'Nothing,' he snapped, but then he seemed to correct himself as he put on a smile and said, 'I just couldn't sleep, that's all.'

'Aw, you seem really tense,' said Maddy.

'No, I'm fine. Honestly. I suppose I've just got a lot on with the business and house-hunting and what have you.'

'I can help you with your house-hunting if you like,' she said. 'I could—'

'No, no. It's OK,' he replied, quickly. 'I need to concentrate on the business first. Don't worry, I'll be fine. It'll all work out.'

He smiled again but the smile seemed forced. Maddy was concerned but she didn't know what else to say that would be of help, so she left him while she went to the bathroom.

When she came back Aaron was lying on the bed. Maddy snuggled into him and started to nod off. She was almost asleep when she felt him move and then heard his feet touch down onto the floor and his footsteps pattering across the room. The last thing she heard was the bathroom door swinging open before she went back to sleep.

When Maddy awoke Aaron seemed much more relaxed. He had already showered and switched on the kettle in the room.

'Would you like a coffee?' he asked, walking across to the dresser wearing only his boxer shorts.

'There's something else I'd like first,' said Maddy, patting the bed beside her as she eyed him appreciatively.

Aaron didn't disappoint her and for over an hour they carried on making love.

Once Maddy was showered and dressed they sat contentedly drinking coffee and eating biscuits from the tea tray.

'I suppose we'd best get you home,' he said.

'Yes, I've got work to do, I'm afraid,' said Maddy.

'What, on a Sunday?' he asked.

'Yes, I'm afraid so. I have to make the most of the time when Becky's at her dad's. And I suppose you'll have a busy day ahead too, what with the business and the house-hunting.'

'You're right there,' he said. 'Erm... Maddy, I forgot to tell you last night, we were so busy talking about other things. I'm afraid my car is in the garage at the moment so I won't be able to drive you back. Do you mind getting a taxi? I'll give you the money for it.'

'No, you won't,' she said. 'You already paid for a meal and drinks last night. Don't worry, I'll get the taxi. It's a shame though. I was looking forward to seeing your Porsche.'

'Ah, well. Never mind. Maybe next time,' he said.

'Nothing major, I hope.'

'What?' he asked.

'Your car. I hope there's nothing major wrong with it.'

'No. Well, I'm not sure yet. It depends what the guy at the garage has to say when I ring him later.'

'OK, well, good luck with it,' she said.

'Thanks.'

'Aaron, before I go, I wondered if you'd like to come back to mine next time. We'll probably arrange it for when Becky's at her dad's the first time, but you'll soon get to meet her.'

Aaron smiled. 'I'd love to,' he said. 'Now, come on, let's get you that taxi otherwise neither of us will get anything done today.'

He walked her down to the hotel lobby, then waited with her until her taxi arrived.

'Bye, see you soon,' she said, giving Aaron a last kiss before she got inside the cab.

All the way home Maddy was on a high. She'd just spent the most wonderful night with the man of her dreams and for the first time in ages she felt deliriously happy.

Aaron stood and watched as the taxi pulled away. He waved until it disappeared from view, then he doubled back to the hotel and strode up to the reception desk.

'I'd like to check out, please,' he said to the receptionist.

'Was everything all right with your room, sir?' the over-eager receptionist asked.

'Yes, it was fine. In fact, will I be able to book the same room for the weekend after next?'

'I'll just check, sir,' said the receptionist, looking at her computer screen and clicking the mouse in front of her. 'Yes, it's still available at the moment,' she said. 'What nights would you like to book?'

'I'm not sure yet.'

'OK. Well, I'd better warn you that our rooms get booked up very quickly so if you would like to stay in the same room it would be best to book as soon as possible.'

'Thanks for the heads up. I'm not sure what my arrangements are yet but I'll ring and book as soon as I know.'

14

It was two days later when Maddy met Clare in The Bank, a city-centre gastro pub, which had been converted from a nineteenth century bank building. She was running late and by the time she arrived Clare's wine glass was already half empty.

'So sorry, Clare. Today has been a mad rush,' said Maddy. 'Would you like another drink?'

'Don't worry about it. I've been admiring the view,' she said, smiling at two men on a nearby table. 'But yes, I'd love another glass of wine.'

Maddy glanced over to the table. 'Not my type,' she said. 'Anyway, I'm a bit busy at the moment.'

Clare laughed. 'Yes, I noticed lover boy's been keeping you busy. I thought you'd never find room in your schedule for me.'

'Aw, I'm so sorry, Clare,' said Maddy, her face full of concern.

'I'm only winding you up, you daft mare. I'm pleased for you.'

Maddy smiled. 'I can't wait to tell you all about him,' she said. 'Let me get the drinks first. I'll be back in a tick.'

Maddy was soon back from the bar carrying two glasses of red and she began telling Clare all about Aaron even before she'd sat down.

'Aw, Clare. He's so lovely. I can't believe my luck. He treats me so nicely. And as for the sex…'

'Yes, you have mentioned that once or twice on the phone,' said Clare, laughing. 'I take it that it's good, then.'

'The best. I've never known anything like it! He's so-o-o-o-o good.'

'You lucky bugger,' said Clare, her eyes drifting over to the men on the nearby table. Maddy followed her friend's gaze and noticed that the men were getting up to leave.

'Damn! Just my luck,' said Clare.

'Never mind,' Maddy said. 'There'll be others.' Then, switching her attention away from the men, she continued talking about Aaron. 'We had a lovely time at the Midland but I'm taking him to mine next time I see him. I'm arranging it for when Becky isn't there. I'm not quite ready for her to meet him yet.'

'What's the Midland like? I've never been inside.'

'Absolutely stunning! I can't believe I've never been before. We should go there for lunch some time. Or even afternoon tea.'

'Sounds great. We'll have to arrange it. Anyway, tell me more about your new man. Have you been out in his Porsche yet?'

'No. Well, we've usually had a drink so we've caught taxis.'

'What about when you stayed at the Midland? Did he not drive you back home?'

'No, his car was in the garage. In fact, you've just reminded me, I meant to ask him if he'd managed to get it fixed.'

'Maybe you'll get to ride in it next time you see him,' said Clare.

'Oh, I hope so,' said Maddy. As she spoke she noticed Clare's eyes wandering around the pub. She laughed. 'Will you behave?' she said, knowing that Clare was on the lookout for men.

Clare switched her attention back to Maddy. 'When are you going to meet his family?' she asked.

'Oh, it's early days. I want to introduce him to Becky first.'

'Don't you think it would be better to meet his family and friends before you introduce him to Becky?' asked Clare.

'Why?'

'Well, she's just a child, isn't she? It might be best finding out a bit more about him before she meets him.'

'What are you trying to say, Clare?' asked Maddy.

'Nothing but… well, it's like you say, it's early days yet and you don't really know him.'

'His family and friends are all in Yorkshire so surely it makes sense to introduce him to mine first?'

'Yeah, if that's what you want. It's your decision, Maddy.'

Maddy paused for a moment, chewing things over in her mind. It was as though Clare didn't trust him. 'I can't understand what you've got against him,' she said.

'Nothing. I don't even know him. I'm just looking out for you, that's all.'

'Well, I'm more than capable of looking out for myself, thank you very much.'

'Steady, no need to get tetchy,' said Clare. 'I didn't mean any harm.'

'It just seems that every time I mention Aaron you're picking fault with him. Why?'

'It isn't deliberate, Maddy. I just don't want you getting hurt again, that's all.'

Maddy didn't say anything further on the subject. There was no point getting into a row about it even though Clare had offended her. For the rest of the night she tried to put Clare's words out of her mind and carry on as normal.

But Clare's words had stung, and when they reached the end of the night and both went their separate ways, Maddy began to dwell on the warning once more. The way Clare tried to put Aaron down at every opportunity, anyone would think she was jealous. Maybe it was because she wasn't having much luck with men herself, thought Maddy. She decided to try and put it out of her mind and not let it bother her. After all, Aaron had been the perfect boyfriend up to now and he hadn't given her any reason to doubt him.

Crystal had stopped by The Rose and Crown to give Gilly her wages. She found him standing at the bar talking to two of the regulars.

'All right?' he asked as Crystal sidled up to him.

'Yeah, I've brought back that money you lent me,' she said.

Gilly held out his hand, keeping up the pretence of a debt repaid and then pocketing her earnings from the previous night. He turned back to the two men standing next to him, but Crystal didn't leave the pub. Instead she hung on, waiting for Gilly to give her some attention.

Eventually Gilly turned back round, his eyes locking with hers. 'What d'you want?' he asked.

'I thought we might have a drink together,' said Crystal, pouting.

Gilly sighed, withdrew some cash from his pocket and called the barmaid over. He bought Crystal half a lager and stuck the glass in front of her. 'That's all you're getting. Can't you see I'm busy?'

Crystal took the proffered drink gratefully. For her it was a small triumph. She didn't get much attention from Gilly these days so she made the most of any minor offering. She never stopped to think about why she put up with his behaviour. Her mind was too focused on trying to get their relationship back on track.

Gilly had never been really respectful to Crystal, but he had given her attention, affection and protection, and for Crystal that had been enough. Being Gilly's woman had elevated her status amongst the rest of the girls, and made her feel special. But now things had changed between them.

For a few minutes Crystal stood next to him at the bar, drinking her drink while he chatted with the other customers. Suddenly all conversation stopped. Gilly looked up at the TV screen at the end of the bar. His two companions also stared at the television.

There was an item on the news that had caught their interest. The report was of a missing man. A Mr Tim O'Brien, aged forty-two, described as tall and well built with dark hair. He had been reported missing by one of his neighbours from the house where he lived in Burnage. The report stated that his car, a red Toyota Avensis, had been found abandoned and burnt out in Ardwick.

Crystal watched in shock as his photograph appeared on the screen, a small gasp escaping from her mouth. It was the man Gilly had killed. He flashed her a warning look and she kept quiet while the report went on to detail when Tim O'Brien was last seen and by whom.

'Jesus Christ! You never know the fuckin' minute, do you?' said one of the customers standing next to Gilly. 'He only lived a few streets from me.'

Other customers began to give their input, drowning out the rest of the news. While they chatted, Gilly turned to Crystal. 'Come on. Let's sit down over there,' he said.

He chose a table well away from the regulars and Crystal knew why. 'Not a fuckin' word about this to anyone,' he hissed. 'As far as they're concerned, this is the first you've fuckin' heard about it.'

'I know,' replied Crystal. 'You've already said. You don't think I'm gonna go spouting off now just because it's on the news, do you?' she asked, affronted.

'Shush,' he warned. 'Keep your fuckin' voice down.'

'All right, all right!'

'Look, this report is only telling us that he's missing. As far as we know the police don't know fuck all else. So, unless they find his body or some other evidence, we're home and dry. You just need to stay calm and not fuckin' blab to anyone. And I mean *anyone*, Crystal.'

'All right! How many times do I have to tell you? I'm not gonna say anything. Otherwise I'd be in the shit just as much as you.'

Crystal gazed at the glass in front of her, which was almost empty. 'We having another, or what?' she asked.

'No, not for me,' he said, standing up and pushing his chair back. 'I'm off.' He took a five-pound note from his wallet and flung it on the table. 'Here, you have another if you want but I'm going. And don't get too pissed. Don't forget, you're working later.'

'Why won't you stay, Gilly? What's wrong?'

'What the fuck d'you think's wrong?' he asked.

Crystal didn't reply. Instead she responded with another question. 'Do you want me to come round to yours later?'

'No!'

He turned away from her and shouted his goodbyes to the regulars just before he went through the door. Then he was gone, leaving Crystal feeling dejected. She grabbed herself another drink but didn't stay at the bar chatting. Instead she sat at the same table, alone, going over everything in her head.

There was no doubt in her mind that Gilly had changed towards her since the night of the killing, maybe even before that. Anyone would think the man's death was her fault, the way Gilly carried on. He rarely came back to hers nowadays, or invited her to stay at his place.

His attitude was worse than ever too, as though he couldn't stand the sight of her. Maybe she reminded him too much of what he had done and he couldn't bear the guilt. And today, when that reminder had been reinforced by the news item, it had seemed too much for him to handle.

And another thing. He seemed to spend a lot of time elsewhere. Before, even when he hadn't stayed with her, she'd generally had a good idea of where he was. He'd be in The Rose and Crown, occasionally straying to another nearby pub. Otherwise, he'd be hanging out in the red-light district keeping an eye on things.

But lately, she had no idea where he got to whenever he disappeared. Perhaps he had taken up with one of the other girls. Maybe Ruby or Amber or one of the others. Crystal went through each of the girls in her mind, weighing up their relative merits and potential appeal to Gilly. She wasn't sure which of them it could be. But, one thing was for sure, if she ever found out, they'd have her to answer to.

As she sat there drinking alone Crystal decided that she would start keeping a closer eye on things where Gilly was concerned. He was her man and she was damned if she was going to let anyone else have him! She vowed to herself that, one way or another, she would find out just what he got up to when he wasn't with her.

15

Maddy took one last look at her dining table, which she had laid for two people with her best china and lead-crystal glasses. In the centre was a food warmer filled with tantalising dishes. She'd cooked Chinese, one of her favourite meals and something she had cooked on many previous occasions, so she knew it would be good. Next to the food warmer stood a bottle of red on a decorative chrome trivet, opened and breathing ready for the arrival of her special guest, Aaron.

As Aaron was still without a car she'd offered him a lift but he had turned it down, insisting he could get a taxi. She was glad in a way because it had given her time to prepare the meal and make sure everything was just right.

After Aaron had given her such a fabulous night on the occasions when she had seen him, she really wanted everything to be perfect. She gazed at her watch for the zillionth time and realised that the rice should be just about ready by now. But before she had chance to check on it, she heard the doorbell ring. That would be him.

Maddy pulled off her apron, revealing a fetching, low-cut top, and dashed to answer the door, the flutter of excitement already making her insides quiver. It was so wonderful to see him standing on her doorstep, looking just as handsome as she remembered and clutching a bottle of red. A smile lit up her face as she thought yet again just how lucky she was.

He smiled back at her and planted a chaste kiss on her lips. She smiled again, knowing he was saving his more passionate kisses for later. He then leant back and his eyes glanced over her appreciatively. 'You're looking just as lovely as ever,' he said. 'And bloody irresistible too.'

'Thank you. You're not so bad yourself,' she quipped, before stepping aside so that he could enter.

As soon as she shut the door he reached out for her but she held him back. 'Just give me a minute,' she said, making her way towards the kitchen. 'I just need to see to the rice before it's ruined. Follow me.'

Once they were inside the kitchen she tended to the rice while Aaron stood and glanced round the kitchen and through to the dining room.

'If you want to sit at the table, I'll be with you in a few seconds,' said Maddy. 'You can pour the wine,' she shouted after his retreating back.

She walked into the dining room to find Aaron looking round the room, two full wine glasses standing on the table in front of him.

'Oh, thanks for pouring the wine,' said Maddy and Aaron's attention immediately switched to her.

She proudly showed off the food that she had prepared, naming each dish as she opened the lids of the food warmer.

'That all sounds delicious,' said Aaron. 'You didn't need to go to so much trouble, y'know. I'd have been happy just to spend the evening with you. All this is just a bonus,' he added, his eyes taking in the food and tasteful crockery and glassware laid out on the table.

'It's the least I could do after that lovely meal you took me for,' said Maddy. 'Enjoy.'

They spent the next half-hour tucking into the delicious meal Maddy had prepared. First they had mixed starters of prawn toast, wontons, spring rolls, chicken wings and crispy seaweed. Then she cleared away the plates and brought out fresh plates ready for them to eat the main course.

As she tidied up Maddy noticed that Aaron hadn't eaten much of the starters and she scraped away the food that remained on his plate. He had drunk a lot of wine though and she wondered if his lack of appetite was because of the sexual tension that hung between them.

She went back into the dining room and Aaron stood up to meet her, taking her into his arms before she had chance to sit down and start on the main course. For a while she responded to his passionate embrace and deep kisses but then she pulled away, giggling like a schoolgirl.

'Come on, cheeky,' she said. 'There'll be plenty of time for that later.'

They sat down at the table; helping themselves to food, but Aaron seemed to toy with his and each time she looked up from her plate his eyes were upon her.

'Aren't you having anything to eat?' she asked.

He smiled. 'I'm not hungry. Not for food anyway. But it's delicious. You were already winning my heart but your cookery skills have just sealed the deal.'

She paused under his intense scrutiny. 'You carry on,' he said. 'Don't let me stop you.'

Maddy's eyes dropped back to her plate and for a while she tried to concentrate on her food, but it was difficult when she was constantly aware of Aaron's amorous gaze.

She giggled again. 'I can't bloody concentrate with you staring at me.'

'Sorry,' said Aaron, sitting up straight and looking around him in an exaggerated manner, an affectionate smirk playing across his lips.

Eventually his eyes settled back on her and they both broke into gales of laughter.

'Are you going to have something to eat?' she asked, smiling.

'No. I told you, I'm not hungry.'

'Well, stop watching me and let me eat mine, then,' she said, laughing.

'It's your own fault,' he said. 'You shouldn't be so ravishing.'

In the end she gave up trying. 'Come on,' she said. 'Let's go through to the living room. We can watch a film and take the wine with us.' As she got up from her seat her eyes took in the discarded food on the table. 'I'll clear this lot up in the morning.' She picked up the bottle of wine from the table, saying, 'Can you get the glasses?'

But the film, like the meal, was left neglected. As soon as they sat down on the sofa Aaron showered her with attention and Maddy felt herself responding to his passionate kisses and gentle embrace. Before long their clothes also lay discarded on the living-room floor and they were making love on the sofa.

'Should we continue this upstairs?' said Aaron as she lay against him, still tingling from the after effects of their lovemaking.

Maddy didn't say a word. Instead she got up from the sofa, took hold of Aaron's hand and led him upstairs to the bedroom, ready for another night of passionate lovemaking with her delectable younger lover. She had only known him for a relatively short period of time but already she could feel herself steadily being pulled towards him.

16

'Aw, I'm so sorry I couldn't give you a lift,' said Maddy the next day as she and Aaron embraced on her doorstep, 'but I've got so much to do before Andy comes back with Becky.'

'Don't worry about it,' said Aaron, running his fingers affectionately along her neck then down to her chest, skirting the tops of her breasts and making her tremble. 'I'll be OK getting the bus.'

'It's ironic really, isn't it, you having to get the bus when you consider what you drive?' she said.

Aaron stared blankly at her until she continued.

'You know, the Porsche?'

Aaron quickly recovered. 'Oh, that. Don't remind me!'

'Yes, it's a shame they found so many things wrong with it.'

'I know. I'm more than a bit gutted but it's not worth spending the money when there are so many parts that want replacing. So, until I get another car, it's public transport and taxis for me.'

'What will you buy?' she asked.

'Don't know yet. Depends what I see. But I might give the performance cars a miss. They're too much bloody trouble.'

'Don't blame you,' she said, reluctantly pulling away from him. 'Anyway, much as I'd love you to stay a bit longer, this isn't getting me any further forward.'

He smiled deliciously and planted another kiss on her lips before he went on his way. Behind the closed door Maddy hugged herself and grinned. She was deliriously happy.

But she was also a bit suspicious. She didn't buy his story about the Porsche and suspected he'd never even driven one. Fancy telling her that just to impress her! As if it mattered to her what car he drove. She should have told him to come in his car next time and that it didn't matter to her what it was. But perhaps that would only embarrass him and make him feel foolish about his white lie.

As far as Maddy was concerned, cars weren't that important; they just got you from A to B. The way Aaron behaved towards her was much more important. And he had been so wonderful, caring and attentive. Besides, it wasn't as if he didn't have any money; he wouldn't have been able to afford to stay at the Midland otherwise. Maybe he felt it was expected of him to have all the trappings that went with his success.

Maddy was getting so attached to Aaron that she didn't want to acknowledge any negatives, so she buried all thoughts of his car and carried on dreaming about a perfect life with her perfect man. She knew she didn't have time to dwell on it anyway. She had work that needed her urgent attention so she forced herself to her desk and switched on her PC.

It was two hours before Maddy allowed herself a tea break. She had been furiously tapping at the keyboard, trying to finish an article that was due in first thing the next day. Maddy knew it wasn't her best work. It was too rushed for that. She should have sent Aaron on his way first thing instead of waiting till way past lunchtime. But she hadn't done; the man was addictive!

Maddy was also tired after another night of passionate lovemaking, and a bit hungover. She really could have done without having to finish this article, but she had no choice and now it was just a matter of getting it done as soon as possible as far as she was concerned.

Hoping her brain might benefit from a five-minute break, Maddy had a walk round the house, stopping to gaze through the living-room window. Aware that the day was marching on, she hoped to God that Andy wouldn't return early with Rebecca. Not having seen her daughter for two days, she couldn't very well ignore her once she came home.

While Maddy was looking out of the window she noticed a car parked on the other side of the road. It was a blue Astra, an older model by the looks of it. Maddy thought no further about it and went back to her work.

An hour later and Maddy took another break. She was so tired that her concentration was waning. Maddy was also aware that time was marching on and she was still nowhere near finishing her article. It was now five o'clock and she would soon have to start cooking as she'd received a text from Andy to say he'd get Rebecca back for teatime.

Maddy looked out of the living-room window again, relieved that there was no sign of Andy yet. But then something else caught her eye. There was that car again; the blue Astra, parked across the road. And there was somebody sitting in it. She didn't recognise it as belonging to any of her neighbours and it seemed strange that the driver would have been sitting there all that time. Unless he'd gone away and come back again.

Curious, Maddy peered inside the car but she couldn't see much from her place at the window. The car was parked facing the wrong way, with the driver's seat on the opposite side of the car, so it was difficult to tell whether it was a man or a woman driver. Whoever it was, they were wearing a baseball cap and had their jacket collar pulled high. At least, it looked like a jacket from where she was standing but it could have been a hoody.

For a few seconds Maddy hovered at the window, puzzled as to why the car was parked there all that time but unsure what to do. The driver glanced in her direction, only momentarily. It was a man, she thought. But it was difficult to tell. Whoever it was, they only turned their head for a minute, then drove off.

Relieved, Maddy went back to her desk, hoping to get some more work done before her daughter returned home. She'd just have to grab them a quick tea and then finish the article once Rebecca was in bed.

Gilly was parked outside Maddy's home, waiting to catch a glimpse of her. It seemed ages before he saw her at the window and then she was only there for a moment before she disappeared again. He looked once more at the immaculate house and as he did so his mind drifted.

He thought with bitterness about the life he could have had if he had carried on along his chosen pathway. It had all been mapped out for him. From a good school in an affluent middle-class area and on to university, then a junior position with a reputable company before working his way up the career ladder.

But he'd blown it after he'd been caught selling dope in his university halls of residence. The university had thrown him out and his parents had subsequently disowned him. He'd tried to tell them it was only a minor drug, but they wouldn't listen. As far as they were concerned he'd brought shame on the family and that was that.

Since then he'd been looking after himself and making a living whatever way he could, and now all he could do was dream about the life he could have had. The sort of life Maddy had. Part of him was enamoured with her; another part resentful. But all was not lost. He'd find a way to get what Maddy had. It was just a matter of time. He'd not quite worked out what his plan was yet, but he'd think of something. In the meantime he would continue to watch Maddy and find out as much about her as he could.

While he sat there daydreaming he eventually saw Maddy at the window again and this time she stayed there for a while. Curious, he turned to face her. Shit! She'd spotted him. He quickly turned away again, hoping she hadn't seen too much of his face.

But it was only a moment's view, with his baseball hat and the top of his hoody obscuring a lot of his face. Nevertheless, he was taking no chances. He started the engine and put the car into gear. Then he was gone. He'd come back another day and hope she didn't catch sight of him this time.

17

Gilly and Crystal were both in The Rose and Crown, but Gilly wasn't with Crystal. He was currently chatting to another of the girls, Amber, at the bar while Crystal sat and watched from a table a few metres away. A couple of the other girls were sitting with Crystal, having a few drinks and a chat before they went to work, but Crystal wasn't really listening to Ruby and Angie, an older prostitute, as they discussed their latest clients. She was too busy watching what was going on at the bar, and she was becoming increasingly annoyed.

She saw Gilly speak to the barmaid. While the barmaid went to fetch drinks, Gilly turned to Amber and said something and Amber giggled in response. Then the barmaid returned with two drinks and Gilly paid for them. He put one of the drinks down in front of Amber. It was a short, golden-coloured, possibly a whisky or a brandy with soda. Gilly's drink was also golden-coloured but darker; he was drinking it straight.

Crystal looked down at her own glass of lager, which was almost empty. The bastard had only bought her one drink since she'd come in over half an hour ago. She'd been trying to make it last, knowing she was short of cash but wary of asking him for more. But now, as she watched him with Amber, her anger was making her bold. She decided she would go to the bar as soon as she had emptied her glass, and ask Gilly to buy her a drink.

'Are you fuckin' listening?' asked Ruby, catching Crystal's attention. 'Or are you too busy watching them?'

'What? Yes,' said Crystal, looking at Ruby, although she hadn't heard a thing she had said.

For the next ten minutes Crystal joined in the conversation with Ruby and Angie. She didn't want to upset Ruby. Nobody upset Ruby if they knew what was good for them. She had a vile temper and took offence at next to nothing, and you never knew just when she was going to turn on you.

Having the excuse of an empty glass, Crystal was just about to get up and go to the bar when she saw Gilly down the remainder of his short and leave the pub, tapping Amber affectionately on the back before he went. Crystal got up from her seat and rushed out of the pub after him. Sod Ruby! Gilly was off somewhere again and she wanted to find out where.

Crystal was outside the pub just in time to see Gilly getting into his car. She shouted his name but he either didn't hear or he chose to ignore her. Unperturbed, Crystal dashed out into the road. A car swerved to avoid her and she heard the driver hurling abuse. It slowed her down though and by the time she was out of the way of the car, she saw Gilly driving off. She chased after him but it was too late. The car was too fast and he was soon well away.

Crystal stood outside the pub for a few moments, confused. There was no doubt in her mind that Gilly was up to something, but she couldn't understand what. She still had an inkling that Gilly was playing around with one of the other girls, and the way he had acted with Amber made her even more suspicious. What she didn't get was why he was going off elsewhere. Unless that was for her benefit and he had secretly arranged to meet Amber later.

With that thought in mind, Crystal went back into the pub in a rage. By this time Amber had moved from the bar and was sitting with the other girls having a laugh. Crystal was so angry that she was determined to tackle Amber whether Ruby was there or not.

'Just what the fuck do you think you're playing at, Amber?' she demanded.

All the girls stopped talking and looked up at her.

'What you on about?' said Amber.

'You and Gilly. I'm not stupid! I saw what you were like with him. Going to yours later, is he?'

'No!' said Amber, with attitude.

'Don't tell fuckin' lies!' said Crystal. 'I saw what you were like with him. Shoving your fuckin' tits in his face.'

'Bollocks!' said Amber. 'You're just fuckin' jealous cos you're not his favourite any more.'

'I fuckin' am,' said Crystal. 'He's still my bloke so you can keep your fuckin' mitts off.'

As she issued her warning, Crystal waved her fist in Amber's face. Amber quickly pulled her head back. Then

Ruby got up and stood between them, her tall frame dominating Crystal's personal space.

'Back off, Crystal,' she warned. 'You don't fuckin' own him! If he ain't interested in you any more then he ain't fuckin' interested. Right?'

Crystal knew better than to pick a fight with Ruby so, despite her anger, she lowered her fist and stepped back.

'I'm going to work,' she said, turning away from the girls.

As she walked out of the pub Crystal was seething with anger. It was bad enough that Amber had flirted blatantly with Gilly in front of her, but to have Ruby turning on her was just too much. Crystal was gutted about Gilly. She knew she was losing him and it seemed as if there wasn't a damn thing she could do about it.

But she wasn't giving up without a fight. As she made the short trip on foot to Minshull Street, Crystal went over everything in her head. He was still seeing her, but his visits were becoming less frequent. Did that mean he was seeing someone else as well? He was certainly flirting enough with Amber. But if he was seeing Amber then where did he keep disappearing to in his car? It just didn't stack up.

Deep down she knew that he'd changed towards her ever since he'd killed the man that had abused her. But why was that her fault? She hadn't asked him to drive the man out to the country and then threaten him! So, distancing himself from her didn't seem fair.

Eventually she decided that if she was to uncover what Gilly was up to then she would have to start by tackling him about it. He wouldn't like it but tough! He was her man and it was about time she found out just what the hell he was up to.

18

Aaron walked into the offices of the car-hire company to pick up the car he'd ordered over the phone. It was a BMW and at the lower end of the range, but he was familiar with the model and decided it would be OK. There was no way he was hiring a Porsche; that would have been far too expensive.

The clerk behind the desk went through the documentation with him then got him to sign a form. 'Come on, I'll show you where it's parked,' he said, leading Aaron out of the office.

Aaron glanced over the car. It looked good. He'd opted for the red model as it was more eye-catching than some of the others. They also had a few of them in stock, which meant that he could hire the same type and colour of car each time, and just swap the number plates for a set of his own while he had the car. The clerk gave him a quick rundown of how everything worked, then handed over the keys.

'Thanks,' said Aaron, grinning.

He got behind the wheel, ready to start the car. The dashboard looked good too and so shiny new, he was impressed. Hopefully Maddy would be impressed too, as long as he remembered to remove all the hire-company stickers. Then he could easily pass it off as his own.

By the time Gilly walked into The Rose and Crown the next night Crystal had already worked herself up into a state. She was dreading confronting him but knew it was something she had to do. His lack of interest was getting to her and she knew she wouldn't settle until she'd had it out with him.

When she saw him walk to the bar she left the girls she'd been sitting with and joined him. He looked down at her, spotted the half-empty glass of drink in her hand and turned back to the barmaid.

'Don't bother asking if I want one, will you, Gilly?' she said, sarcastically.

Gilly turned back around and glared at her. 'What you fuckin' on about? You've already got one!'

'Yes, but it's half empty.'

'Tough! Now get off my fuckin' case and let me get served.'

He turned back to face the barmaid who was waiting to take his order, and ignored Crystal. As she stood next to Gilly she noticed people looking at her, and felt humiliated. They'd obviously noticed the way Gilly had spoken to her and the way she was being ignored. Gradually her embarrassment faded and was replaced by anger. *How dare he snub her!*

Once Gilly had got his drink he turned towards her once more. 'Are you still fuckin' here?' he asked. 'What do you want?'

'A word.'

'Well, go on, then, but make it fuckin' snappy! There's other people I want to see in this pub as well as you, y'know.'

'Amber isn't here!' she snapped.

'What the fuck are you on about?' he demanded, pulling his shoulders back and glaring at her once more.

Crystal visibly flinched, almost losing her nerve at the sight of Gilly hovering menacingly over her. She glanced over his shoulder, spotting two customers behind him, paying rapt attention to the heated exchange, and knowing that he'd be even more annoyed if she showed him up in front of other people. 'I – I think we'd best go outside to have a chat,' she said.

Gilly slammed his pint on the bar. 'Go on, then,' he said, nodding his head towards the doorway then following her out. 'But this better be fuckin' good if you're dragging me outside.'

All the way to the door, Crystal could feel her heart pounding. Now that she'd broached the subject she knew she had to go through with it, but she also knew that Gilly wasn't going to be pleased.

Crystal stepped onto the pavement then turned until she was facing Gilly, who failed to stop quickly enough, so that they were almost touching. As she prepared to speak he stayed where he was, invading her personal space. He scowled at her as he waited to see what she had to say.

'Sorry, Gilly, but they were all nosying at the bar and I didn't think you'd want them to hear our private business.'

She was capitulating already.

'Just fuckin' get on with it, will you?' he said.

'OK, well, to be honest, I didn't like the way you were flirting with Amber the other day,' she began, pausing to assess his response before continuing.

Gilly pulled his chin back and sniggered in disbelief. 'Are you for fuckin' real? You mean to say you've brought me out here just to tell me that?'

'N-no,' said Crystal. 'It's not just that.' She could hear her next words forming inside her head as though her mind wanted her to voice them despite her trepidation. 'I, well, it's just, I wanted to talk to you about how you've been with me lately.' She rushed the words out but she'd started now so she pushed herself to finish. 'It's not been the same, Gilly,' she said, her tone pleading. 'You hardly ever come back with me these days and when I saw you with Amber, well, I wondered, y'know, if you were seeing her.'

'No, I'm not!' he snapped. 'But even if I was, it's none of your fuckin' business. You don't own me and I can do what the fuck I want. Now stop wasting my time over shite. I've got a fuckin' pint on the bar going flat.'

He turned away from her and started walking back into the pub. Feeling brave, Crystal called after him. 'What about where you keep going in your car?'

He swivelled round, and Crystal could see by the look on his face that he was furious. 'What the fuck do you know about that?' he demanded, grasping hold of her top in both hands and pushing her roughly against the pub wall.

'N-nothing,' she said, gasping with fright as her back slammed against the coarse bricks. 'I just wondered where you keep going. I thought you might be seeing someone else.'

'What the fuck if I am?' he shouted, ramming his fists harder into her shoulders as he pinned her back. 'And how the fuck do you know I go out in my car?'

'I've just seen you once or twice, that's all.'

'Have you been fuckin' following me?'

'No, no! I've just seen you drive off in your car, that's all,' she cried.

He released his right hand and slapped her sharply across the face several times until tears sprang to her eyes, and she lifted her hands to cover her stinging face.

'You must have fuckin' followed me out of the pub!' he yelled.

'No! I mean, only because I was going out to work anyway. I just happened to see you get in your car, that's all.'

He grabbed hold of her top again and held her fast against the wall, bending until his face was only a few centimetres from hers. 'From now on,' he said, through gritted teeth, 'you mind your own fuckin' business about where I go. Is that clear?' He relaxed his hold then pushed her back again to emphasise his words. When Crystal stared back in shock, he repeated himself. 'I said is that fuckin' clear?'

'Yes,' she said.

'Right. Well, you make sure you keep your fuckin' nose out in future. If I want to be with you, I will, and if I don't, I fuckin' won't. Do you get that?' he yelled into her face.

By this point her legs had gone weak and it was only the force of Gilly's hold that kept her standing still. 'Yes,' she sobbed. 'I'm sorry. I didn't mean it.'

He let go of her and looked at her with distaste. 'I'm going back to drink my pint and you can stay out of my fuckin' way before I really lose it!' he said, before walking away.

Crystal took a few seconds to compose herself before following him back into the pub. This time she sat at the table of girls and avoided the bar area where Gilly was standing. Nevertheless, as she had walked back inside The Rose and Crown she'd felt as though all eyes were upon her. Even though no one had witnessed what had just happened outside the pub, they could probably tell from her flustered appearance and the look of fury on Gilly's face.

Crystal had achieved nothing but upset and humiliation. Her confrontation with Gilly had been a waste of time. Rather than finding anything out, all she'd got off him was a few good smacks. But why shouldn't she ask him where he got to? He was supposed to be with her when all was said and done.

As she mulled things over Crystal became angry with herself for backing down when he was so obviously in the wrong. Not only that, Gilly's reaction told her that he was definitely up to something that he didn't want her to find out about. Eventually, feeling dejected as well as angry, she decided that if Gilly wouldn't tell her where he got to then she'd just have to find out for herself by following him. But that would be difficult without money. She didn't have a car at the moment so the only way she had of following him would be by taxi.

Crystal couldn't risk involving anyone else. After her previous confrontation with Amber and Ruby, and now this latest set-to with Gilly, she didn't want to make an even bigger fool of herself. No, it was best if she did this alone. As things stood she couldn't afford taxis, but she'd soon get round that one by pocketing some of her earnings and not telling Gilly. Stuff him! If he'd treated her better, then she wouldn't need to follow him in the first place.

The more she thought about it, the more determined Crystal became that, one way or another, she was going to find out just where Gilly went to whenever he disappeared in his car for hours.

19

Maddy answered the door to find the handsome face of Aaron smiling back at her.

'Your carriage awaits, madam,' he said, turning to the side and waving his hand with a flourish towards the shiny red BMW that was parked on the road.

'Very nice,' said Maddy.

'Yes, I'm happy with it. I mean, it's not as good as the Porsche but it'll do for now.'

'I wasn't talking about the car,' said Maddy, grinning as she turned and walked back up the hall.

Aaron stepped inside and shut the door before following her. As they walked he grasped one of her buttocks in his hand. 'You're cheeky,' he said. 'And you know what happens to cheeky girls, don't you?'

Maddy chuckled. 'Ooh, I can't wait.'

'Well, you'll have to,' said Aaron. 'Grab your coat. I want to take you out in the car. I've got something to show you.'

Within fifteen minutes they were sitting inside Aaron's car in the middle of Trafford Park.

'So, what do you think?' asked Aaron.

Maddy looked out of the car window. Across from them was a large warehouse. Erected from red brick, it had pale grey metal sheeting covering the top part of the building and dark grey metal shutters. Maddy could see a small wooden door next to the enormous shutters and a tiny window with a metal grille. The building wasn't exactly aesthetically pleasing and she wasn't sure what he wanted her to say.

'Erm, yeah. It's big, isn't it?'

Aaron laughed. 'Yeah, and it's got kitchen space, an office and toilets. I think it'll be perfect for the business.'

'Ooh, can we take a look inside?' asked Maddy.

'Not on a Sunday, no. But I've already checked it out and it's great. I just wanted you to see it too, even if it is only from the outside.'

'It sounds fine,' said Maddy.

Aaron leaned across and kissed her. Then he said, 'And it's not a million miles from where you live.'

Maddy smiled. 'True,' she said. 'Now, are we going back to mine for a bit before we have to get ready for Becky coming home?'

'Sure,' he said. 'But before we do I want to stop off at the supermarket to get some flowers for you both.'

'You don't have to,' said Maddy.

'I want to,' said Aaron, laying his hand on her inner thigh as he leant over for another kiss. 'Besides,' he added as he pulled away again, 'I want to make a good first impression on your daughter, don't I?'

Maddy was secretly pleased. She desperately wanted Aaron and Rebecca to get on and was glad he was making an effort.

Despite Maddy's best intentions, the pull of Aaron was too much. Within five minutes of arriving home they were upstairs in bed, the flowers discarded on the coffee table. After another session of ardent lovemaking Maddy glanced across at the bedside clock.

'Bloody hell!' she said, jumping out of bed and picking her clothes up off the bedroom floor where she had left them. 'Becky's due home any minute. We can't let her see us like this.'

While she rushed round, pulling her clothes on and frantically trying to smooth down her hair, Aaron remained in bed, smiling at her. 'Chill,' he said. 'She's not here yet, is she?'

As if in response to his words the doorbell sounded. 'Shit! She's here,' said Maddy, throwing Aaron's jeans at him. 'Get some bloody clothes on quick.'

Maddy dashed out of the bedroom and down the stairs, stopping to check her appearance in the hallway mirror. She glanced back to see Aaron trudging behind, slowly buttoning up his shirt.

'Quick,' said Maddy. 'Get in there.' She nodded towards the living room then gave him a few seconds to settle while the doorbell chimed urgently and the sound of Andy's voice met her ears.

Hoping she'd given Aaron enough time to make himself decent, she swung open the door and smiled at her daughter and ex-husband.

'God, Mum! We've been waiting ages,' said Rebecca.

'Sorry, love,' said Maddy, bending to plant a kiss on top of Rebecca's head. 'I was in the bathroom.'

She bid a hasty goodbye to Andy then turned her attention back to Rebecca, who was busy trying to remove her shoes. 'I've got someone I'd like you to meet,' she said, before opening the living-room door.

To Maddy's delight, Aaron was standing on the other side of the door with a bunch of flowers in each hand and a big beaming smile on his face. He handed the first bunch to Maddy, who thanked him, then he turned his attention to Rebecca.

'Hi, you must be Becky,' he said, handing her the second bunch of flowers.

Maddy could see from the expression on Rebecca's face that she was thrilled to receive the flowers. At eight years of age it wasn't something she was used to.

'Thanks,' she gushed. 'Nobody's bought me flowers before.'

'Why not?' asked Aaron.

Rebecca screwed up her face. 'I think it might be because I'm just a kid.'

'Well, I think you're a young lady, and every lady should receive flowers.'

Rebecca smiled coyly at him. 'Can we put them in vases together, Mummy?' she asked.

'Course we can, love,' said Maddy, following Rebecca through to the kitchen.

As Maddy passed Aaron, a look of acknowledgement passed between them. She was thrilled at Rebecca's reaction and knew that Aaron had played her just right, making her feel grown up and special. She also knew that, like her, Rebecca had immediately taken to Aaron. The man was irresistible! He had only known her daughter a few moments and yet he was already beginning to work his magic.

20

'Jesus, is that the time? I must get back,' said Maddy, edging her way out of bed while checking her watch.'

It was a week later and Maddy was at the Midland hotel with Aaron.

'Relax,' said Aaron, moving over to her until she could feel his breath on her back. 'It's Sunday and Becky isn't due back till this evening, is she?'

'Yes but...' Maddy began but stopped when she felt Aaron lift her hair and plant tiny kisses on the back of her neck, sending shivers all the way down her spine. 'I've got loads to do before she gets back,' she continued till Aaron cupped her breasts and began gently stroking her nipples. She relaxed as she lost herself to the exhilarating thrill that swept through her body.

'Have I ever mentioned just how gorgeous you are?' he whispered.

Maddy giggled. 'Once or twice,' she said.

Just as she was beginning to surrender the sound of her mobile phone ringing seemed to pierce the air and she reached over to the bedside table to grab it.

'Shit! It's Annette Willoughby, the editor from *Glimmer* magazine,' she said on seeing the name on the screen.

'Ignore it,' said Aaron.

'You're right,' said Maddy, replacing her mobile on the bedside table. 'Who the bloody hell rings on a Sunday, anyway?'

'Exactly,' said Aaron.

It was a while later before Maddy and Aaron were showered, dressed and ready to leave the Midland hotel. Aaron ran her back home in his BMW and for the duration of the journey Maddy sat back in her seat, making the most of the opportunity to rest before she got home.

While Aaron drove, Maddy decided to check her phone, alarmed to find a message from Andy, which had been sent an hour and a half earlier. His mother had been taken ill and rushed to hospital. Unsure of just how ill she was, he wanted to go and see her as soon as he could but preferred not to take Rebecca with him just in case it was bad news. He asked if it would therefore be all right to bring Rebecca back as soon as possible.

Maddy rang him straight away, 'Andy, I'm sorry, I've only just got your message,' she said. 'I'm on my way home.'

'OK, I'll bring Becky back now,' he said.

'How is your mum?'

'I don't know,' Andy replied. 'They haven't told us anything yet.'

'Aw, well, please give her my good wishes, won't you?' said Maddy. 'I'll see you in a bit.'

She cut the call and put the mobile back in her handbag.

'Bad news?' asked Aaron, taking his eyes off the road for a moment and raising his eyebrows quizzically.

Maddy quickly explained what had happened. When they arrived home she gave him a chaste kiss on the cheek and turned to get out of the car.

'Is that all I'm getting?' he asked, pretending to be affronted.

'Sorry, love, but they'll be here any minute and the house is a tip.'

Maddy waved him goodbye and rushed up the garden path. She opened her front door but, rather than the fresh homely smell that usually greeted her when she walked in, there was an unwelcome odour of unemptied bins and alcohol.

She raced through the house, disturbed to take in the state of the place. Somehow it hadn't seemed that bad on Saturday morning when she'd had Aaron distracting her. In the living room the cushions had been scattered wantonly about the furniture rather than arranged neatly. Her cardigan lay draped over the arm of the settee, a pile of DVDs was stacked haphazardly on the coffee table and the smell of stale beer filled the room.

Maddy sniffed the air as she wandered round the room trying to detect where the smell was coming from. To her consternation she found two empty lager tins at the side of the sofa, one of which lay upturned in a small pool of beer where the dregs had leaked out of it.

Her mind switched back to Friday night. She had stayed in with Aaron, watching a film while they ate Chinese takeaway and drank beer. Feeling tipsy by the end of the night, she had gone to bed fully intending to clear up the mess the next day. But the following morning Aaron had grown bored waiting for her to get ready so they could go out for the day. At his insistence she'd left most of the mess from the previous night, thinking she would have plenty of time to clean the place up when she returned home on Sunday.

She bent to retrieve the discarded cans and rushed through to the kitchen to put them in the bin. But here the smell was worse. The bin hadn't been emptied for several days and, as well as the greasy odour of Chinese food, there was another, stronger smell coming from the bin. Something had obviously gone off since she'd last emptied it.

In the sink, Friday's pots lay half submerged in water. She'd quickly dumped them there instead of taking the time to load the dishwasher while she'd rushed to leave the house with her impatient lover.

For several minutes Maddy rushed round the house trying to tidy as much of the mess as she could before Rebecca returned home. As she made her way through each of the rooms, she noted with dismay that a thin layer of dust also clung to the furniture.

Maddy had managed to make a good start on tidying up before the doorbell rang. She headed for the door, stopping in the hallway to check her appearance and smooth down her top. She was delighted to see Rebecca standing there with Andy beside her. As soon as Maddy opened the door Rebecca dashed inside, shouting bye to her father as she sped down the hall.

'What's got into her?' Maddy asked, laughing.

'There's something she wants to watch on the TV apparently.'

'Aah, right.'

'She's looking forward to watching her princesses DVD later too.' He chuckled, despite the obvious strain he was under. It was a shared joke between them that Rebecca would watch the same DVD over and over till everybody but Rebecca was tired of seeing it. 'Anyway, she's all yours,' he said, smiling. 'I'm off to the hospital now. Maybe I'll have a well-earned rest while I'm there. She's worn me out.'

Maddy smiled. 'You must be getting old, can't take the pace any more.'

'Dead right. She's been a bundle of energy.' Then he turned to go, saying, 'See you next week.'

'OK, see you then,' said Maddy, adding, 'I hope everything's OK with your mum.'

'Thanks,' said Andy before walking away.

Before Maddy went to join her daughter, she briefly scanned the street, thoughts of the blue Astra now dominating her mind. But there was no sign of it, just a red car further up the road. But as she looked she thought she saw the bare outline of a driver inside it and he seemed to be wearing a baseball cap. Maddy dismissed the thought almost as soon as it had entered her head; she was obviously getting a bit carried away with herself. Instead of dwelling on it she shut the door and went in search of her daughter.

Gilly sat in his car watching Maddy's home. He'd swapped the blue Astra for a red Honda Civic and parked a short way down the road in the hope that Maddy wouldn't notice him again.

As he watched, Gilly saw a car drive up to the gate and a tall, good-looking man of about forty get out of it with a young girl. Then they walked up the driveway and knocked on the door. Gilly had never seen the man at the house before and he presumed he must be her ex-husband dropping her daughter off.

He saw Maddy answer the door, her hair loose and falling in waves round her pretty face. She was wearing fitted jeans again, which clung to her firmly rounded hips, and he felt the desire stirring within him, imagining himself grasping hold of those hips as he penetrated her and she screamed with delight.

The girl went into the house straight away but Maddy stayed there chatting with her ex for a while. Gilly felt irritated as he watched them sharing a joke and saw her flick her hair about, tantalisingly, and the ex was smiling, putting on the charm and trying to impress her with his humour.

The man obviously still wanted her. How could he not? She was stunning! Gilly could feel his irritation shifting up into anger. *Wanker! Who did he think he was? She wasn't with him any more so why the fuck did he still think he could have her?*

And her! She was flirting too! Why? Why would she want to be fuckin' laughing and joking with a man she had divorced? He couldn't understand it; unless they were still seeing each other. That happened sometimes. Couples who couldn't live with each other any more ended up splitting up, but the desire was still there and they still fucked. Sneaking around when they thought no one would know. The bastard ex, waiting till the daughter was at school before he popped round for a quickie.

I bet she'd be fucking him now if her daughter wasn't there. Bitch! Slut! She's just like all the other women. She might wear nice clothes and keep herself looking good but deep down she's no different from all the others. Willing to do whatever it takes to get what she wants out of men.

He tried to bite back his anger. Maybe she wasn't fucking the ex. Maybe she was just flirty like that. But he didn't like it. He'd thought she was different from the other women. But she wasn't that different after all...

21

'Hiya, love. Have you had a nice time?' Maddy asked Rebecca when she found her in the living room.

'Yes, what time is it?'

'Don't worry, you haven't missed your programme. You've got plenty of time before it starts.'

For the next quarter of an hour Rebecca regaled her with tales of her weekend but Maddy found it difficult to focus, her mind straying to other things. Apart from the state of the house, she had got behind with her work. She had two in-depth pieces that needed returning to editors by the end of the next day and, although one of them was almost finished, she hadn't even started the other.

'Will you take me there too?' she heard Rebecca ask and Maddy switched her attention back to her daughter, who was staring doe-eyed at her, in eager anticipation.

'What? Where?'

Rebecca sighed in exasperation. 'I've just told you. That restaurant near the DIY store.'

'What? Which one? Yeah, course I will, love.' She smiled fondly at her daughter. 'Have you got any homework to do, Becky?'

'No, I did it at Dad's.'

'OK. Do you want to watch TV, then, or would you rather play on the PC in your room?'

Rebecca's face dropped. She didn't say anything but the glum look on her face gave away the disappointment that Maddy didn't seem to want to spend any time with her.

'OK.'

She stood up and shrugged, then stomped off to her bedroom. Maddy felt a stab of guilt. She hadn't seen Rebecca all weekend and now here she was packing her off to her room as soon as she got home, but she'd make it up to her when she had more time. For the moment though she had work that needed doing and that had to come first if she was going to keep a roof over their heads.

She walked over to her workstation and plonked herself down on her office chair. Working was the last thing she felt like doing, especially on a Sunday, but she'd already neglected it in the week due to the amount of time she'd spent with Aaron. She would much rather be snuggled up on the sofa with her daughter watching TV and, as well as feeling guilty for neglecting Becky, Maddy was overtired. Aaron was a voracious lover and she caught little sleep when she spent the night with him.

The first thing she needed to do was to phone *Glimmer* magazine. She picked up her mobile and noticed that since the call this morning Annette Willoughby had also sent her a text asking her to get in touch urgently. It didn't bode well and Maddy braced herself as she selected Annette's phone number on her mobile then hit the call button.

'Hi, Annette, it's Maddy. How are you?'

'Fine,' the woman replied curtly before coming straight to the point. 'It's about that last article you sent to me. I've had chance to read it over the weekend and I'm afraid it's not what we're looking for.'

'Oh,' said Maddy, trying to take in her words. 'Why's that?'

'Well, to be honest, Maddy, I'm afraid it's just not up to your usual standard and certainly not of the standard we require. The level of detail is lacking, some of the language is unnecessarily long-winded and I was disappointed to find several grammatical and typo errors. It's certainly not the type of thing we would have expected from a seasoned professional like you.'

'I see,' said Maddy, slowly, as she frantically tried to come up with an explanation. 'I'm afraid I was a bit stuck for time with that one. I've had a lot on and I know it's no excuse but perhaps I should have got back to you and asked for more time.'

'We gave you three weeks to write the article as it was, and we had magazine deadlines to meet, Maddy.'

'I know. I'm so sorry. Would it help if I had another look at it to correct the errors and see if I can make the language more succinct?'

'Not really. Apart from everything else, the angle is all wrong for our readership. I would have thought you'd have known what our readers were looking for.'

'OK. What about a rewrite?'

'No, I'm afraid it just won't be possible. Like I say, we've got magazine deadlines to fill. We just wouldn't have time to make it work. As it stands, we'll have to substitute the article with fillers.'

Maddy was beginning to wonder about the purpose of the call if Annette didn't want her to put things right, but Annette's next words made her reasoning clear.

'There isn't anything you can do to put this right, Maddy. You've let us down badly but, because you've worked so well with us in the past, I thought I'd give you the courtesy of letting you know that we won't require your services in future. That also applies to the other magazines in the group, not just *Glimmer*.'

'Oh,' said Maddy, stuck for something more concrete to say as the harshness of Annette's words hit her.

'I'm sorry, but we need writers we can rely on,' Annette added to fill in the void of silence.

The reality of the situation was beginning to sink in for Maddy as she realised what impact this loss would have on her finances. Feeling desperate, she made one last-ditch attempt to win Annette round. 'Is there anything at all I can do to put it right? I'll even write the next article for free to prove that I won't let you down.'

'No, I'm sorry; we can't take that risk, not when we have such strict deadlines to meet.'

Again Maddy stayed silent and, when she failed to come up with any further assurances, Annette thanked her for her past work and terminated the call. Maddy was devastated. The Sunshine group had been a major employer for the past seven years. She'd done lots of good work for them, often putting in extra hours if they called for an article at a moment's notice, and this was all the thanks she got? One bad article and they let her go, just like that.

Curious, Maddy pulled up the article on her computer screen. She remembered writing it after Aaron had stayed over. At the time she'd been preoccupied with thoughts of her delectable lover and in a bit of a rush because she'd spent too much time with him again. But surely the article couldn't have been that bad?

Then Maddy began reading the article and she cringed as she took in the number of basic errors she had made. Too instead of to, wander instead of wonder and a couple of typos where she'd hit the wrong keys in her rush to get the article finished. There were several long rambling sentences too, which would have benefitted from tightening up. She'd thought she'd checked the article at the time but perhaps she had been too tired to concentrate.

She knew there was no point correcting it now, not after Annette Willoughby had flatly refused to accept any more work from her. So she quickly shut down the document and tried to put it out of her mind, knowing she had other matters she needed to tend to.

Maddy turned her attention to the two pieces of work she needed to finish for the end of the next day. She decided to start work on the one that hadn't been touched. If possible she wanted to get the first draft finished that day, so that she could have another look at it the following day with a fresh mind and then polish it up.

But when Maddy looked at the brief she was disturbed to note that a lot of research was required. She only had scant knowledge of the subject matter and, although she was tempted to skim through the research and make assumptions, she knew it was too risky, especially as she'd already lost one valuable client that day. Besides, that just wasn't her style. If she hadn't let herself get so far behind with her work in the first place, then she would never have even considered that as an option.

Growing exasperated, she turned her attention to the article that she had almost finished. For several minutes she tried to read through the article but was finding it difficult to focus. Annette's harsh words flitted through her brain and she was full of regret at allowing herself to return substandard work. She kept reading a couple of paragraphs and realising none of what she had read had registered, so she returned to the beginning of the document.

Just as she was trying to read through it for the third time, Rebecca appeared by her side. 'Mum, I'm bored. Can we watch my princesses DVD, please?'

'What about the TV?' she suggested again. 'Isn't your programme still on?'

'No, it finished ages ago and I missed it while I was on the computer.'

Maddy was short with her. 'Go and find your DVD, then. You know where they are.'

'But I want you to watch it with me.'

'No, Becky. I can't. I've told you, I'm too busy.'

'But, Mum, it's Sunday. You always watch DVDs with me on Sundays.'

'For God's sake, Rebecca! Will you just do as you're bloody well told?' Maddy snapped.

As soon as she said the words she realised she had been unnecessarily sharp with her daughter and when she saw the hurt expression on Rebecca's face she tried to backtrack.

'Look, Becky, I'm sorry for shouting at you, but you know not to interrupt me when I'm busy working. Now will you please just do as I ask?'

But her apology was too little too late, she realised, as she watched Rebecca walk away with her shoulders slumped. Maddy tried to return to the article but it was no use, she was overtired and still upset by the call with Annette bloody Willoughby. Eventually, realising she would get no further; she decided to leave it for the day. She'd get an early night and face the task with a fresh mind tomorrow.

But she knew that although she'd manage to finish this article, there was no way she would make a good job of the other one in just a day. It was an in-depth piece, requiring a lot of research, and, as she thought about it, she realised that there was only one alternative left to her: she'd phone the magazine and ask for a few days' extension. Then she'd just have to pull out all the stops next week to do a good job of it as well as all the other work she had to get through.

She switched off the computer and went in search of her daughter. At least if she could make it up to Rebecca, then she would have achieved something today. The promise of ice cream after tea and the offer to watch Rebecca's favourite DVD did the trick and Maddy settled on the sofa next to her.

But even as she watched the DVD Maddy's mind kept wandering. She knew that the amount of time she was spending with Aaron was impacting negatively on other aspects of her life. And as she sat there she vowed to herself that she would spend less time with him. Surely he'd understand when she explained to him how she was getting behind with her work? Wouldn't he?

22

Crystal went out to the red-light district much earlier than usual on Sunday. She knew Gilly wouldn't have expected it, so she would therefore be safe to pocket the earnings from a couple of additional clients. Her plan was to then head back to The Rose and Crown and see what Gilly was up to.

If Gilly did his disappearing act again she would follow him. She'd earnt enough to pay for a taxi and make up for some earnings she would lose later in the day while she was pursuing Gilly.

She found daytime working a strange and more threatening experience. At night-time she knew a lot of the clients whereas in the daytime she didn't, and these clients seemed a different type. They were bolder; the sort of men who didn't feel the need to operate under cover of darkness, as though they didn't give a damn who saw what they were up to. Then there were others who were so desperate to live out their sick fantasies that they couldn't wait until later.

But Crystal had learnt over the years to have her wits about her when she was working. She knew the signs to look out for. The smell of booze on a client's breath. An overly aggressive attitude. Quibbling over price before she'd even got in the car. They were all warning signals and her reaction would usually be to avoid those clients and send them on their way. There were too many people ready to take advantage, and regular abuse was all part and parcel of a prostitute's life.

Although Gilly did his best to protect them, he couldn't be everywhere. When he'd killed the man who had abused her, she'd felt safer on the streets at first. But she'd soon realised that it didn't make that much difference. Other clients weren't aware of the threat of revenge if they stepped out of line so they carried on as normal.

Her mind went straight back to Gilly. To think, he'd killed that man for her. He might not be as attentive as he used to be but that was probably because it had freaked him out and, as far as Crystal was concerned, Gilly was still her man.

She was relieved to leave Minshull Street later that evening and get back to The Rose and Crown with her earnings safely tucked away. Crystal had timed it so that she returned before the timeframe in which she had previously seen Gilly leave the pub and get in his car and she was relieved to see him standing at the bar. He bought her a drink, unaware that tonight she could easily afford to buy her own.

To Crystal's dismay it was over an hour before Gilly left the pub. While she was standing at the bar he asked her twice when she was going to work. She knew that he was getting irritated at the loss of earnings while she was in the pub drinking, so she moved away from the bar where he couldn't get at her so easily.

Eventually she was rewarded by the sight of Gilly draining his pint and preparing to leave. Before he set off he turned to Crystal and two of his other girls who were sitting at a table with her.

'Time to go, girls,' he said. 'I want you out of here as soon as you've finished that drink.'

'It's OK, we're going,' said Crystal.

She left the remainder of her drink on the table as she dashed after him.

'Bloody hell, Crystal,' shouted one of the girls. 'You don't have to go that quick. At least finish your drink first.'

But Crystal ignored her. She wasn't rushing to work, she was rushing to catch up with Gilly before he and his car disappeared altogether. As she suspected, he crossed the road, heading in the direction of his car, which was parked further along. Before he had even got inside the car Crystal spotted a taxi and flagged it down.

'We're following that car,' she said, feeling as if she were in a film. 'But wait till he sets off and stay well back. I don't want him to spot us.'

The taxi driver turned round and looked at her uncertainly. 'Don't worry, I'll pay you for your trouble,' she said.

She was relieved when he turned back and set off just in time for her to keep tabs on Gilly. As she settled down in the back seat of the cab she felt a mixture of relief and dread. Tonight she would finally find out just what Gilly was up to. But whether that would be a good thing, she just wasn't sure.

It was ages since Clare had seen Maddy and she'd put off ringing her, knowing that their last meeting had been a bit fraught. But Maddy was her friend and she was worried about her. Clare felt that Maddy was making a big mistake rushing into things with Aaron. She had a bad feeling about him but, just to keep the peace, she decided not to say anything negative when she rang her friend. With that in mind she picked up the phone and made the call.

'Hi, Maddy, how are you?' she asked, trying her best to sound cheerful so she could get things back on track with her friend.

'Oh, not too bad, y'know.'

'You sound a bit down. What's the matter?'

'Nothing. It's just that, well, it's a bad time, to be honest. I'm watching a DVD with Becky.' Then Maddy whispered, 'I've already been a bit short with her today so I'm trying to make it up to her.'

'Oh, I see. That's not like you.'

'I know, but I've had a bit of a bad day.'

'Really? What's wrong?'

'Oh, it's not what you think. Me and Aaron are fine.' Maddy's voice had adopted a sing-song tone but then she became serious again as she said, 'No, I had a nasty call from *Glimmer* magazine. They weren't happy with the article I submitted. They wouldn't even give me a chance to put it right. Not only that, but they've refused to accept any more of my work in the future, and that applies to all the magazines in the Sunshine group.'

'Really?' asked Clare, becoming concerned. 'But weren't they one of your biggest clients?'

'*The* biggest.'

'Why didn't they like the article?'

'Well, if I'm honest, it wasn't up to my usual standard. I did it in a bit of a rush. I'd been with Aaron and left myself a bit short of time.' Then she giggled. 'The man's bloody insatiable but *so* hard to resist. Anyway, you would have thought they'd have given me a second chance after all the good work I've sent to them in the past. But no.'

Clare was surprised at the flippancy of her friend's words. Maddy had always prided herself on the quality of her work but she didn't seem to care any more. It wasn't like her to be snappy with Rebecca either. Clare knew it was since Maddy had been seeing Aaron that she'd let things slide but she had promised herself that she'd try not to criticise. So, instead of expressing her disquiet, she said, 'What will you do?'

'There's not much I can do about the Sunshine group. She was adamant she didn't want any more work from me. The nasty bitch! Anyway, there's always other magazines. It's not as if I haven't got a good portfolio to show them and I've got contacts in the industry.'

'Well, good luck with it, Maddy. I hope you manage to find a replacement. Anyway, do you fancy meeting up next week? It's been ages since we've had a get-together.'

'Aw, I'm sorry, Clare, but I'm really up against it next week. I've got tons of work on. In fact, I'm already going to have to ask for an extension on one piece of work tomorrow.'

'Oh, I see,' said Clare, trying to keep the disappointment out of her voice, but failing.

'I know what you're thinking,' said Maddy. 'I *have* been spending too much time with Aaron and I think what's happened today with *Glimmer* magazine has made me realise that. I'm going to have to start seeing a bit less of him, but it's difficult when I just want to be with him all the time. Anyway, while I'm thinking about it, I'll ring him tonight after Becky's gone to bed and tell him we need to see less of each other.'

'Bloody hell, Maddy, you have got it bad,' said Clare, trying to sound jovial.

'I know.' Then Maddy paused before saying her next words. 'You're wrong about him, y'know. He's lovely. He treats me so well and even Becky thinks he's wonderful.'

'Oh, so she's met him, then?'

'Yes, and he was brilliant with her; he had her eating out of his hand in no time. And he's taking us to meet his family in Yorkshire soon.'

'Oh, that's good,' said Clare, but her voice didn't reflect her positive words.

'Yeah, it is,' said Maddy. 'Anyway, I'm sorry to rush off but Becky keeps looking over at me. She wants me to get back to watching her DVD with her.'

'OK, well, I'll let you go, then,' said Clare.

'OK, but I promise I'll be in touch soon when things are less hectic and we'll arrange a get-together.'

'All right, bye, then,' said Clare.

Then she heard Maddy saying goodbye, but she cut the call even before she'd finished that one word. Clare sat reflecting on the call. She was concerned for her friend. She'd seen her fall head over heels before and it usually ended badly. Previously, Clare had been there to help her friend pick up the pieces and Maddy had always been resilient enough to bounce back.

But somehow this time was different. She had never seen her friend so smitten that she neglected her work or grew snappy with Rebecca. It was as if Aaron had got her under his spell. And, aside from all that, there was something about Aaron that she just didn't trust. It all seemed a bit of a mystery. Why was he living in a hotel? Why tell Maddy he had a Porsche when he so obviously didn't? And would he really take Maddy and Rebecca to meet his family or was he just spinning her another yarn?

Clare felt that Maddy was making a big mistake where Aaron was concerned but what could she do about it when Maddy refused to have a bad word said about him?

23

As the taxi carrying Crystal made its way out of the city centre it got stuck at some traffic lights. The red Honda Civic had already shot through the lights just as they were changing from amber to red.

'Shit!' said Crystal, leaning forward in her seat so she could try to keep tabs on the car.

By the time the lights changed to green Gilly's car was no longer in view.

'Where to now?' asked the taxi driver.

Crystal desperately hoped they might still have a chance of catching Gilly. 'Straight ahead. As fast as you can,' she said. 'We might catch him at the next lights.'

'I'll go as fast as I can but I'm not breaking the speed limit. I can't risk losing my bloody licence,' said the taxi driver, who was already put out because they were pursuing a vehicle.

They soon arrived at another set of traffic lights and the taxi drew to a stop. Crystal leant forward again, scanning the queue of traffic in front of them, but there was no sign of Gilly in his red Honda.

'Shit!' she cursed again.

'You still wanna carry on?' asked the taxi driver.

'No, it's a waste of time,' she said. 'Turn back. We'll go back to The Rose and Crown.'

'All right, I'll turn first chance I get but it might be a while unless I find a side road.'

'OK,' said Crystal, resignedly. 'Eh, what about here? Can't you turn here?' she asked as the taxi driver passed a petrol station on their left.

She looked back at the petrol station, dismayed as the taxi driver muttered, 'Too late, love.'

It was while she was gazing at the petrol station forecourt that she spotted it. A red Honda Civic. Could it be Gilly?

'Quick. Turn around!' she yelled at the driver. 'He's back there, at the petrol station.'

The driver checked his rear-view mirror and tutted. Fortunately there was a side street just ahead and the driver turned sharply into it. The taxi's tyres screeched as he then did a speedy turn in the road.

'Right or left?' he asked.

'Wait! Let's see if he passes,' said Crystal, fully expecting that Gilly would carry on heading in the same direction rather than go back to the city centre. After all, if he had just come out for petrol, there were plenty of petrol stations nearer to the city centre than this one.

It was only a few seconds later when they caught sight of the red Honda as it passed them. Crystal recognised Gilly in the driving seat and quickly ducked so he wouldn't see her.

'Quick! Go now,' she ordered the taxi driver. 'It's definitely him.'

For the next fifteen minutes they kept pace with Gilly, staying a couple of cars behind so that he wouldn't spot Crystal. Eventually they went through the centre of Urmston and towards Flixton. Crystal knew the area but only because she had a regular client who lived near the hospital and he always insisted she spent the night at his house. She couldn't think what business Gilly would have in such a nice area though.

Then the Honda stopped in a tree-lined road full of detached houses. The taxi driver had already spotted it before she spoke.

'Do you want me to stop further up?' he asked, guessing that she didn't want to be seen.

'Yeah, just there on the right,' she said.

They were just about near enough for her to see what Gilly was up to but not too near that she would be seen. She swivelled round in her seat and, keeping her head low, she watched.

'I hope you realise the meter's still ticking,' said the driver.

Crystal tutted. 'Yeah, it's all right. I'll pay you whatever it costs.'

For a few minutes nothing happened. Gilly stayed inside his car. He seemed to be watching a house on the other side of the street. But why? Crystal wasn't sure. She continued watching till the driver interrupted her again.

'How long we staying here?' he asked.

'Shush!' she said. 'I've told you, I'll pay you whatever it costs. I'm not going now we've come this far.'

She carried on looking out of the back window. Then, suddenly, the Honda started up and she ducked again so Gilly wouldn't spot her as he passed by. Once the car was way up the road, she sat up straight again.

'You wanna carry on following him?' the driver asked.

Crystal paused a moment, unsure what to do next. But she decided against continuing to follow Gilly. Somehow, whatever business he was on, she had a feeling it was connected to the house he had been watching. Curious, she wanted to have a look at the house to see if she could find out anything more.

'Wait here a minute,' she said. 'I'm just going to check something out.'

'Look, love, it's twenty-six quid already. How do I know you're not gonna do a runner once you get outside?'

She tutted again and pulled some money out of her handbag, then gave him three ten-pound notes. 'Here. Keep the change,' she said.

Crystal then stepped from the cab, which zoomed off down the street.

'Bastard!' she cursed when the driver didn't wait for her. Now she was stuck in the middle of Flixton with no way of getting back to Manchester. She supposed she'd better do what she'd set out to do, which was to find out just why the hell Gilly was interested in that house. Then she could look for a bus stop or taxi rank so that she could get back to town.

Crystal walked in the direction of the house, staying on the other side of the road while she glanced over. To her surprise she saw a woman walk to the gate and peer down the road as though looking where Gilly's car had got to. Recognising the woman, Crystal quickly hid behind a parked car.

For a moment she continued watching from her safe vantage point, hardly believing what she was seeing. It was the journalist! But why? What business did Gilly have with her and why the hell would he sit in his car watching her house?

It wasn't long before Maddy walked back up her drive, making sure the gate was bolted before she walked away. Then she went inside and shut her front door. Crystal took a mental note of the house number then walked down the street to check the name of it before finding her way to a main road where she might have chance of catching a bus or taxi.

All the way back to town she puzzled about what she had seen. Was Gilly into house break-ins now? Or did he perhaps have something going on with the journalist? No, that couldn't be right; otherwise he'd have knocked on the door instead of just watching from his car.

Crystal had no idea what Gilly was up to but, whatever it was, she sensed that it wasn't good. After mulling things over for a while Crystal came to the most likely conclusion that Gilly had a thing for the journalist.

She recalled him telling her to allow the journalist's second interview and the way he had kept glancing over through the bar's mirror while the interview was taking place. At the time she'd thought it was because he didn't trust the journalist, but then he'd followed her out of the pub. In fact, from what Crystal remembered, he couldn't get out of the pub quickly enough. Suddenly it all seemed to fit. Maybe something had taken place between them.

Crystal also recalled how beautiful the journalist was and the smart clothes she had worn. Even today when, from what Crystal could see, Maddy was wearing little make-up and a lounge suit, she still looked stunning. When Crystal had met Maddy she hadn't given her appearance that much thought, readily accepting that Maddy was from a different world. Now though, as she thought about Gilly's interest in the journalist and the way he had treated her ever since Maddy had come on the scene, she grew jealous.

But Crystal was wary of challenging Gilly until she found out more, especially since he had already slapped her around for asking where he went in his car. It was obviously a touchy subject with him, so she decided to keep the information to herself for a while.

No matter what his reasons were, though, for following Maddy, it wasn't right. He was supposed to be in a relationship with her and, as Crystal seethed with anger at his betrayal, she decided that somehow she'd find a way to get her own back.

24

It was only a day after Maddy's last date with Aaron when he turned up on her doorstep again late in the evening. The day had been frantic. Maddy had rung and asked for an extension on the article she was behind with and, although the magazine editor had granted it, he wasn't at all pleased. For the rest of the day she had worked hard to make a good start on the article, knowing that she had several others she needed to finish that week too. And she really didn't want to upset any more editors.

When she heard the doorbell ring, she automatically checked the time by the living-room clock. Twenty-five to ten. Who could it be at this time? In view of the strange cars she had seen parked outside a few times recently, Maddy was a bit unsettled.

She inched the door open, making sure the security chain was in place, and was surprised to see Aaron standing there carrying another bunch of flowers and a box of luxury chocolates.

'Aaron?' she asked. 'What are you doing here?'

He smiled. 'Well, aren't you going to let me in? Anyone would think you weren't pleased to see me.'

'Of course I am,' said Maddy, releasing the chain and opening the door. She allowed him to plant a kiss on her lips and step inside the hallway before she added, 'But I thought we agreed on the phone last night that we would see less of each other so I can catch up with my work.'

He looked a bit put out. Then he said, 'I know, but when I got up today I realised that it's exactly one month since we started seeing each other. And I couldn't let an important day like that go by without seeing you.'

He handed her the flowers and she smiled. 'Aw, Aaron, you're so sweet. That's really thoughtful of you.'

'I've brought you these too,' he said, pressing the box of chocolates into her other hand. 'You're the best thing that's happened to me in a long time.'

'Thank you, but you shouldn't have. You're always buying me things. Seriously though, Aaron, I love being with you, but I'm so far behind with my work and I really need to catch up.'

He kissed her and said, 'Stop fretting. I'll leave early in the morning so you can get on with it. You'll soon catch up; I've got every faith in you. Anyway, haven't you already caught up with some of it today?'

'Well, yes, but it's just the tip of the iceberg really. I'll have to work flat out all week if I'm to get anywhere near caught up with all the work I've got on.'

'Do you want me to go, then?' he asked, staring at her with those irresistible blue eyes, and Maddy could feel herself weaken.

'No, it's OK,' she said, resigned to the fact that he would be with her for the rest of the night but also dismayed because she knew it would be another late one. That meant she would be overtired again the following day when she really needed to be on top of things. But she didn't tell him what she was really thinking. Instead she said, 'Becky will be disappointed she's missed you tonight. She'll be fast asleep by now.'

'I didn't come here to see Becky,' he said, grasping her buttocks firmly. 'Now, are you going to get inside and let me ravish you or do we have to do it out here in the hallway?'

Later they were lying in bed after another session of passionate lovemaking. Maddy had her head on Aaron's chest and was feeling content. 'Oh, I meant to ask,' she said. 'How did you go on with that warehouse?'

Aaron hesitated before answering. 'Oh, erm, somebody had beaten me to it, I'm afraid.'

It was only a moment's hesitation but, nevertheless, Maddy had noticed it. 'Oh, that's a shame,' she said. 'What will you do?'

'Well, it's a bit of a pain really. I'm sure there'll be something else suitable but, obviously, having to take the time to view other properties will put me behind a bit.'

'Aw, that's a shame,' she repeated. 'It would have been perfect for you as well, wouldn't it? What about houses? Have you viewed any yet?'

'No, I told you, I need to sort out the business first. It's not just a warehouse I need. There's loads of other things I need to sort out like stock and staff, and all kinds of other stuff that I won't even bore you with.'

Maddy could sense a bit of irritation in his tone. She guessed he must have been getting hassled with it all, especially after he had lost the warehouse that he really wanted. Deciding not to add to his stresses, she changed the subject.

'I've been thinking, now that you're getting to know Becky, why don't we take her with us to meet your family next weekend?'

'No, I can't do next weekend.'

'Oh, why not?' she asked. 'I'm sure Becky would love to meet them, and I'm looking forward to it too.'

'For fuck's sake!' he snapped. 'You know how busy I am with everything. Now, will you just stop asking me questions all the time?'

For a moment Maddy didn't speak, too shocked to respond.

Then her reaction seemed to bring him to his senses. 'Listen, I'm sorry, Maddy,' he said, stroking the back of her head. 'I didn't mean to snap like that but it's just that I'm so busy with everything and I don't need any more mither.'

She sat up and looked straight into his eyes. He shifted uncomfortably at the intensity of her gaze but she continued staring. 'Do not ever speak to me like that again,' she said slowly and deliberately.

'I know,' he said. 'I shouldn't have and I'm sorry. I promise I won't do it again.'

'You'd better not,' said Maddy, 'because I won't stand for it. I don't like being spoken to like that; I don't like it at all.'

Aaron pulled his head back and held his hands out. 'Sorry, sorry,' he repeated, smiling.

His jovial manner worked to mollify her and she lay back down with her head on his chest. He moved his hand round until it grazed her breast, then he began fingering her nipple till she could feel a wave of desire.

'I know what you *do* like,' he said. 'Should we focus on that instead? I don't think I like angry Maddy,' he teased.

She giggled and tapped him lightly on the arm. 'You're incorrigible,' she said.

'Would you like me to get even more incorrigible?' he asked, laughing and sliding his hand down her body till he reached the top of her legs, then slid his fingers inside her vagina. Maddy became lost in the moment as he worked his magic yet again.

His angry reaction had momentarily sown a seed of doubt for Maddy but he'd soon won her round and, in her own mind, she quickly excused his outburst.

25

Maddy awoke to the shrill buzzing of her alarm at 7.00 the next morning. She prised herself away from Aaron and reached over to switch it off. As she lay back again, she felt the weight of Aaron's arm land on top of her and for a moment she was tempted to stay in bed with him. She was so tired! But then she thought about the amount of work she had to get through and that was enough to get her out of bed.

She flung on her dressing gown and tiptoed out of the room. Then she woke Rebecca up and got her ready for school, leaving Aaron sleeping. She knew Rebecca would want to chat to him and risk being late for school if she found out he was in the house so she decided not to tell her.

Once she had returned from the school run she switched on her PC, grabbing the chance to start some work while Aaron was still in bed. It was 10.20 a.m. before she heard him stir and within minutes he was standing alongside her, peeping over her shoulder at the article she was writing.

'Morning, gorgeous,' he said.

'Hello, sleepy head,' said Maddy, looking up at him while she continued to type. He looked irresistible; his hair all tousled and his lovely blue eyes heavy with sleep. 'Let me just finish typing this sentence, then I'll go and make you a cuppa,' she said.

He kissed the top of her head. 'OK, thanks.'

Maddy was torn. She was in the middle of an article and would have loved to continue it while the ideas were fresh in her mind. But she also wanted to be with Aaron, who was now sitting on her sofa waiting for his cup of coffee. She quickly jotted down a few notes so that she wouldn't lose track of where she was up to when she returned to her PC. Then she dashed through to the kitchen and made them each a drink.

When Maddy returned to the living room Aaron was tucking into a banana that he had helped himself to, while flicking through her CD collection. She put his drink down on the coffee table, near to where he had been sitting on the sofa. Then she sat on the armchair, not wanting to get too near to him and risk being further distracted from her work.

He turned round and flashed a beaming smile at her. Then he sat down and finished eating. Leaving the banana skin on the coffee table, he patted the seat next to him. 'Come and sit here,' he said. Then he picked up his cup of coffee and took a gulp.

'No, it's OK,' said Maddy, smiling back at him. 'I need to get back to work in a minute.'

'Aah, right. Do you want me to go, then? I can take a hint.'

Maddy felt awful for neglecting him but she knew she had to be disciplined with herself if she was to have any chance of catching up with her work.

'Sorry. I'd love you to stay a bit longer, but you know how it is.'

'OK. OK. I understand.' Then he laughed. 'Your work is far more important than entertaining the demands of your randy young boyfriend.'

'Well, I wouldn't have put it quite like that,' she said, sharing the joke.

'It's OK,' he said, putting his cup back on the coffee table although it was still almost full. Then he stood up. 'I'll go and leave you to your work.'

Maddy resisted the temptation to tell him to stay until he had finished his drink. Instead she got up and walked out of the room with him. Inside the hallway he turned to embrace her before he opened the door to leave. She looked up at him and their lips met. As she returned his passionate kiss she could feel his hands roaming up and down her body. She quickly pulled away before she became lost to his charms once more.

A wide beaming smile lit up his handsome features. 'You sure I can't persuade you back to bed?' he asked, his hand still resting on her buttocks while his finger drew tiny, tantalising circles that sent shivers right through her.

She smiled back. 'No, cheeky! I've told you—'

'I know, you've got work to do,' he said, his voice imitating hers.

'Yes, and so have you, don't forget,' said Maddy, smiling at him. She reached over and unlocked the catch on the door while continuing to smile. Then she said, in mock irritation, 'Come on, pest, out.'

He held up his hands as if in surrender, 'OK, OK. Mustn't get on the wrong side of the hotshot journalist.'

Then he was gone and she went back to her PC, taking a moment to reflect before returning to her work. She had been right the previous night when she had called him incorrigible. But he was also irresistible! It wasn't only his looks; it was the way he was with her, most of the time anyway. He made her feel so special, showering her with affection, bringing her little gifts, paying her compliments. And as for the sex. Wow! He was such an unselfish lover, who took the time and care to focus on her needs.

But before she could become too carried away with thoughts of Aaron, she switched her focus back to the article she had been working on. She quickly read through the notes she had written so that her mind could switch back into writing mode, then she started tapping away at the keyboard.

Maddy worked flat out till mid-afternoon. It was only when she had finished another article and stopped to look at the clock that she realised it was three o'clock and she still hadn't eaten. No wonder her stomach was rumbling. She hadn't even had a coffee break since her mid-morning one with Aaron. Thank God Andy had agreed to collect Rebecca from school and keep her till seven o'clock so that she could work later and get more done. She had felt guilty asking him at first, in view of what he was going through, but when she'd spoken to him he'd told her that his mother was over the worst and already starting to recover well.

She broke off for half an hour and grabbed herself something quick to eat. She was exhausted; it must have been around two o'clock in the morning before she'd got to sleep and then she was up at seven after already having had a heavy weekend. She grabbed herself another coffee, hoping it would keep her alert for a few more hours as she still had a lot of work to get through.

As soon as she broke off from work her mind drifted back to Aaron, who was never far from her thoughts. But this time she wasn't thinking about how wonderful he was; she was thinking of how he'd snapped at her the previous night.

It had shocked her, especially when he had used bad language. She'd never seen him like that before, and she hoped it was a one-off. Still, at least she had let him know she wouldn't stand for it so perhaps he wouldn't try it on again.

For Maddy it was as if somebody had taken an artistic masterpiece and scrawled a red jagged line across one corner of it. Up until yesterday their relationship had been flawless but now it was marred. Why did he have to act like that and spoil things? Perhaps, like her, he had just been tired and overstressed. After all, he still had a lot of things to sort out.

But then, if he was so busy, why wasn't he in a rush to leave this morning? Surely there were things he should be getting on with? Perhaps he wasn't as self-disciplined as her when it came to work. She knew a few people like that; they took everything in their stride and then had a last-minute panic when things weren't done. Maybe he was one of those types.

Thinking about it, she didn't really know him that well yet.

Her eyes zoomed in on the lovely flowers he'd bought for her. Then there were the chocolates as well as all the other little gifts he'd brought, and the considerate way he'd made Rebecca feel all grown up by bringing her flowers too. Quickly dismissing the few negative thoughts, she instead thought again of everything that was good about Aaron.

Once she had taken her break, Maddy returned to work, thankful that the coffee had woken her up a bit. For a few more hours she continued to work on her PC till the insistent ringing of the phone grabbed her attention. Curious as to who it could be, she instinctively looked at the clock. She realised what time it was just as she answered the call.

'I've brought my princesses DVD to watch, Daddy,' said Rebecca, pulling the DVD out of her rucksack. 'Will you watch it with me later?'

Andy wasn't exactly thrilled at the thought of watching a princesses DVD. Maddy would usually watch that sort of thing with Rebecca. But he liked to make the most of his time with his daughter so instead of a flat-out refusal he thought he'd talk her into watching another DVD instead.

'Didn't you watch that one on Sunday with your mum?' he asked, recalling the way Rebecca often chatted about how much she enjoyed watching DVDs with her mum and how the princesses one was her favourite.

'Not all of it. Mum was busy and then she was on the phone with Clare,' she said.

'Really?' he asked, knowing it wasn't like Maddy not to spare time for her daughter. 'What was she busy doing?'

'Working, on her computer.'

'Oh. On a Sunday?'

'Yes. Mummy's always busy working or being with Aaron.'

Andy felt a little perturbed on hearing this. He couldn't understand why Maddy would be working on a Sunday, especially after Rebecca had already been with him most of the weekend. Then she'd also asked him to pick up Rebecca tonight so she could catch up with some work. Why was she so behind? Unless, of course, she was spending all her time with this new man.

Rebecca must have picked up on his disquiet as she said, 'I like Aaron though. He makes Mummy laugh except when she's working. Then she sometimes shouts at me. Aaron doesn't shout at me. He brought me some flowers.'

'I see,' said Andy. 'Well, he sounds very nice.'

His words disguised his true feelings. He was perturbed at the fact that Mandy had been shouting at Rebecca. He was also never happy when Maddy was seeing someone, but there was no way he was going to let his eight-year-old daughter know any of that. He couldn't hide those feelings from himself though. Apart from being a little jealous at the thought of his ex-wife with someone else, he always worried about Maddy introducing new men into Rebecca's life.

He knew he had no right to deny Maddy a chance at happiness. It was his fault the marriage had failed when all was said and done, and he would always feel guilty about the hurt he had caused Maddy. A part of him still cared about her, and he just hoped she wasn't making a big mistake.

He looked at the clock. 'I don't think we'll have much time to watch DVDs anyway, Becky. Mummy will be here any minute.'

He noted that Maddy was in fact forty minutes late, which wasn't like her at all. Once again a feeling of disquiet niggled away at him. Sensing that something wasn't quite right, he picked up the house phone and dialled Maddy's number. It took a while for her to answer the phone but when she did she sounded disconnected, as though she had other things on her mind.

'Hi, Maddy. It's Andy. I was just wondering if you are coming to pick Becky up soon.'

'What? Oh, bloody hell! Is that the time?'

'Yes. It *was* seven we agreed, wasn't it?' asked Andy, even though he was pretty sure it was.

'Yes. Yes, of course. I'm so sorry. I got so carried away with the article I was writing that I lost all track of time. I'll be round as soon as I can.'

'OK, see you soon,' said Andy.

He put the phone down and tried to put all thoughts of Maddy out of his mind so he could focus on Rebecca while she was still with him. Maybe he was overreacting where Maddy was concerned. After all, her parenting skills had never given him cause for concern in the past. Perhaps she just had a lot of work on and was feeling overstressed.

He decided not to voice his concerns to Maddy when she came to collect Rebecca, knowing she would see it as a criticism. It was important to stay amicable for Rebecca's sake, but a niggling doubt had taken root in the back of his mind and it refused to go away.

26

The next evening Gilly was on edge when he arrived in The Rose and Crown. He knew a fix would make him feel calmer, which was why he'd arranged to meet his dealer there. Ignoring Crystal and some of the other girls who were sitting at a table, he went straight to the bar and ordered a drink. The last thing he needed was Crystal bothering him when he was already feeling strung out.

He had a quick look round the room but was disappointed to find that his dealer hadn't arrived yet and it wasn't long before Crystal sidled up to him at the bar and whispered into his ear.

'You got any gear?'

He glared at her, annoyed that she was mentioning it at the bar. His arrangement with his dealer was his secret and he didn't want anyone else finding out. Although the landlord turned a blind eye to most things, even he wouldn't be happy at people dealing drugs in his pub.

'Shush,' he said, his eyes flashing her a warning look. 'Not now. Later.'

Crystal took heed of his warning and went back to join the other girls.

It was only ten minutes later when his dealer arrived but it seemed longer. Gilly was still tense and as he stood at the bar he felt nauseous and shaky, his limbs twitchy.

His dealer headed towards the bar. Gilly had spotted him through the bar's mirror even before he drew up alongside him. He strutted through the pub high-fiving his mates and trading flirty looks with the women, most of whom gazed longingly at him.

He had the kind of good looks and charisma that drew everybody in, and a dazzling smile to go with them. Gilly suspected that he indulged in a few drugs himself, but he could tell from his appearance that he wasn't dependent on the drugs he peddled, unlike most of his clientele. His boyish good looks were still intact and a sharp contrast to the sallow complexions and facial sores of many of the women he passed. He also dressed stylishly in the latest designer gear.

'You took your time,' said Gilly, but the man just smiled in that overconfident way he had and then ordered them both a drink.

Usually Gilly would wait a while before doing the deal but not today. As he tried to make small talk with his dealer, he could feel himself becoming irritated with him. The cocky, smart-arsed bastard!

Gilly put his pint down on the bar, trying to stay cool as he announced, 'I'm going outside for a cig.' It was his way of letting his supplier know that he would be in the men's toilets.

Inside the gents Gilly was relieved to find that he was alone and for some minutes he waited for his supplier. While he waited two customers entered but each time Gilly kept out of the way, hiding in a cubicle, until he heard them go out again. He felt jumpy and fidgety but knew he had to wait. His dealer would never leave the bar area at the same time as him. It would look too suspicious.

Eventually he heard the door opening again and dashed into a cubicle. Then he heard his name being called and he sighed with relief and went to join his dealer.

'Thank fuck for that,' he said. 'I thought you'd never take the hint. Let's just get it over with. You got any coke ready?'

'What? To take now?'

'Yeah, course. I need a fuckin' fix, mate,' Gilly said.

'Not in here. It's too risky.'

'I don't give a shit. Just give me the gear then you can fuck off out of it. You don't need to stay.'

His supplier quickly carried out the deal and left. Gilly went straight into a cubicle and opened up the small container of white powder. He licked his forefinger, dipped it in and placed it under his right nostril, inhaling deeply so that he could get as much of the powder into his system as possible. Then he repeated the action on his left nostril, and waited for it to take effect.

Within a couple of minutes he felt the rush. His anxiety disappeared; he was on a high, confident, full of energy and ready to take on the world. He left the gents and strode to the bar.

When Crystal went back to join her friends at the table, she kept a watch on Gilly, who was standing at the bar. He had snapped at her and she didn't like that at all. She could tell he wanted a fix; his limbs were twitchy as though he was unable to settle, and he was irritable. But she wanted a fix too. She waited for him, making small talk with her friends, while she watched him leave the room, followed some time afterwards by his dealer.

He avoided eye contact with her as he walked away from the bar, which annoyed her even more. The way he treated her was bad enough. The only reason she tolerated it was because she was in love with him, and he *did* look after her. He kept her in drugs and took care of any aggravation. But now she knew what else he got up to, it was just too much.

When he passed within a couple of metres of her table, she looked at him with distaste. How dare he chase another woman when he's with me, she thought, and then ignore me as though I don't matter?

Eventually Gilly came back into the room and went straight to the bar, where he carried on drinking his pint. Crystal continued to wait; she knew he'd give her a sign just as soon as he was ready. It wasn't long before he finished the last of his drink, said goodbye to his cronies then nodded at Crystal on his way out. She dashed after him, eager to get hold of some gear.

Outside she found him in the side street. He was buzzing, bouncing around on his feet with a big wide grin on his face. 'Got some good shit here,' he said, taking her into the shadow of a doorway so he could hand over her share. 'I'll take it out of your money tonight,' he said.

'OK, thanks.'

'You off now?' he asked after Crystal had taken a quick snort.

'Yeah, I was just waiting for some stuff.'

'OK,' he said, patting her on the behind. 'Be good.'

Then he went back into the pub and Crystal set off for her night's work. She'd noticed the change in him and realised he had probably taken something while he was still in the pub. He'd even been a bit affectionate with her, if the pat on the backside could be considered affectionate, which was as good as it got with Gilly these days.

Only a few days ago she would have been grateful for his change in attitude and for that one small sign of affection. But not now. Because what she knew changed everything. And although his interest in the journalist upset her, having something on Gilly also gave her a certain amount of control.

She now knew all about what he got up to and was determined to use that information to her advantage. What exactly she would do, she wasn't sure yet. She feared Gilly's reaction if she faced him with it, so she'd have to find some other way of hitting back at him without him knowing. Somehow, she'd make sure she got her revenge though.

27

Aaron was looking forward to spending a night in Maddy's company again. He regretted being snappy last time he saw her, a few days ago, and had vowed to himself that he would keep his cool this time. The non-stop questions were getting a bit much, but he had been thinking about how to deal with the situation and had come up with an answer.

He smiled as he rang Maddy's doorbell, carrying a bottle of her favourite wine. Within seconds she was standing on the other side of the door, but his smile slipped when he noticed Rebecca standing next to her.

'Hi!' she greeted, kissing him on the cheek.

'Hiya,' Rebecca echoed, excitedly, but he didn't return the greeting. Instead he passed Maddy the bottle of wine and stepped into the hallway.

'Ooh, lovely. My favourite,' she said.

Damn! he thought. Why is the bloody kid here?

They went inside and Rebecca gushed about a new book her dad had bought her. 'Can I show it to Aaron, Mummy?' she asked.

'Course you can, love,' said Maddy, and Rebecca rushed upstairs to find it.

'What's Becky doing here?' he asked Maddy, failing to hide his disappointment.

'Andy couldn't have her. He had to collect his mother from the hospital and settle her back into her own home.'

'He's got a nerve, hasn't he? You've had her all week!'

'Not really. His mother has been quite ill and he has her for me often enough, which has helped us to spend more time together. Anyway, you and Becky get on, don't you?'

'Well, yeah,' said Aaron, suddenly realising how much he had let his disappointment show.

He walked over to Maddy and placed his hand on her waist, his lips only centimetres from hers. 'She's a great kid but I suppose I just wanted you all to myself,' he said, feigning cheerfulness. 'Can I help it if you're so bloody desirable?' he asked before kissing her passionately.

Maddy soon pulled away. 'Don't. Becky will be back down any minute.'

As if on cue Rebecca walked into the room and took her book over to Aaron. He pretended to be interested in the bright pink book with a picture of a cat on the front.

'I'll go and get some glasses for the wine,' said Maddy, smiling in amusement. 'I'll fetch us a few nibbles too.'

Once Maddy was out of the room, Aaron thrust the book back at Rebecca. 'It looks like a good book,' he said. 'Why don't you go and read it in your room?'

He could see a look of confusion on the child's face. She had obviously been expecting to stay in their company. *No chance,* he thought. He didn't want a kid cramping his style. He had come here to spend time with Maddy, alone; not with her kid in tow.

'I don't want to,' said Rebecca. 'Will you read it to me, Aaron? Please?'

'No! Do as you're told and take it up to your room. Me and your mum want to spend some time alone.'

'But...' she began, until Aaron flashed her a warning look. 'Mum!' she called, turning away from him.

Aaron quickly grabbed her by the wrist before she had chance to go in search of her mother. 'I said go up to your fuckin' room!' he snarled, noticing the look of terror on the child's face as she turned back and looked at him.

For a moment she tried to pull away but he tightened his hold on her wrist, twisting the delicate flesh till it brought tears to her eyes. Once he had her full attention, he said, 'Now, are you gonna do as you're told and stay in your room?'

'Yes,' cried Rebecca.

He let go of her wrist and as she walked away, he added, 'And not a fuckin' word about this to anyone, if you know what's good for you!'

Rebecca fled the room in tears just before Maddy returned carrying a tray of snacks on which she'd also placed two glasses of wine. 'Where's Becky?' she asked.

Aaron shrugged. 'Dunno, gone back to her room, I think. Probably didn't want to be down here with us boring grown-ups,' he joked.

'Oh,' said Maddy, giggling then putting the tray down on the coffee table. 'I could have sworn I heard her call my name.'

'No. She didn't say anything,' said Aaron. 'Just went upstairs.'

Aaron could see a puzzled expression on Maddy's face as she took a step towards the living-room door. He knew she was going to go after Rebecca so he stopped her. If she saw her daughter had been crying it might give the game away.

'Eh,' he said, watching her hesitate then sneaking up behind her, pulling her hair to one side and kissing the back of her neck. 'She's fine. Don't worry. If she wants anything she'll soon come down and let you know.'

He continued to work on Maddy, placing his hands on the backs of her shoulders then working them down and sliding them round to her breasts. He carried on kissing the back of her neck while slipping one hand inside her bra and gently caressing her nipple till he heard her sigh with pleasure.

'Did I ever tell you you've got the most perfect breasts?' he whispered into her ear as he caressed each one in turn.

He succeeded in grabbing her attention for the next few minutes until she insisted on going to see if her daughter was all right. He hoped to God that the kid didn't say anything, but if she did then he'd just have to brazen it out and deny everything.

It was a few minutes later when Maddy came back downstairs. In the meantime Aaron had selected a DVD from Maddy's collection and put it into the player ready to watch.

'I can't think what's got into her,' Maddy said. 'She says there's nothing wrong, but she doesn't look very happy. In fact, I could swear she's been crying but she says she hasn't. She's in a horrible mood too.'

'Well, maybe she's just a bit jealous at having to share you with me; you know what kids are like.'

'Hmm,' said Maddy. 'You might have a point there. She did get a bit like that when I was seeing Rob.'

'She'll come round to the idea eventually,' said Aaron. 'Now, will you stop worrying and come and sit down?' he added. Then he nodded at the glass of wine she'd left on the coffee table. 'Look. You've hardly touched your wine. Come and relax. Becky will be fine.'

'I do hope so,' said Maddy. 'I don't like to see her like that.'

'Course she will. You know what they're like at that age. Anything could have set her off. She'll probably be fine later.'

'I suppose so,' said Maddy. 'She's almost a pre-teen now so maybe this is just a taste of what's to come.'

Aaron laughed. 'Yeah, you women can be a handful...' He then patted the seat to the side of him. 'Are you coming to sit down, then? The DVD's good to go.'

Maddy snuggled up next to Aaron. She looked at the DVD case on the coffee table, an action film, but she didn't say anything.

'I've heard it's good,' said Aaron.

Maddy tutted in mock exasperation. 'Go on, then. I've seen it before but I don't mind watching it again.'

For the first half-hour Aaron enjoyed watching the film, cuddled up with the woman of his dreams, and drinking quality wine, but then she started with the questions again.

'Can we go to the Midland next time I see you?' she said.

'Why?' he asked. 'You've got all your home comforts here.'

'Well, I just thought it would be nice. We've been here the past couple of times so it would make a change. Plus, we could go out in Manchester and not have to worry about catching a taxi back.'

Aaron laughed.

'Why are you laughing?'

'Nothing. It's just… well… it's probably still a novelty for you, isn't it? And, I must admit, I was like that at first. But when you're staying there all the time the novelty soon wears off and you're glad to get away from the place.'

'Really? Why?' she asked.

'Well, there's the noise for one thing. You know what it's like when these drunken people come in late at night waking everybody up?' His tone was jovial, laughing at the fact that they had had a couple of late boozy nights at the Midland themselves. 'But then you get the early risers as well,' he continued. 'About half six it starts: showers going, people chatting, alarms going off. It's a pain at times. Then there's the staff. Did I tell you about that cleaner who walked in on me when I was stark naked?'

Maddy laughed. 'No, you didn't,' she said. 'I bet you made her day.'

'It was bloody embarrassing, I tell you. I wouldn't mind but instead of saying sorry and shutting the door again, she stood staring at me for ages.'

'I told you, you probably made her day,' Maddy teased. 'How old was she?'

'Only a young girl.'

'There you go, then.'

Aaron sniggered before carrying on. 'Seriously though, it can be a pain at times. But if you want to go, then we'll go, no probs.'

'OK,' she said. 'We still haven't visited your family either.'

He could feel himself becoming irritated with all the probing. He loved his time with Maddy, but he wished she could just enjoy their time together like he did, and shut the fuck up about his family, business, houses and all that shit. But, despite his irritation, he didn't want to snap at her again so instead he said, 'I know, but you know how busy we've both been. I'll sort something out soon, I promise.'

He then kissed her on the lips to put an end to the conversation and they went back to watching the film. Aaron was satisfied that she was happy with his answers for now, but he'd also decided that a return visit to the Midland was needed soon. An occasional visit would be OK, just to keep her sweet and make sure she didn't suspect anything. But he'd need to do something about the family situation soon...

28

The following evening Aaron went to visit someone in The Rose and Crown. It was quiet in there so he didn't have to fight off the over-amorous women he usually attracted whenever he walked into the pub. But he was pleased to find that the person he was here to see was sitting at a side table, alone, waiting for him as arranged.

'I'll get us both a drink,' he shouted to Angie, an aging prostitute. 'What are you having?'

'I'll have a double vodka and coke, seeing as how you're buying,' she shouted back, laughing raucously at her own words.

Aaron bought the drinks then went to join Angie at the side table. Angie was considerably older than most of the other girls who worked the streets and, although she was skinny, her flesh was nevertheless sagging. She had a crinkled cleavage, enhanced by a gravity-defying push-up bra, and a complexion ravaged by drugs and cigarettes.

Angie was surprisingly well spoken for a prostitute but her voice had become husky, which Aaron presumed was down to heavy smoking. He guessed that her background was in vast contrast to the life she now led but he had never bothered asking her about it.

'What can I do for you?' she asked.

Her tone was flirty. Aaron looked across at her and cringed at the thought of doing anything intimate with Angie. He decided to come straight to the point and get this done with as soon as possible.

'I've got a job for you,' he said. 'I'll pay you, but I want it done properly and not a word to anyone.'

'Ooh, sounds interesting,' said Angie, edging forward then resting her head on her hand and attempting to stare into his eyes.

'Stop pissing about! This is fuckin' serious,' he said.

Angie sat up straight in her chair. 'OK, run it by me.'

Aaron then spent a few minutes explaining exactly what he wanted Angie to do and when he wanted it doing. Then he added, 'Her name's Maddy and she's got an eight-year-old daughter called Becky. You got that?'

'Yes, sure.'

'Well, don't forget their names. It's important.'

'OK, that's fine,' said Angie. 'How much?'

'Fifty quid.'

Angie's eyes lit up. 'Sounds good to me,' she said, holding out her hand.

'No,' he said. 'You'll get it once the job's done.'

Then he finished his pint and left The Rose and Crown.

The following Saturday night Maddy was out with Aaron.

'I've got something exciting to tell you,' he said as soon as she walked into the city centre bar where they had arranged to meet.

Maddy's eyes lit up, as she anticipated what he might have to say.

'I've found another warehouse,' he announced.

'Really?' she asked, smiling. 'Is it as good as the other one?'

'Better.'

'Great. Where is it?'

'Witney industrial estate.'

'Brilliant! That's really handy.'

'I know,' he said. 'That's why I chose it. Because it's near to you.'

Later, Aaron kept to his promise and brought Maddy to stay at the Midland hotel. She was buzzing from a wonderful night out where they'd had a meal at a top restaurant with plenty of wine. Afterwards they had a few drinks in a lively bar and danced to some great tunes.

As soon as she got inside the room she flung off her clothes and lay on top of the bed. 'I'm ready for you,' she said, giggling.

'Hang on,' said Aaron, who then pulled a backpack out from beneath the bed and unzipped it. 'I've got something that will really help you have a good time.'

'What's that?' she asked, a smile still painted on her pretty face.

He withdrew a polythene bag from the backpack, then put his hand inside it and pulled out a small container. He took the lid off and dipped his finger into some powder, which he then held to his nose and snorted.

Maddy shot up in the bed. 'Shit! Is that what I think it is?'

'Shush,' said Aaron, then whispered, 'It's coke. Why don't you try some?'

'No. Not a chance!' she said.

Aaron sidled up to her, his face serious. 'Maddy, don't believe all the scare stories. It's absolutely fine, honestly. I take it and it doesn't do me any harm.'

Maddy was alarmed and flummoxed.

'How often do you do that?' she asked, still in shock.

'Just every now and again. I'm not an addict or anything. I mean, you've never seen me take it before, have you? And I've been with you for weeks. I can take it or leave it. It's just recreational. Loads of people take it, especially middle-class professionals. Why do you think they used to call it the yuppie drug?'

'I… I don't know,' she said.

Aaron grinned at her. 'It's great stuff, honestly. And it's brilliant for sex. You'll have the best time of your life on this, trust me. If you think I've made you feel good up to now, that's nothing to how you will feel!'

Maddy still wasn't sure. But he was so convincing and part of her wanted to experience it.

'It'll take you to a whole new high,' said Aaron, adding to her thoughts.

'What if I take it, just once?' she asked. 'Will I become addicted, and have to carry on taking it?'

'Will you heck!' he scoffed. 'I told you; they're just scare stories from killjoys. If you try it once and don't like it, you never have to take it again. But, I guarantee, you *will* like it, and the sex will be out of this world.'

Maddy looked at him, still undecided. But he'd just taken some, and he seemed all right. 'How do you feel?' she asked.

'Fine. It's just starting to kick in.' Then he lifted his face as though looking at the sky, 'Wonderful!' he said.

'OK,' she said. 'But only a little bit. Let me do it myself.'

She dipped her finger cautiously into the container and withdrew a tiny amount then held her finger up, gazing at it curiously.

'That should do fine,' said Aaron. 'Just place your finger to your nostril and sniff.'

Maddy did as he suggested then waited. And waited. 'I don't feel any different,' she said.

'You will do. Give it a few minutes.'

'OK, but what do I do in the meantime?'

'Anything you want,' said Aaron, who began running his hands gently up and down her body.

Within minutes the effects kicked in. 'Wow, that's wonderful!' she said.

Aaron laughed. 'What did I tell you?'

'I mean, even better than ever.'

'Told you,' he said as he ran his tongue down her body till he found her clitoris and Maddy squealed with the pure thrill of it.

They carried on for hours, euphoric with synthetic pleasure. Maddy couldn't get enough of Aaron, and, with all her inhibitions lost to drink and drugs, she indulged in new sexual experiences that she would never have tried otherwise. It was one of the best nights of Maddy's life, and one that she was eager to repeat.

29

The following morning Maddy was still on a high and they continued to make love once they had both woken up. They were lying on the bed in a post-coital state of pure relaxation, having a pleasant chat, when Aaron's phone rang. He looked at the screen on his phone, which was on the bedside cabinet, then sprang up out of bed.

'Shit! I need the loo,' he said, heading to the bathroom. 'It's my mum. Can you take it for me, please, Maddy?'

'What do I say?' she asked.

'Just tell her I've gone to the bathroom and hold her off till I get back. I'll only be a minute.'

Maddy sighed, a little uncomfortable at having to speak to Aaron's mother, who she had never met. She shifted over to the other side of the bed and looked at the screen, which, sure enough, showed the caller's name as Mum. Then she pressed the call receive button. 'Hello, Aaron's phone,' she said.

The woman on the other end of the line sounded surprised at hearing a woman answer her son's phone.

'Oh, hello. Is Aaron not there?'

'No, I'm sorry. He's in the bathroom at the moment but he won't be long if you want to hang on a minute.'

'Yes, that's fine,' said the caller who sounded middle-aged, fairly well spoken and with an accent that was difficult to place.

'You must be Maddy,' said the woman.

It was Maddy's turn to be surprised, as well as flattered that Aaron's mother seemed to know who she was. That meant he must have talked about her to his family.

'Yes, that's right,' said Maddy.

'How are you? I've heard a lot of good things about you.'

'I'm good, thanks. I hope you are too.'

'Yes, I'm very well. I've heard a lot about your daughter too. Becky, isn't it? I believe she's as good as gold.'

Maddy was feeling a little embarrassed at being showered with praise by a complete stranger. 'Oh, she has her moments.' She laughed. 'But then, don't all children?'

'Oh, yes. I could tell you plenty of tales about Aaron when he was a child. Anyway, it will be lovely to meet you and your daughter when Aaron brings you to Yorkshire. I'm looking forward to it.'

'Me too,' said Maddy before Aaron returned from the bathroom and she passed him the phone.

For a few minutes he chatted to his mother. Maddy could tell that she was asking after his welfare. It sounded as though the conversation might go on for some time so Maddy decided to give Aaron some privacy while she went to take a shower.

Her good mood continued while she showered and got herself ready. She hoped she had made a good impression on Aaron's mother, who had sounded so nice, and it was reassuring to know that Aaron had been talking to his mother about her. After all, he was the man of her dreams and she intended for him to be a major part of her life for a long time to come.

Later that day Andy was at home with Rebecca waiting for Maddy to pick her daughter up. As the time approached seven, he had an unsettling feeling that Maddy was going to be late again.

The end of Rebecca's visits were always a bit awkward. For one thing, he usually knew that it would be a few days before he saw her again. So, even if they'd had a great time together, he would always feel disappointed at having to say goodbye. He could sense the build-up in Rebecca too and, although she no longer cried as she used to in the early days, she was always in an odd mood. It felt as if her excitement at the prospect of seeing her mother was tinged with disappointment at having to leave him.

Apart from that, he could never decide what to do with Rebecca when Maddy was due to pick her up. Whatever activity they started would be interrupted by Maddy's arrival. Even TV wasn't a safe option as Rebecca would be disheartened at having to leave a programme part way through. And he hated letting her down in any way; the divorce had already caused her enough pain and he'd always feel guilty about that.

Rebecca seemed to reflect his thoughts when she asked, 'What time is Mummy coming?'

'Seven,' he said, noticing that it was already five to.

Rebecca had noticed the time too. 'She'll be here soon, then, won't she, Daddy?'

'Yes,' he said.

But Maddy didn't arrive at seven and Andy had to keep reassuring his daughter that she wouldn't be long. When it got to ten past seven he decided to give it five more minutes before ringing her to find out where she was.

It wasn't the first time Maddy had been late recently and, along with other things surrounding Maddy's new relationship, he was worried about the effects it was having on his daughter. And, if he was honest with himself, he was a little bit worried about Maddy too. What Rebecca had told him during this visit had caused him particular anguish and he felt he had no alternative but to speak to Maddy about it.

It was a few seconds later when he heard the doorbell and he and Rebecca raced to answer the door. He found Maddy on the other side, looking a bit dishevelled and apologising profusely for being late. It was the usual excuse: she'd had a lot of work to catch up on that day and had lost track of the time. He presumed she mustn't have been able to get through her work during the week for whatever reason.

While making her excuses Maddy gushed about what a wonderful time she'd had in Manchester on Saturday night and was he familiar with such and such a bar, which was a great place to go. Andy feigned interest but he was really more concerned about the effect her busy new lifestyle was having on his daughter.

Rebecca seemed a little subdued when her mother arrived. She didn't rush to tell her all her news as she would normally have done. Instead she looked up at her mother and gave her a wan smile.

'Becky, I need to speak to your mother,' said Andy. 'Would you mind waiting in the car while we have a quick word?'

Maddy raised her eyebrows inquisitively while Rebecca nodded and made for the car, dragging her feet.

'It's about something Becky told me,' said Andy. 'She told me that Aaron has been swearing in front of her. When I asked her what he said she clammed up and just said "really bad words". I'm not very happy about it, Maddy. You know we don't use that sort of language in front of Becky. She's just a child.'

Maddy's mood soon changed, her tone strident as she retaliated. 'Hang on a minute! I think you're jumping the gun a bit,' she said. 'Aaron has *never* sworn in front of Becky.'

'Why would she lie about something like that, Maddy?'

'Right, so you're assuming that I must be lying, is that it?'

'Well, one of you is, and I don't think it's Becky.'

'Are you sure you haven't got the wrong end of the stick here, Andy?'

'Not at all; I could tell she wasn't lying. In fact, she seemed quite upset about it.'

'So, are you saying that I must be lying, then?'

Andy shrugged. 'Well, like I say, one of you must be. To tell you the truth, Maddy, I'm more than a bit concerned. Becky doesn't seem herself recently and, to be honest, neither do you. From what she tells me you don't spend as much time with her lately and you always seem to be running late these days—'

Maddy cut him short before he could say anything else. 'How dare you? How dare you judge me and how I am with

Becky? I was the one who had to hold everything together when you destroyed our marriage because of your carry-on with that tart. And now that I've found a bit of happiness, you don't bloody well like it, do you?'

Andy held his hand out in supplication, conscious of how heated the conversation had become, and not wanting either Rebecca or the neighbours to overhear.

'This isn't helping Becky,' he said. 'I think we should discuss things another time, but I can't pretend I'm happy with your current situation, Maddy.'

'You're just bloody jealous,' she continued. 'Aaron is wonderful with Becky, and that's what you can't stand, isn't it? Well, if you didn't want another man in Becky's life then you shouldn't have done what you did, should you?'

Over her shoulder Andy could see Rebecca opening the car door then stepping out. He nodded in her direction, hoping Maddy would take the hint and calm down in front of her daughter.

'I'll see you next weekend,' he said to Maddy, 'but please think about what I've said.' Then he shouted to Rebecca, 'Bye, sweetheart, see you soon.'

Maddy scowled at him before turning and walking away.

When she was gone, Andy thought about the cross words they'd exchanged. He hadn't wanted it to become so heated, especially in front of his daughter. Up to now he and Maddy had managed to remain amicable, but, where Rebecca's welfare was concerned, he couldn't just sit back and say nothing. The trouble was that he had hurt Maddy in the past and, although he'd thought she had buried the hurt a long time ago, it was still there, and, on days like today, it would quickly rise back to the surface along with all the bitterness and resentment that went with it.

Andy had a bad feeling about this Aaron character. Something wasn't right about him and he hoped that Maddy would soon come to her senses and end the relationship.

30

The Rose and Crown was busy when Aaron arrived, which wasn't ideal. There were many women in the pub, most of them rough-looking, and as he walked through the bar he could see some of them preening themselves and trying to catch his eye. He ignored them as he searched for Angie, who he spotted on a table full of working girls.

Aaron walked over to her. 'Can I have a word?' he asked, then he walked out of the pub, expecting Angie to follow him.

'Let's go for a walk,' he said once they were outside the pub. 'I don't want anyone listening.'

'You're looking smart tonight,' she commented. 'Going anywhere nice?'

Aaron ignored her question. He wasn't in the mood for small talk, especially with someone like Angie. He didn't actually want to be seen with her at all, but she had been perfect for the task she'd carried out and now he just wanted to pay up.

As they walked down the road, he spoke. 'Well done,' he said. 'She fell for it hook, line and sinker.'

Angie smiled. 'Good, glad to hear it.'

He pulled five ten-pound notes from his wallet, folded them in his hand and then surreptitiously passed them to her.

'Thanks,' she said, laughing. 'It's the easiest fifty quid I've earnt for a while. Let me know if you need my services again.' She smiled and raised her eyebrows provocatively.

'You can go back to the pub now,' said Aaron, not wishing to stay in Angie's company any longer than necessary. He found the mere sight of her repugnant and her flirtation irritating.

He could see the disappointment in her face but he didn't care; he just wanted rid of her. But Angie wasn't so easy to get rid of.

'How come you want her to think I'm your mum anyway?' she asked.

'What did I fuckin' say to you when I asked you to do the job?' he snapped. Her confused expression made him even more annoyed. 'I said no fuckin' questions. You just do what I pay you to do and keep your fuckin' nose out of my business. OK?'

'I was only asking,' said Angie.

'Well, don't! And, you've to keep this to yourself, all right? I swear that if I hear you've breathed a word of this to anyone, I'll fuckin' have you! Do you understand?'

'Yes,' she said, her voice now a mere whisper, but he could tell by the expression on her face that his words had got through to her.

'Right, now fuck off!'

Angie turned back towards the pub without saying another word while Aaron carried on in the opposite direction. He was livid with her but at least she'd done a good job. And now that Maddy believed him he just had to keep thinking up excuses to delay the visit to Yorkshire.

Maddy was delighted when Aaron turned up at her home that Saturday afternoon. It was the first time she'd seen him for days. For once she'd resisted the temptation to see him during the week, knowing they both had a lot to do. What she didn't admit to herself was that Andy's words of a few days ago had perhaps also affected her.

She'd spoken to Aaron on the phone during the week, telling him about her row with Andy but not going into too many details as she hadn't wanted Rebecca to overhear her. But now they were alone, she couldn't wait to confide in him.

'Put your jacket on. We're not stopping,' he said as soon as he walked into the hallway.

'Oh,' she said, looking at him, her lips pouting and her manner sultry. Then she drew closer, grasping his shoulders between her hands as her breasts rubbed against his body. 'Haven't you missed me?'

Aaron laughed. 'Of course I have but there'll be plenty of time for that later. There's something I want to show you first and I think you're gonna like it.'

'Ooh, sounds good.' She giggled.

Aaron took hold of her hand. 'Come on,' he said. 'I can't wait to show you.'

'Wait a minute. I haven't got my jacket yet or put my shoes on.'

Aaron waited in the car, then watched as Maddy stepped into the vehicle, her tight-fitting skirt riding up to expose a tantalising amount of flesh as she curled her legs inside. He smiled and started the engine.

'What's all this about your ex-husband, then?' he asked as they set off down the road.

'Oh, he seems to have got a bee in his bonnet.' She sighed in irritation. 'Like I told you on the phone, Becky is supposed to have told him that you swore at her.'

'I'd never do that, Maddy.'

'I know. You told me. I can only think Becky lied about it for some reason, but I can't think why. It isn't like her. Then again, she is showing signs of jealousy like she did when I was with Rob. So perhaps it's down to that. I did tackle her about it and she swears she didn't say anything to her father. In fact, she looked a bit put out by the fact that he had told me what she said.'

'Well, to be honest, Maddy, we have been spending a lot of time together.'

Maddy looked at him, shocked, and he could tell she was expecting him to cool things off. 'Oh, not that I'm complaining,' he quickly added. 'But you can understand it in a way. She's become used to having you to herself and probably doesn't like to share you. Kids can get like that. It's understandable.'

'Well, it's not on,' she said. 'I'm entitled to a life too and she'll just have to get used to it.'

Aaron had been testing her to see how much she valued his company, and by the sound of things she wasn't going to let even her daughter come between them.

'What are you smiling at?' she asked, pulling him out of his reverie.

'Oh, sorry. It's just nice to know that you won't let anything come between us. I didn't mean to smile. I know it can't be easy for you if Becky's playing up a bit.'

'Oh, she's not playing up, not really. Andy might even have got the wrong end of the stick. But then he really started getting on my case, telling me Becky wasn't herself these days and neither was I. Oh, and I'm always on the last minute, apparently.'

'Really?'

'Yes. How dare he? What I do with my life is my own bloody business.'

'Too true,' he said. 'You sure he isn't a bit jealous too?'

'Possibly. I don't think he likes the idea of me being with someone else, but he should have thought of that before he started knocking about with that tart, shouldn't he?'

'Dead right. Don't let him get to you, Maddy. Like you say, you're entitled to a life and you're a brilliant mother. Becky's very lucky to have you.'

Maddy smiled and patted him affectionately. This time he resisted the temptation to smile back. It was important that she thought he was taking her seriously and supporting her. Her ex-husband could go to hell! He might think he was still pulling her strings, but Aaron knew that, where Maddy was concerned, *he* was the one in control.

31

Aaron and Maddy were still inside his car, heading towards Stockport. Once they'd passed through the town Aaron drove on for a while longer. As they sat in silence he could tell Maddy had a lot on her mind and, sure enough, after a few minutes she wanted to offload again.

'Aaron,' she began. 'Thanks for being patient and agreeing not to see me for a few days this week.'

'That's OK, no problem,' he cut in. 'As long as it makes you happy, Maddy; I'll do whatever it takes. You know that.' Then he quickly added, 'Not that I haven't missed you, but I hope it's given you chance to catch up with things.'

'Yes, it has,' she said. 'I'd sooner have been with you, but I need to earn a living at the end of the day.'

'No worries,' he said. 'Stick with me and, you never know, you might be able to give up work one day.'

Maddy flashed a surprised grin at him then said, 'Don't get me wrong, I love what I do. But sometimes I just feel so bloody overwhelmed with everything. I love being with you and why shouldn't I be? But then there's my job, Becky, the house and everything else. Most of the time I'm run off my feet. Anyway, I hope it's given you chance to catch up with things too. Maybe next week we can spend a little more time together.'

'Sounds good,' he said, evading her comment about him catching up with things but quick to notice her reaction when he'd mentioned the possibility of her giving up work in the future and he knew the comment had hit home.

'Anyway, we're almost there,' he said as they drove along Bramhall Lane.

A couple of minutes later and they were turning into the car park at a new housing development. 'It sounds as though you could do with cheering up so maybe this will do the trick,' he said, peering through the windscreen at the executive homes.

Her eyes followed his and she smiled. 'Wow! It looks lovely,' she said.

'I know. I found it on the Internet. I'm looking forward to seeing the properties myself. I've only seen them online but they looked great.'

They walked into the sales office where an eager agent greeted them. 'Hello,' she said, peering up from her desk when she heard the door open. 'What can I do for you?'

'We'd like to do some viewings,' said Aaron.

'Aah, right. Do you have an appointment?'

'No, we called in on spec,' said Aaron.

'Oh, I see. Well, I'm afraid we only do viewings by appointment. This is an exclusive development so we like to run checks on prospective buyers' financial status. I'm sure you understand.'

'Oh, that's a pity,' said Aaron. 'I've been busy all week, tied up with my businesses, so I've only just had chance to pop by. But I did manage to take a look online and your top-of-the-range home would suit us down to a tee.'

'Aah, the Maple?' she asked. 'Perhaps I could make an appointment for you to view it.' She began flicking through the pages of her desk diary.

'Ooh, not sure,' said Aaron, looking at the screen on his phone and pressing a few buttons. 'Let me see when I'm next free... Ooh, I'm afraid I couldn't fit in a viewing for at least two weeks. My business is in central Manchester, you see, and I just wouldn't have the time to drive here and back in the week. Then the weekends are tied up with transferring stock from my Yorkshire branch over to Manchester.'

He could tell by the look on the agent's face that she was suitably impressed. 'Is there no way you could squeeze in a viewing before then?' she asked. 'These houses will go very fast so it's best to get in early.'

'Not really,' he said, then he made a show of looking pensive before he turned to Maddy. 'How about that other development we talked about?' he asked. 'We could always go there, then come back here in a couple of weeks if we don't find anything. Their five-bedroomed house did look particularly nice online. A business colleague of mine bought one recently and he says there's a good chance of us getting a price reduction, what with being cash buyers.'

To his relief Maddy played along with his act. 'I suppose so, but I wouldn't have minded seeing this one while we're here,' she said.

'You sure you can't squeeze us in today?' he asked again. 'I hate to let my partner down. She's used to the best,' he said, enjoying the pretence.

While he was talking he had been watching the look on the agent's face. The obsequious smile had vanished and she had started instead to look concerned; it was obvious to Aaron that she hadn't sold many houses lately. At these prices they were probably slow to shift.

'Perhaps we could,' she said, consulting her diary again. 'I've got another viewing to the Maple in a quarter of an hour. Perhaps if you're quick we could do it before then.'

'Sure,' said Aaron, striding over to the desk and waiting while she searched for the keys to the property.

When she had located them, she gave them brief instructions of where to find the show home. Then she held out the keys for Aaron to take.

'And please don't let anybody know that you viewed without an appointment,' she added as she dropped them into his hand. 'It isn't something we usually do.'

'No problems,' said Aaron, smiling. 'Your secret's safe with me.'

As soon as they were outside and out of the agent's view, Maddy burst into laughter. 'I can't believe you,' she said. 'You can really pour the charm on when you want to,' she teased.

'You know me,' said Aaron. 'Charming is my middle name,' to which Maddy responded by laughing some more. 'It's not as if I can't afford it, is it?' he said. 'Sod their petty rules. I haven't got time to come back just to keep them happy. Anyway, I really wanted to show it to you today. You needed cheering up.'

Maddy smiled at him. 'Aw, you're so sweet,' she said.

They spent the next ten minutes looking round the plush executive home. Maddy marvelled at the luxury fitted kitchen, modern bathrooms and high-end furnishings and Aaron could tell she was impressed. She might have had a lovely home but it was nothing compared to this one.

When they finished looking round, Aaron locked the front door and turned to walk back to the sales office. 'Well, what do you think?' asked Maddy.

'Very nice,' he said. 'Just the sort of thing I'm looking for.'

'Are you going to buy one?' she asked.

'Not yet. I'm still busy kitting out the new warehouse so I don't want to get bogged down with all the paperwork, not to mention decorating, buying furniture and all the rest of it. I just wanted to give you an idea of the sort of thing we'll be looking for once everything else is sorted.'

The 'we' was deliberate and he noticed how her face lit up as he said it. They went back into the sales office and Aaron made his excuses before they walked away. Inside the car he turned to her before starting the engine. 'Well, I'm glad that seems to have done the trick,' he said. 'You look much happier than you did earlier.'

'I know, I—'

'Shush,' he said, pressing his finger to her lips before silencing her. 'Forget about your worries for now. I want you to be happy. So, today we're going to have a good time.'

Aaron took his finger away from her lips and reached towards the glove compartment. He opened it up and took out a small container and placed it inside her hand, folding her fingers around it.

Maddy went to open her hand to check what it was but he stopped her. 'No, not here,' he said. 'Put it inside your handbag. It's just a little something for you. I know things have been stressful for you lately and I feel a bit responsible as I've been taking up so much of your time. This will help to pick you up if you need it. Next time you're feeling a bit low, stressed out or just overtired, take some. It'll make you feel better.'

'No, I couldn't,' she said as she tried to pass it back to him.

'Why not?' he asked. 'You've had it before and it didn't do you any harm. In fact, if I remember rightly, you rather enjoyed it.' He gazed intently at her, noticing her flush at his words, and he grinned wickedly.

'Seriously, though, it won't do you any harm, as long as you only take a bit and don't make a habit of it. It's my little present to you and I'd be offended if you refused it.'

She looked shamefaced, 'OK, thank you,' she said, placing it reluctantly inside her handbag.

As they drove back Aaron became immersed in his own thoughts. He was pleased Maddy had believed him when he'd feigned interest in the house, and she'd even gone along with his little lie to entice the sales clerk into letting them have a viewing.

She'd also believed Angie was his mother, and taken the coke he'd offered her. He was happy with the way things were going and, where Maddy was concerned, it was all so easy.

32

It was the following evening. Aaron had left that afternoon to go back to the Midland and Rebecca had returned from her father's and Maddy thought she'd take the opportunity to have a chat with Rebecca while they were alone. She was concerned that Rebecca might have been telling lies about Aaron and she wanted to find out why that might be.

'Becky,' she said, as she popped her head through the door of her daughter's bedroom. She walked over and sat down on the bed beside her. 'I want us to have a little talk. It's about what you said to Daddy about Aaron. Do you remember? You told Daddy that Aaron had been swearing at you.' Rebecca nodded but didn't say anything so Maddy continued. 'Why did you say that, Becky?'

Rebecca looked at her, wide-eyed, then lowered her head and shrugged.

'You know it's not a nice thing to say, don't you?'

Rebecca kept her head down but nodded again.

'Then why would you say that, Becky?'

Her daughter still kept her head lowered and didn't react so Maddy gently took her chin and lifted it until she was facing her. 'Come on now, Becky. Tell me. I want to know.'

Her daughter just stared at her, but didn't speak. She looked uncomfortable, her eyes flitting about, unable to maintain eye contact, and Maddy took it as a sign of guilt.

'Come on, Becky. I'm waiting. Aaron didn't really swear at you, did he? Aaron never swears at you.'

As Maddy watched her daughter she saw her eyes fill with tears and Rebecca tried to pull away from her.

'Do you not like Aaron, Becky?'

Her daughter still didn't reply. 'If you're bothered by me spending so much time with Aaron, then tell me. Are you, Becky?'

For a few moments Rebecca remained silent, and Maddy continued to hold her chin so that she was facing her. She fixed her with a stony stare, refusing to budge until her daughter spoke. She noticed a tear fall onto Rebecca's cheek and tried to ignore her feelings of guilt as she waited for an answer.

'No,' said Rebecca, in the tiniest of voices.

'No, what? No, you're not bothered about me spending so much time with Aaron or no, you don't like him?'

'No, I don't like him,' said Rebecca, her bottom lip jutting out sulkily.

'Why, Becky, when he's always been so nice to you?'

When Rebecca didn't reply, Maddy sighed and said, 'You know Mummy is allowed to have her own friends, don't you, Becky? It doesn't mean I love you any less.'

Rebecca nodded slowly but didn't speak, and Maddy persisted. 'So what is it that's bothering you, Becky? Why did you tell Daddy that Aaron swore?'

Rebecca shrugged again but she still didn't say anything further. Maddy resigned herself to the fact that her daughter wasn't going to open up, so she changed tack. 'Right, I want you to promise me, Becky, that you won't go telling such tales to Daddy again. It's naughty to do that, do you understand?' Rebecca nodded again. 'Right, well, let me hear you promise you won't do it again,' Maddy persisted.

'Yes,' mumbled Rebecca.

'Yes, what?'

'Yes, I promise,' she said, her eyes downcast and her voice barely a whisper.

Maddy let go of her daughter's chin and stood up. 'Right, well, let that be the end of it,' she said, then she left her daughter alone and returned to the living room.

Maddy was still troubled. She had been determined to find out why her daughter was telling tales, but she had given nothing away. Perhaps it was like Aaron had said: she was seeking attention because she was feeling a bit jealous. Unless Aaron *had* sworn at her. But Maddy quickly dismissed that thought.

No, Rebecca was obviously telling little fibs and, Maddy thought, it was the last thing she needed. Up until now, she and Andy had managed the arrangements for Rebecca's care amicably and Maddy didn't really want to get into a situation where she and Andy were at loggerheads. She'd just have to hope that things settled down.

Her thoughts soon switched to Aaron and, as she thought about the previous night that she had spent with him, a shiver of excitement ran through her body. The sex had been phenomenal; the best yet. They'd used cocaine again and, although Maddy promised herself that she wouldn't make a regular habit of it, she loved the added buzz that it gave her. It was only a few hours since Aaron had left her company but already she was eager to see him again.

Maddy had dropped Rebecca at school that morning. Since their discussion the previous day, Maddy hadn't mentioned Rebecca's little fib again. She'd decided to let it go and hope that there were no further incidents, but she couldn't help noticing how subdued Rebecca was.

Now, as she ploughed through her work, Maddy was trying not to think about her concerns. It was mid-morning when she heard the sound of the letterbox clattering. That will be the postman, she thought, noticing that it was his usual time for deliveries and then hearing the mail land on the hallway carpet.

Deciding it was time for a coffee break, Maddy flicked the switch on the kettle, then retrieved her mail while she waited for it to boil. She quickly sorted through her letters, which were mainly junk with the exception of one from the building society. Curious, she opened it and was alarmed to find that they were demanding payment for last month's mortgage, which hadn't been paid. *Surely that couldn't be right,* but she decided to check to be on the safe side.

Maddy strode over to her computer and signed into her online banking account. She was alarmed to find that, not only had her mortgage payment not gone through, but she was also a further three hundred pounds overdrawn. Not quite believing her eyes, she scanned through the figures on the screen, checking that there hadn't been some sort of error. But everything seemed to be in order except that her outgoings exceeded her income.

Maddy never went overdrawn! She usually earned far in excess of her outgoings so she didn't need to worry about bills, feeling confident they would be covered. But now, as she stared in shock at the figures on the screen, she realised that she had let things slide. It was a long time since she had checked her bank balance. She had been so busy lately that it was yet another thing she had neglected, and she needed to put everything else to one side while she chased up some outstanding payments.

Maddy checked the spreadsheet on which she recorded all her income and compared it to her bank account. There was only one company that hadn't paid her and that was for a small amount, which wouldn't have impacted her account that much. But as she checked she saw that her income for that month was well down on previous months.

It was with startling clarity that Maddy realised her lack of production, together with the business she had lost, had caused a drastic reduction in income. Maddy felt a rush of adrenalin as panic gripped her. She'd never been in debt in her life! The fear of losing her home was too big a worry for Maddy and she knew she had to work much harder if she was to get her bank account out of the red.

When Crystal woke up that Monday morning Gilly was still snoring gently beside her. She quietly slipped out of bed, knowing that Candice would soon be up and wanting her attention. It was the first time Gilly had come back to her place for ages. At one time he'd have been back several nights a week after she'd said goodbye to her last customer, but not now.

The sex had changed too. He used to be really attentive but now it was beginning to feel as if he were just another client, there to satiate his own needs regardless of how she felt. But the difference was that Gilly was the man she loved and it was her love for him that made her stick by him. She wished, not for the first time, that he didn't have this hold over her.

Crystal knew the change in Gilly had something to do with his interest in the journalist. The way he sat in his car outside her house for ages just wasn't normal. But she knew better than to challenge him about it. He'd probably go ape shit if he knew she was on to him. So, for now, she'd put up with it but not for long.

33

When Maddy arrived at school to collect Rebecca on Thursday of the following week, she was disappointed to find that all the parking spaces had been taken. As usual recently, Maddy was running late. She had been trying to utilise every spare minute to get as much work done as possible, having got behind again due to the amount of time she had been spending with Aaron. Unfortunately, while she was busy typing up an article, she'd become so engrossed in her work that she had lost track of time.

She passed by the school building looking out for any available space in which to park her car. Nothing. After she had passed the school she turned left but was disconcerted to find that this road was jam-packed too.

Eventually Maddy found a space but it was several streets away. She parked the car then ran till she got to the top of the street. She rounded the bend and continued running. In the distance she could see a few parents with their children.

Damn! thought Maddy. They were already on their way home and she was still a few minutes away.

By the time Maddy arrived at school she was almost ten minutes late. The yard was empty and Maddy knew she'd find Rebecca inside with her teacher, Miss Lazenby. Maddy knew the drill by now; it was the third time she'd been late in as many weeks.

She walked into the classroom, her face flushed and her hair messy. Rebecca was at the back of the classroom writing in an exercise book while Miss Lazenby sat at her desk at the front attending to some paperwork. Rebecca looked up from her work as Maddy walked in, but she remained seated, waiting for her teacher's permission to leave her desk.

'I'm so sorry,' said Maddy, directing the apology at Miss Lazenby as she made her way towards Rebecca.

Miss Lazenby, usually very pleasant and forgiving, gave a weak smile before she spoke. 'Mrs Chambers, could I have a word, please?' Then her eyes flitted to Rebecca. 'Can you carry on with what you're doing for now, please, Rebecca? I need to have a word with your mother.'

'Certainly,' said Maddy and she started to make her way over to Miss Lazenby's desk, but the teacher got up from her seat.

'I think outside might be better,' she said, and Maddy could tell from her posture and body language that this was going to be an awkward discussion.

They stood outside the classroom, near enough for Rebecca to find them if necessary but far enough for her not to hear the conversation. Miss Lazenby came straight to the point, her eyes twitching nervously as she spoke.

'Mrs Chambers, do you think you could start arriving at the proper time to pick Rebecca up?' she asked.

Maddy wasn't sure why she was making such a big deal of it, knowing that teachers rarely went home as soon as the pupils finished. Nevertheless, she felt duty bound to apologise again. 'Yes, yes. I'm sorry,' she said. 'I was a bit late setting off and it was impossible to get a parking space so—'

Miss Lazenby cut her off, appearing anxious to say what she had to say as soon as possible. 'I'm afraid this is the third time in three weeks. Perhaps you could leave home a little earlier or ask someone else to collect Rebecca if you aren't able to do it.'

Maddy was embarrassed at being addressed in this manner. She felt like a naughty schoolgirl. 'No, no, it's OK,' she said. 'I can collect Becky. I'll make sure it doesn't happen again.'

She raised her hand ready to push the handle on the classroom door, but Miss Lazenby wasn't finished yet. She cleared her throat before continuing.

'Erm, there is another matter I need to discuss with you.'

Maddy recognised the severity of her tone and raised her eyebrows inquisitively.

'I'm afraid we've noticed some changes in Rebecca's behaviour,' said Miss Lazenby. 'She doesn't seem to be engaging as much in the classroom and has become a bit distanced from the other children.'

'How do you mean?' asked Maddy.

'Well, it's difficult to pinpoint but she seems troubled, as though she has something on her mind.' For a few seconds there was an awkward silence between them until Miss

Lazenby asked, 'Is there anything you're aware of that might be troubling her?'

Thoughts of Rebecca's claims about Aaron swearing flashed through Maddy's mind but she quickly decided not to mention that. She didn't want to give the school reason to think that all wasn't well at home. Anyway, it probably wasn't even relevant.

'No,' said Maddy, but she was slow to react.

'Are you sure?' asked Miss Lazenby. 'Is there anything at all that might have upset her?'

'No, not at all,' said Maddy with conviction, trying to compensate for her initial slow response. 'Are you sure it isn't something at school? And what exactly is the problem?' Maddy asked, becoming defensive. 'What do you mean by distanced?'

'Well, like I said, it's difficult to pinpoint. It's more a feeling that she doesn't seem as happy as usual. Not always joining in games with the other children, sitting quietly on her own, that sort of thing.'

'Well, I would have thought it's a good thing that she sits quietly. At least she isn't being disruptive.'

'Yes, I appreciate that, Mrs Chambers. I wasn't suggesting that she's disruptive. It might be something and nothing, but I just felt that I should make you aware of it, that's all. If you can think of anything, anything at all, please let the school know.'

'Yes, I will do,' said Maddy, reaching once again towards the door handle.

Before she had chance to push the door open, Miss Lazenby added a few quick words. 'And if you could please get to school on time, Mrs Chambers. I'm sure it would be better for Rebecca if she sees you in the playground when all her friends' parents arrive.'

Now Maddy realised what the big deal was. She was so busy thinking about the teacher's reaction to her being late that she hadn't thought about the effect on Rebecca. As the realisation hit her, she felt a stab of guilt, picturing Rebecca's eager little face as she waited for her to arrive. The look of disappointment when she realised that her mother was late, yet again. And her slumped shoulders as she trudged dejectedly back to the classroom.

'Yes, of course I will,' said Maddy, dashing into the classroom to hide her look of shame and embarrassment at being rebuked by a woman ten years her junior.

When Maddy arrived home she decided to have a chat with Rebecca and see if she could get her to open up about what was troubling her. But, just like their last chat, Rebecca remained tight-lipped. Maddy tried to tell herself that if Rebecca really was troubled then she would have told her about it, and part of her was more focused on returning to that article she had left. If she was quick she might just finish it before teatime.

It took longer than she'd thought and by the time she had typed the last word it was turned five o'clock. The thought of cooking a big meal at this time didn't really appeal so she decided to settle for a quick dinner of beans on toast. It wouldn't do them any harm for once.

After Maddy had finished dishing up their dinner she gave Rebecca a shout, and she came trundling down from her room. Straight away, a look of disappointment flashed across her face when she saw the meagre meal set out before her.

'What's the matter?' asked Maddy.

Rebecca remained standing, looking contemptuously at the meal. 'You said we were having cheese and onion pie,' she said.

Maddy remembered her promise to make Rebecca her home-made cheese and onion pie. 'I said I'd do it if I wasn't too busy, Becky, but unfortunately I haven't had time. I'll make it for you another night. Now sit down, please, and eat up.'

'No. You won't make it. I know you won't. You're always too busy since Aaron started coming here.'

'It's got nothing to do with Aaron,' said Maddy. 'I need to work to make a living otherwise you wouldn't have all the nice things you take for granted. And, as I've told you before, Mummy is allowed to spend time with her friends. Now do as you're told and eat your food.'

'I don't want it!' shouted Rebecca, who then fled to her room in tears.

After a few seconds in shock, Maddy stormed after her, furious by now. 'Don't you dare leave the table! Get back here at once,' she shouted up the stairs.

But when Becky didn't reply she followed her to her room. There she found her face down on her bed, the sound of her sobbing stifled by her pillow, which she clutched to her face.

For a moment Maddy felt sorry for her, knowing that it hadn't always been easy for her since the divorce, but she knew she couldn't afford to let her get away with such behaviour.

'Becky, are you going to come and eat your dinner or do I have to punish you?'

When Rebecca still wouldn't come downstairs after several minutes Maddy felt she'd have to take action. 'Right, you're grounded for a week and that means no netball club either.'

She walked out of Rebecca's room without waiting for a response, worried that she might weaken if she saw the disappointment on her daughter's face.

By the time Maddy returned to her own dinner it had gone cold and after a half-hearted attempt she left most of it. She was already feeling bad. Her daughter wasn't having a good time of it; first she turned up late to pick her up again and then this. As the guilt ate away at her she couldn't help but wonder if she was somehow responsible for her daughter's behaviour.

Maddy decided that maybe she was neglecting her a bit lately and promised herself, yet again, that she would try to see less of Aaron and spend more time with her daughter. She only hoped she could keep to that promise and avoid Aaron's temptations.

Later, when Rebecca was in bed, Maddy tried to get some more work done. But it was difficult to concentrate; she was bogged down with tiredness, strung out and had too much on her mind. She was also upset about Rebecca. Eventually, when her brain wouldn't focus, she thought about the words Aaron had spoken as he had given her his gift. *Next time you're feeling a bit low, stressed out or just overtired, take some. It'll make you feel better.*

At the time, she had accepted the gift to please him without any intentions of using it. But now, as she thought about the buzz she gained from something so seemingly innocuous as a bit of white powder, she was sorely tempted, knowing it would make her more alert and perhaps awake enough to do some more work. But she managed to resist, for now.

34

The following morning Maddy was glad that Rebecca seemed in a better mood as she got ready for school. Maddy was planning on dropping her at the school gate before driving into Manchester, where she was due to attend an editorial meeting with a major client. After the meeting she had arranged to meet Clare for lunch.

For once Maddy was well ahead of schedule as she waited in the hallway for Rebecca to put her shoes on. Once Rebecca was ready Maddy opened the front door, smiling at her daughter as she did so, but when she swung the door open she was alarmed at what she saw and the smile soon slipped from her face.

The word *bitch* was emblazoned across the front door in thick red marker pen. A whimper escaped Maddy's lips as she took a sharp breath and her hand shot up to cover her mouth.

'What is it, Mummy?' asked Rebecca, approaching Maddy so she could take a look.

Maddy quickly stood in front of the letters but they were so huge that her slim frame failed to conceal them all. The letter B and half of the letter H were still visible. Rebecca looked at them curiously, trying to figure out what they said.

'It's graffiti,' Maddy said, becoming agitated. 'Nothing for you to worry about; I can get rid of it. Go and wait at the car while I lock up. And don't look at it. It's a rude word.'

Maddy stood in front of the graffiti, facing the door. Wanting desperately to hide it from her daughter, she pulled a tissue out of her handbag and dabbed it with her tongue till it was moist. Then she took the tissue to the door, rubbing at the letters frantically in the hope that she could at least get rid of part of it before they set off for school. But it soon became clear that it wasn't going to shift easily. And she really needed to get to school. She couldn't be late again.

Maddy paused for a moment, undecided. Then her worry about being late won over her concerns about the graffiti. She'd have to take Rebecca to school and sort the graffiti out later, she thought while she locked the door, her hands trembling. She felt sullied and upset. But at the moment she was more concerned about her daughter's reaction if she saw what was written.

Maddy swung round, trying to obscure most of the word while checking that her daughter kept her gaze ahead of her.

As she walked towards the car Maddy clicked her key fob to open the doors. 'Get inside the car and ignore it,' she said, regretting that, yet again, she was a bit sharp with Rebecca.

She watched as Rebecca opened the car door and stepped inside, then Maddy walked round to the driver's door and got in. As she started the engine she glanced across at her daughter, whose head was now turned towards the house.

'I said don't look at it!' yelled Maddy and Rebecca automatically obeyed by turning her head face forward.

But it was too late. She could tell by the shocked expression on her daughter's face that she had seen it. Neither of them spoke. Maddy felt too ashamed and didn't know what to say that would make it seem better. Rebecca, Maddy guessed, probably didn't want to hear her acknowledge that she had seen it.

A few minutes later Maddy dropped Rebecca at school, her mind preoccupied throughout the journey with worries about who would do such a thing. She wondered if it could have been her ex, Rob. Or even her ex-husband? *No. It wasn't really Rob's style, and Andy would never do that even if they had had a few cross words recently.*

Then she thought that perhaps it was someone acting the fool on the way home from the pub. But even so, it was a terrible thing to do. And why her? Why bitch? Did they even know her? She wondered whether anybody could really dislike her so much that they would be watching her home, waiting for a chance to do something so nasty to get at her.

When Maddy left Rebecca at the gate she stooped to give her a customary kiss. Then, in an attempt to reassure her, she said, 'Try not to think about what you saw. It'll be gone by the time you get home.'

Rebecca shrugged, something she seemed to be doing a lot of lately, but she didn't speak. Instead she rushed across the school yard, seeming anxious to break away from her tainted mother.

Maddy decided to go back home and try to remove the graffiti before she went to her editorial meeting. If she was quick then she would still make the meeting on time. It was important to her to get rid of the graffiti as soon as possible. She thought of all her neighbours and passers-by seeing the word 'bitch' on her front door and the judgements they would make as a result of it. And she knew she wouldn't feel at ease until it was gone.

It was only when Maddy was on the way back from school that she realised there might be a link between the graffiti and the strange car she had seen parked across from her house. Then there was the other car parked further up the street, which also seemed to have a driver sitting inside, watching. The thought struck terror into her. What if she had upset someone? There could be someone out there now who had it in for her. Getting enemies wasn't unheard of in her profession, after all.

She stopped herself before she got too carried away. The parked cars were probably just a coincidence. She couldn't brush aside the graffiti quite so easily, but she told herself that it might have been a one-off. It wasn't necessarily personal, just some drunken layabout with nothing else better to do. Maddy decided that the best thing she could do would be to get rid of it as soon as possible and then just forget about it.

As soon as she reached home Maddy parked up and went inside the house in search of something with which to clean the ink off her door. She tried washing-up liquid, kitchen cleaning spray and even disinfectant but nothing would clean it away. The perpetrator had obviously used a permanent marker pen.

For a long while she stood outside the house rubbing frantically at the bold red letters, feeling humiliated and exposed. In her mind she pictured numerous eyes watching, boring right through her and seeing the rot within.

The neighbours would be forming their opinions of her: a different person from the one they had come to know. The brazen divorcee, working her way through a series of younger lovers. And, through her debauched lifestyle, attracting the unwanted attention of someone venomous enough to scrawl such a hateful word on her door.

She knew she shouldn't care what people thought, but she did. So much of her lifestyle was about giving the right impression. The consummate journalist turning up to editorial meetings in a smart suit and conducting herself professionally while she tried to sell her ideas to the influential staff of high-profile publications. And she was bloody good at it. She'd grown used to being well respected. Until now.

Suddenly her rambling thoughts jolted her memory. The editorial meeting. Shit! She'd become so engrossed in trying to remove the ink that she'd let it slip her mind. And one look at the word on her door told her that her efforts had been futile. She glanced at her watch. There were only fifteen minutes till the meeting started. She had no chance now of getting there on time once she'd managed to drive to Manchester and park the car.

Feeling despondent, she decided to ring the magazine and cry off the meeting on some pretext or other. The editor wasn't impressed. Maddy's excuse of an upset stomach was unconvincing, especially at this short notice, and the editor let her know it. He was brusque on the phone and kept on emphasising repeatedly how disappointed he was. For the second time in two days Maddy felt patronised and belittled.

With the awkward call behind her, she sat down to have a moment's reflection. Maddy was worried, knowing that she couldn't afford to lose another major client. She was having a bad enough time of it as it was and was still struggling to get her bank account out of the red. And as she sat reflecting on the disastrous turn her life had taken lately, she found herself in tears.

It took her by surprise at first. She couldn't remember the last time she had been reduced to tears. Probably when she had discovered her husband's infidelity. Even when her relationship with Rob had ended, she hadn't cried about it. She had known she was better off without him.

But as the crying continued she let the tears fall, giving her a release from all the anguish of the last few weeks. When she had cried herself out she felt silly and weak. Why had she let something as trivial as a bit of graffiti upset her like that? After all, she had so much to be grateful for: a lovely daughter, nice home, good job and now a wonderful boyfriend too.

As she counted her blessings it made her feel much better about things and, in a moment of clarity, it occurred to her to look on the Internet for a solution to removing permanent marker pen. She quickly grabbed her iPad and was amazed to find that alcohol and toothpaste were recommended, both of which she had in stock.

Still anxious to remove every trace of the ink, she dashed outside and set about the task and was relieved to find that the marks came away much more easily. When she had finished she looked at her nice clean door, and she felt calm again.

She decided not to tell Aaron. What was the point? He wouldn't be able to do anything about it, and she didn't want him to think badly of her because of what someone else had written. Besides, she knew how caring Aaron was – he'd probably insist on coming round and staying and that wasn't what she wanted.

At the moment she knew she had to focus on her work and her daughter. So, she would put the incident behind her and hope that it was just a one-off.

35

Clare was in the Bank where she had arranged to meet Maddy for lunch. She arrived at 12.20 p.m., ten minutes before they were due to meet, so she got herself a drink while she waited. She sat down and scanned the menu, looking at her watch once she'd decided what she wanted to eat. It was still only a minute past half twelve so there was time yet for Maddy to get there.

Clare glanced round the pub. It was full of business types, men in suits and officious-looking women, with the exception of a few tables where the clientele were more casually dressed. She guessed that the latter were friends meeting for lunch like her and Maddy. While her eyes scanned the room she noticed that she was the only person sitting on her own.

As the minutes ticked away Clare began to feel self-conscious. She caught a few curious glances from the people on a neighbouring table. They probably thought she'd been stood up.

Clare couldn't resist checking the time on her watch again. Almost a quarter to one. She wanted to ring Maddy but knew she was in a meeting, and Clare didn't want to disrupt it. Besides, Maddy would probably have her phone on vibrate so she wouldn't be disturbed.

When Clare's glass became empty she returned to the bar and came back carrying a second glass of wine. She looked at her watch one more time. Turned five to one. Maddy was almost half an hour late now. Clare flicked through her texts to make sure she had got the meeting time right. Yes, Maddy should definitely have been there by 12.30.

Clare fired off a text to Maddy; surely that wouldn't disrupt the meeting. The most they'd hear would be a ping and maybe that would be enough to remind Maddy of where she should be.

As Clare looked up from her phone she caught the gaze of a lady on the next table, who flashed a sympathetic smile. She managed a faint smile in return, but she didn't feel like smiling. Clare was becoming angry. How dared Maddy stand her up like this, whatever her reasons?

Finally, Clare decided that if Maddy hadn't shown up or called her by the time she had drunk her wine she would give her a call and to hell with the consequences. She was getting a bit tired of Maddy messing her around. Since Maddy had met Aaron she hardly saw her any more and when she did she was usually late. Even when she rang her, it seemed as though Maddy couldn't get off the phone quickly enough.

Clare soon finished her second glass of wine. She fished in her bag for her phone, then made the call. After two glasses of wine and over three quarters of an hour sat stewing, Clare wasn't in the best frame of mind when Maddy answered.

After a tense start to the day, Maddy decided to stop dwelling on the graffiti and the fraught call to the magazine editor, knowing she had other things to do. For the latter part of the morning she threw herself into her work, which helped to take her mind off things.

Maddy worked solidly for over two hours until her rumbling stomach reminded her that it was lunch time. She checked the clock on her PC, noticing that it was well after 1 p.m., and finished what she was doing so she could take a break. Maddy was just checking out the contents of her fridge when the phone rang.

The ringing phone, along with her rumbling stomach, suddenly jolted her memory. Damn! Clare. She had completely forgotten that she should have met her for lunch. She dashed over to her phone and answered it, then braced herself while she awaited Clare's reaction.

'Maddy! What the hell's happened to you?' Clare demanded, and Maddy could tell straight away that she wasn't very happy.

'Clare, I'm so sorry!' said Maddy. 'I completely forgot. You wouldn't believe the morning—'

But Clare butted in, her tone hostile. 'Save it!' she said. 'I don't want to hear your lame excuses. It's bad enough that you never have time for me these days and that you're always late when we do meet. But to stand me up altogether is beyond the pale. Just what the hell is going on with you, Maddy?'

Maddy tried to cut in but Clare wasn't finished yet. 'You're missing appointments, losing work, you've no time for your friends and you're even short with Becky. It's like I don't even recognise you any more.'

Maddy could feel herself becoming annoyed on hearing Clare's words. *How dare she pass judgement? She was meant to be her best friend.* 'Now, just a minute,' she said. 'Fair enough, I didn't make lunch, and I've apologised for that. But there's no need to bring Becky into it or my work life, for that matter.'

'What do you expect, Maddy? I've been sat here like an idiot for the best part of an hour, and all because you can't be bothered to show up!'

'It isn't because I can't be bothered. I've had a lot on my mind this morning, if you must know. But you haven't even given me a chance to explain.'

'Go on, then, enlighten me,' was Clare's sarcastic retort. 'I can't wait to hear this.'

Maddy made as if to speak but before she had chance to get the words out she felt tears cloud her eyes again. She would have liked to confide in someone about her troubles. Someone close. But not like this. She wanted sympathy, not someone pouring scorn over her words.

'Well?' Clare prompted.

Maddy knew she'd have to give Clare something to appease her. Hearing how angry she was, Maddy knew their friendship depended on it.

'I'm sorry,' she said again, her voice catching. 'I didn't go to the editorial meeting. I didn't get as far as Manchester. I didn't even get further than the front door.' Then the catch in her voice developed into a tremor at thoughts of the front door. 'I... something cropped up.'

'Yes?' said Clare, and Maddy could tell she was already mellowing. 'What is it, Maddy?'

Maddy took a moment to calm herself before she said, 'Somebody had written the word "bitch" on my front door. In massive letters. And in bloody permanent marker. Bright red! I had to get rid of it. I couldn't have Becky coming home and finding it still there. I think she already saw it this morning as it is. And the magazine editor wasn't too pleased when I had to cancel the meeting. I'm worried I might lose that magazine too.'

'OK, OK. Calm down,' said Clare. 'It's probably just some idiot with nothing better to do.'

'That's what I thought at first,' said Maddy. 'But there's something else.'

'What?' asked Clare, and Maddy could hear a lingering note of irritation in her tone.

'There was a car. Well, more than one. But at least one that I know of. Somebody was sitting in it watching my house. I didn't mention it before because you might have just thought I was being paranoid but now this has happened too—'

Clare cut in. 'How do you know they were watching the house?'

'It was obvious. He was there for ages.'

'He? So, it was a man?' asked Clare.

'I think so, but it was difficult to tell. He had a baseball cap on and his jacket pulled up round his face. He was parked across the road so it was a bit too far to see from the living-room window. The second time the car was parked further up the street. But it was a different car.'

'OK. So, two cars?' asked Clare, and this time Maddy could detect a hint of scepticism in her voice.

'Yes, but it might be the same person.'

'Look, Maddy, don't you think you're getting a bit carried away?' Clare said. 'I mean, how many times has this happened?'

'Twice. Well, twice with the second car and once with the first. But he could have been there other times for all I know.'

'Um, are you sure it isn't somebody looking for Aaron?'

'No! Why would it be?'

'Well, it just seems strange that these things have started happening since he came on the scene, that's all. Do you think he could have a jealous ex-girlfriend still sniffing around?'

'Not that I know of,' said Maddy, becoming defensive.

Suddenly Maddy felt annoyed. She knew she couldn't expect Clare's sympathy after she had stood her up, but why did she always seem to pick any opportunity to have a go at Aaron? Maddy couldn't see any point in continuing the call with Clare in this frame of mind. She'd had enough of being patronised in the last two days and it was obvious Clare thought that she was either losing it or that she'd brought these troubles on herself.

'Look, Clare, I'll have to go,' she said. 'I've got a lot of work to do. Like I said, I'm really sorry. But I've got a lot on my plate at the moment.'

She put down the receiver without waiting for Clare's response, then took a few deep breaths and tried to steady her rapidly beating heart. But she couldn't calm down. Anxious thoughts were flitting through her head. Clare's anger. The graffiti. Rebecca's problems at school. Her work situation. And the thought that a stranger could be watching her even now. Full of hatred and malice, and plotting against her.

It was impossible to feel calm with everything that was going on. Her heart was still hammering inside her chest and her muscles felt as taut as piano wire. She thought again about ringing Aaron but decided against it. He had enough going on in his life. The last thing he needed was an emotional call from an overwrought girlfriend. Then she thought about the present he had given her, and his words kept playing over in her head. *Take some. It'll make you feel better.*

She tried to resist but, eventually, when her troubled thoughts refused to go away, she capitulated. *Maybe, just a little bit. As long as I don't make a habit of it, what harm can it do?* She recalled again how good the coke made her feel and this time she gave in to temptation.

36

By the time Maddy picked Rebecca up from school she was
feeling much calmer. Despite the bad start to the day, she
had managed to make a lot of progress with her work. It
was early when she arrived so she waited in the car until
it got nearer to home time. As she sat there she did a lot of
thinking.

There was no point worrying about the graffiti, which
was gone now anyway. She couldn't do anything about
it and she hoped she'd forget about it with time. Neither
could she do much about Clare, other than give her time to
calm down and then make a concerted effort to be on time
in future. But she could do something about her daughter.
Maybe she had been neglecting her a bit lately. She'd got so
carried away with all the attention from Aaron that she had
overlooked her daughter's needs and, as she thought about
it, she felt a little ashamed.

So Maddy decided that this evening she would lavish
attention on Rebecca. She was going to her dad's for the

weekend so Maddy would make the most of the few hours she had before Andy came to collect her. Then perhaps Rebecca would go to her father's in a better frame of mind and tell him what a good time they had had rather than telling fibs about Aaron.

She also decided that when Andy came to drop her off on Sunday she would try to build a few bridges with him. After all, it was in Rebecca's best interests that they all got along well together. She'd suggest that he took a weekend off while she did something special with Becky. He deserved it after his mother's recent health scare and it would give her more opportunity to give her daughter some much-needed attention.

Perhaps she'd suggest to Aaron that the three of them went somewhere together; possibly Blackpool or a theme park. Rebecca would like that and it would give her and Aaron a chance to bond a bit more. She'd run it by Aaron first, just to be on the safe side, although she was sure he'd be thrilled at the idea.

Rebecca looked a little morose when she walked out of the school gates but Maddy tried not to let it worry her, knowing that her daughter would soon cheer up once she knew what she had planned.

'Hi, love, have you had a nice day?' she asked, and Rebecca mumbled a reply that Maddy didn't quite catch.

They soon reached home and Rebecca's cursory glance at the front door told Maddy that she hadn't forgotten about the nasty word that had been there that morning. Thankfully it was now gone and Rebecca didn't mention it.

Maddy waited until they got inside before she told Rebecca her plans for the evening. 'When you're ready we'll do some baking,' she said. 'I thought we'd start with your favourite, cheese and onion pie. Then, once we've finished that we can make some jam tarts.'

'Really?' asked Rebecca, her face lighting up.

'Yes, really,' laughed Maddy. 'We can have a jam tart each after tea and then you can take the rest with you to your dad's.'

'Brilliant,' said Rebecca. She had already removed her coat and shoes. 'Can we start now?'

'Yes, course we can,' said Maddy, smiling. 'But let's wash our hands first.'

By the time Andy arrived to pick Rebecca up she was full of smiles. She dashed to the door with Maddy as soon as the doorbell rang, clutching a plastic container full of jam tarts.

'Look, Daddy, look what I've made,' she said, removing the lid from the container and holding it out for him to examine. 'Can we have some when we get to yours?' she asked.

'Yeah, course you can,' he said, smiling. 'They look scrummy.' He looked at Maddy, the smile still on his face, and she smiled back at him. 'See you Sunday after tea,' he said.

'OK, see you then,' said Maddy. 'Have a good time, Becky,' she added, hugging her daughter and kissing the top of her head before Rebecca pulled away and headed down the drive with her dad.

Maddy shut the door with a smile. The jam tarts seemed to have done the trick and she could see that Andy was impressed. She was relieved that he seemed to have mellowed towards her. The last thing she needed was to be at odds with Andy.

Once they were gone she went to get showered and changed. Then she'd reapply her make-up. She was expecting Aaron to arrive later and she wanted to look her best.

Two hours passed and Maddy was ready, an opened bottle of red on the kitchen worktop awaiting his arrival. It wasn't long before she heard the doorbell ring for the second time that evening and she rushed to answer it. She was pleased to see Aaron on her doorstep, looking as handsome as ever and wearing a lovely smile, his hair glistening in the light that streamed out of the hallway.

He held out the bottle of red wine that he was clutching, then leant towards her and planted a kiss on her lips. 'You look gorgeous,' he said.

'Thanks,' said Maddy, pleased that she'd chosen her sexy black top with her jeans.

Maddy didn't tell Aaron about the graffiti and instead, once they were settled with a glass of wine each, she decided to broach the subject of taking Rebecca to Blackpool the following weekend.

'I was thinking,' she began, her forefinger tracing a line along the side of his face as she spoke. 'Why don't we have Becky next weekend? We could have a lovely time, maybe go to Blackpool or somewhere else if you fancy. It would give you a chance to get to know her a bit better. And, if I'm honest, I haven't been spending as much time with her lately as I should.'

His face seemed to darken momentarily before he replied, 'Yes, that sounds good.'

'What do you fancy? Blackpool? Or somewhere else?' she asked.

'No, Blackpool's fine,' he said. 'In fact, if we've got her for the whole weekend, why don't we take her to the zoo as well?'

'Yeah. That would be great,' she said. Then she bent towards him and gave him an appreciative kiss. 'I'll let Andy know when he brings Becky back on Sunday. I'm sure he'll be fine about it, but I thought I'd run it by you first to make sure you're OK with the idea.'

'Yes, fine,' he said. 'Why wouldn't I be?'

Maddy shrugged then Aaron pulled her nearer to him. 'Listen, anywhere is fine for me. As long as I'm in your company, I don't care.'

'Aw, you're so sweet,' she said.

Maddy was now snuggled up to Aaron on the sofa, her back resting on his chest with his left arm draped round her breasts, and she couldn't see the pained expression on his face or read the thoughts running through his mind.

37

It was the following Saturday. Aaron had suggested using his car to take Maddy and Rebecca to Blackpool on the Saturday and Chester Zoo on the Sunday, knowing Maddy would be pleased at his offer to drive. He had just arrived at Maddy's home and parked his car up.

When Maddy answered the door she looked ravishing, her hair loosely tied up, just the way he liked it. She had jeans on and a fitted top that hugged her curves. How he wished it could have been just the two of them.

If it weren't for the kid he'd have had Maddy upstairs before she knew it. As he pictured her hair falling out of its clasp and hanging loosely round her shoulders while he thrust deep inside her, a smile crossed his lips.

'You're looking pleased with yourself,' Maddy commented.

'I always am when I see you,' he teased as he leant in for a kiss.

Maddy pulled away. 'I'm nearly ready, just a few more things to put in the bag before we set off.'

Aaron laughed. 'We're only going to Blackpool, not on an Arctic expedition.'

'I know but I always like to pack a few snacks and things. You never know when they might come in handy. I've already packed the swimming costumes and towels. I hope you've got yours.'

Aaron rolled his eyes as she gazed back at him. 'Hey, that's what it's like when you've got children,' said Maddy. 'You might have your own one day, and then you'll understand.'

Aaron just smiled in response, but his smile was forced. There was no way he was having kids. It was bad enough having Rebecca in tow. He didn't need any more. They were nothing but parasites, and these days they were all bloody spoilt and got too much of their own way. As far as he was concerned children were just an inconvenience and they should learn their place, just as he'd had to do when he was a kid.

'I won't be long,' Maddy continued. 'Have a sit down while you're waiting. Becky's in there watching TV. I'm just going in the kitchen for something.'

She led him to the living room and then carried on through to the kitchen. Rebecca was occupying a seat in the middle of the sofa so he opted for an armchair.

'Hi, you all right?' he said as he plonked himself down.

Rebecca looked up at him but didn't smile. 'Yes, thanks,' she said, turning quickly back to face the TV screen.

Aaron assumed that she wasn't pleased at having him in the house. After all, he'd put her in her place last time he'd seen her and she wouldn't have liked that. This kid was obviously used to getting her own way. Well, there was no way she'd get it with him.

'You could have fooled me,' he said. 'What's with the miserable face?'

'I'm not miserable,' said Rebecca, without looking at him, her voice whiney and annoying.

Aaron got up out of his seat and walked across to her. He saw her flinch as he sat down by her side, and she shuffled further across the sofa. He held out his hand, roughly cupping her chin, his handsome face clouded with menace. 'Look at me when I'm talking to you!' he snapped, pulling her chin round to face him.

She looked up at him, her eyes wide with fright. 'That's more like it,' he said. 'Right, now, for starters, let's have less of the attitude.'

'I'm not giving you attitude,' said Rebecca, trying to pull away.

'Look at me when I'm talking to you,' Aaron snapped, roughly pulling her chin till her eyes were again facing his. He could see the fear on the child's face and was glad that he was now getting through to her. 'Secondly, stop ignoring me. And thirdly, me and your mum have gone to a lot of fuckin' trouble to make this weekend nice for you so the least you can do is show some gratitude. So put a fuckin' smile on your face and stop being so miserable.'

Aaron could hear Maddy walking through to the living room so he quickly let go of Rebecca's chin and sat back in his seat, replacing his sneer with an amiable grin.

'Right, I'm ready,' Maddy said.

'Great stuff. Let's go, then,' said Aaron, flashing Rebecca a warning look before her mother drew close enough to notice.

The child responded by getting up from the sofa, running over to her mother and enthusiastically hugging her. 'Come on, then, Mum,' she said.

Aaron smiled smugly. At least the kid knew how to do as she was told. There was no way he was going to let her ruin things for Maddy. Bloody kids; they were a pain. Especially spoilt kids.

Once he and Maddy were together properly the kid would have to learn to do as she was told, and when that time came he'd let her know that he wasn't going to let their lives be ruled by a kid.

'Ooh, look at that one,' said Rebecca, pointing to a small monkey that was pinching food from another one, then quickly scampering through the trees to escape.

Maddy and Aaron laughed as they caught the bemused expression on the face of the other monkey. What made it even funnier was the fact that the smaller monkey had now got away with the same trick twice.

It was Sunday and they were at Chester Zoo. Maddy was happy to see Rebecca enjoying herself so much. They'd already had a fabulous time at Blackpool the day before, going on the rides and in the Sandcastle Waterpark before collecting shells on the beach. Then they'd gone back to the Midland, just so she could show Rebecca the lovely hotel where Aaron was staying. Rebecca had been suitably impressed, gazing in awe at the beautiful surroundings.

And now they were enjoying the delights of Chester Zoo. Aaron had been fabulous throughout the entire weekend, apart from having to nip out on Saturday evening to tend to some business. He'd bought them sweet treats and patiently taken them wherever they'd wanted to go. Nothing had been too much trouble for him, from running them around in his car to joining in with all the rides and other amusements. In fact, he'd seemed to enjoy the rides just as much as Rebecca, if not more.

As Maddy watched Rebecca squeal in glee at the antics of the monkeys she turned and smiled at Aaron, who returned her smile. The weekend had been perfect and she couldn't remember a time when she'd been happier. Andy had always been so stuffy when it came to funfairs and the like, not like Aaron, who threw himself right into the action.

By the time they were on their way home Maddy was on a high and even Rebecca seemed much happier. Although she'd been a bit moody at the start of the weekend, she'd soon cheered up once they'd set off for Blackpool. Aaron had been wonderful and had even insisted on paying for everything. Although Maddy had politely protested, she was actually relieved because she couldn't afford to let her bank account go any further into the red.

At last, things seemed to be going right for Maddy. She'd had a run of bad luck lately but maybe all that was finally at an end.

38

Andy was having a busy day at work. He was a sales manager for a manufacturing company in Trafford Park. He'd spent the morning in meetings, first with senior management then with his own sales team. The meetings with senior management were always a bit tense. He'd sit there, trying to defend himself and his team, while the company directors fired questions at him about sales figures and performance.

Having got all that out of the way, he was currently trying to catch up with his emails. He'd only just started scrolling through them when his phone rang.

'I've got a Mrs Scott on the phone for you,' announced his secretary.

Andy didn't immediately recognise the name but, nevertheless, he asked his secretary to put her through.

'Mr Chambers,' came the confident voice on the other end of the line. 'It's Mrs Scott from Hope Street primary.'

Now he knew who she was: the head teacher at Rebecca's school. A feeling of dread came over him as he realised there must be something very wrong for her to ring him at work. And why wasn't she ringing Maddy? She was listed with school as the first point of contact.

As if anticipating his thoughts, Mrs Scott quickly added, 'Nothing to worry too much about, Mr Chambers. I just thought it best to have a word with you, that's all.' Then she paused, as if thinking carefully about which words to choose, before she carried on speaking. 'Rebecca's teacher, Miss Lazenby, has been speaking to me about your daughter. It seems that she's not quite herself lately.'

'How do you mean?' asked Andy, immediately becoming concerned.

'She's been a bit withdrawn, not taking part in activities and choosing to sit alone at break times rather than mix with the other children.'

'Oh,' said Andy, unsure how else to respond.

'Like I say, we don't want to worry you too much but, according to Miss Lazenby, Rebecca has always been so enthusiastic and upbeat in the past. I wondered if you might know whether something could be troubling her?'

Andy knew that Rebecca had been upset about her mother's boyfriend swearing in front of her but there was no way he was going to share that information. He didn't want the school to think they were a dysfunctional family.

He hesitated before replying, 'No, nothing that I can think of.'

Mrs Scott picked up on his hesitation. 'Are you sure, Mr Chambers? Anything at all?' she asked.

'No. Nothing,' he said.

'Very well. Miss Lazenby has already spoken to Rebecca's mother about it a week or so ago and she couldn't think of anything either. According to Miss Lazenby things haven't changed much with Rebecca since then. She also had concerns about lateness, but I believe that's all sorted out now.'

'Lateness? You mean Becky's arriving late for school?'

'No, it's more a case of Rebecca's mother arriving late to collect her,' said the head teacher. When Andy didn't respond she added, 'But, like I say, that seems to have been resolved now. And I wouldn't worry about your daughter's lack of participation. I'm sure it's something and nothing. Children can sometimes get like that at Rebecca's age. It will probably blow over, but I just felt that we should inform you in case you might be aware of anything.'

'No, sorry. But thank you for letting me know,' said Andy.

'Not a problem, Mr Chambers. We'll keep an eye on Rebecca for the time being and let you know if things don't improve.'

'Yes, please, if you would. Thank you.'

By the time Andy had finished the call, he wasn't just concerned; he was furious. If Maddy had known about this for over a week then why the hell hadn't she said anything? He was Rebecca's father and had a right to know these things. And why the hell was she arriving late to collect Rebecca from school? It was bad enough that she kept her waiting when she was at his house. But late for school as well? It was ridiculous!

His fury soon turned into worry. It bothered him that his daughter had become withdrawn and he couldn't help thinking that it might have something to do with her mother's latest boyfriend. He recalled how troubled Rebecca had seemed about Aaron swearing. What if there was more going on that he didn't know about?

He switched his attention back to his emails, trying to take his mind off the worrying call while he focused on work. But it wasn't forgotten. As soon as he arrived home he was determined to give Maddy a ring and find out just what the hell had been going on.

Maddy had also been hard at work all morning and had just taken a brief lunch break. Before going back to her computer she took a quick look out of the living-room window, a habit she had got into lately. It was there, again. The same red car.

Curious, she went to the front door and took a few steps down the drive. Then nerves got to her. Should she go and see what the driver wanted or should she leave things? Maybe she should inform the police. But what would she tell them? She didn't really have much to go on, apart from the fact that a strange car was parked outside, and she didn't want to be accused of wasting police time.

For a few moments she was undecided but then she finally resolved to challenge the driver, despite her nerves. It was the only way she would put her mind at ease, but she'd make sure she locked her front door first.

She turned back, grabbed her keys from the hall and stepped back onto the drive. She was locking the front door when she heard the sound of an engine starting up. She quickly spun round and dashed down the drive, but the driver was turning the car round ready to drive off. By the time she got to the gate the car had shot off up the road at speed, the tyres screeching noisily. She tried to read the number plate but was perturbed to find that it had been blanked out.

How strange! thought Maddy as she walked back to her door. Why was the driver so eager to get away as soon as she started walking down the drive? Why weren't his number plates visible? And why did he take the trouble of turning the car round? There was only one reason she could think of for the latter. If he'd driven past her house instead she would have seen him.

Once she was indoors she realised how much the incident had shaken her. There was no doubt in her mind now that she was being watched.

Maddy was so worried that there was no way she could go back to her work. She needed to confide in someone. But who? Andy was a no-no. He didn't feature in her life now except where Rebecca was concerned, and he wouldn't want Rebecca staying there if Maddy had a stalker. And she couldn't ring Clare while things were still so bad between them. Maybe she should ring her parents. But then she decided against it. They were in their sixties and it wouldn't be fair to worry them.

That left only one person. Aaron. Although she had still only been with him for a little less than three months she felt close enough to confide in him. The only thing that had stopped her before was that she hadn't wanted him to think her foolish, but now she felt that it had gone beyond that stage. There was no doubt in her mind that something sinister was going on, and he was the only person left who she could confide in.

Aaron didn't answer the phone straight away so she kept ringing and eventually he took her call. She explained briefly what had happened, trying to stay calm. But as soon as she spoke her voice quivered.

'I don't know what to do, Aaron,' she said. 'What if they come back?'

'It's all right. Lock all the doors and try not to worry. I'll be there as soon as I can.'

He ended the call, quite abruptly, Maddy thought. But then she realised that he would have wanted to be with her as soon as possible. He had seemed concerned while he was on the phone and she was glad she had rung him. Now she just had to wait.

Maddy was so anxious that the time waiting for Aaron seemed to last forever. While she waited she was constantly on her feet, looking out of the window and repeatedly checking that all the doors and windows were locked. Eventually he arrived.

'Oh, Aaron, thank God you're here,' she said, hugging him when she answered the door, and trying to hold back the tears. She didn't want him to think she was hysterical.

'OK, no worries,' he said. 'Let's get you sat down and then you can tell me exactly what's been going on.'

For a few minutes Maddy detailed what had been happening over the previous weeks, starting with the sightings of cars, then the graffiti and then this latest sighting when the driver had hurried off.

'Jesus, Maddy! Why didn't you tell me?' he said, his face full of concern.

'Well, I thought I was being paranoid at first when I saw the cars. Then, when the graffiti happened, I didn't really want to tell you. I was worried that you might think I'd done something to deserve it.'

'Don't be daft,' he said.

'I know. I know... But when that happened today I knew it wasn't just me being paranoid. And I needed to tell someone.'

'Well, I'm glad you told me,' he said, pulling her towards him.

Maddy pulled back and gazed into his eyes. 'I'm worried, Aaron. What if they do something to hurt me or, worse still, what if they harm Becky?'

He broke away from her and went to get something out of his pocket. 'Here,' he said, handing her a lighted spliff and lighting another for himself. 'Have a few drags of that. It'll calm you down.'

'What is it?' she asked.

'Just dope.'

'Oh, I'm not sure I should, Aaron.'

He laughed. 'It's only dope. You've been taking cocaine for the last few weeks and that hasn't harmed you, has it? So a bit of weed isn't gonna kill you. In fact, it'll make you feel a lot better. Look at you,' he said, taking hold of her free hand. 'You're shaking like a leaf.'

He had such a convincing way about him that Maddy found herself doing as he suggested. And he was right: she did feel calmer after a few drags. Then she passed it back to Aaron. She wasn't really that keen on smoking.

'Right, now that you've calmed down a bit,' he said, 'I think that what you need to do is to ring the police. Open the windows before they get here though. No one's gonna get in while I'm here, and I don't want the police smelling dope.'

'Oh, I don't know. What if they think I'm imagining it?'

'OK, then don't tell them about the cars, just the graffiti. It's vandalism, Maddy. They shouldn't be allowed to get away with it.'

Maddy was conscious of the fact that she'd let herself get overly worked up. Now that she was calmer, she tried to take a more reasoned approach.

'I'm not sure,' she said. 'How are they going to prove it, let alone find the culprits, especially now I've cleaned it all off? No, I think I'll leave it for now. But if anything else happens I'll get in contact with them.'

She felt herself shudder as she thought about the possibility of other incidents. Then she gazed into Aaron's eyes. 'Thank God I've got you, Aaron. You're the only thing that's keeping me sane right now,' she said, with a tremble in her voice.

'Come here,' he said, putting his spliff down, then taking her in his arms and stroking her back. 'Try not to worry. Hopefully, nothing else will happen. But keep your doors and windows locked once I'm gone to be on the safe side.'

She spent the rest of the afternoon in the reassuring company of Aaron, who also offered to go with her to collect Rebecca from school. As they sat in Maddy's living room waiting for school to finish, she found herself voicing her worries again. Maddy knew she was going over and over the same ground, but she couldn't help it. Worry and fear had invaded her brain.

But when the phone rang it soon shifted her thoughts onto other matters. It was Andy. And he didn't sound pleased.

39

Andy came straight to the point when he heard Maddy answer the phone. He wasn't in the mood for niceties. 'I've had a call today from Becky's head teacher,' he said to Maddy. 'Apparently the school are concerned about Becky being withdrawn.'

'Aaaah… right,' said Maddy. 'Yes, I know about it.'

'I know you know. In fact, you've known for a bloody week!' he said, incensed. 'So why didn't you bother to tell me, Maddy?'

'I didn't see the need to.'

'Oh, didn't you? I'm her bloody father, for Christ's sake. And the school obviously thought I needed to know otherwise they wouldn't have rung me at work.'

'There was no need for them to ring you at work. They'd already told me about it.'

'Oh, yes, and what exactly have you done about it? Apart from arriving late to collect Becky from school umpteen times.'

'Now, hang on a minute. I don't have to justify my actions to you. I had a couple of days where I was so busy with work that I lost track of the time, that's all. It won't happen again.'

Andy knew that was nonsense. As far as he knew, there had never been a time in the past when Maddy had been late to collect Rebecca, no matter how much work she had on. So why now? He thought he knew the answer to that one; it was since she had been seeing this latest guy, and it was clear to him that Rebecca had been shuffled down Maddy's list of priorities.

'Well, the school obviously have little faith in you, seeing as how they felt the need to contact me at work,' he said. 'Just try putting yourself in my shoes, Maddy. How do you think I bloody well felt when the school headmistress rang me at work to tell me something you should already have shared with me?'

'Welcome to the club, Andy,' she said, sarcastically. 'It's called being a parent. I often have to break off from work to tend to Becky but, unlike you, I accept that it's all part and parcel of my responsibilities.'

'You're missing the point,' he seethed. 'If you had been looking after Becky properly then there would have been no need for the school to ring me.'

'How dare you?' she yelled. 'I have always done my best for Becky.'

'Have you? Is that why you can't be bothered to pick her up on time and why you seem to prefer the company of your latest foul-mouthed lover rather than your daughter?'

'That was a lie, and you know it! Aaron would never swear in front of Becky. You're just getting on your high horse because your work life has been interrupted,' she said.

Andy realised that things were getting a bit out of hand, and hurling insults at his ex-wife wasn't really getting him anywhere. He took a deep breath, his tone calmer when he responded. 'No. I'm not, Maddy,' he said. 'I'm actually really concerned for our daughter. I think it's more than coincidence that all these things have started since you let this stranger into your life. Are you sure you're up to the job of looking after our daughter?'

'What do you mean?' she snapped.

'Well, if things get much worse, Maddy, then you will leave me with no alternative but to reassess the custody arrangements.'

'Oh, get lost, Andy,' she said before hanging up the phone.

Andy stared at his phone, incredulous. How dared she end the call? He was tempted to ring her back but knew it wouldn't get him anywhere. For a few moments he reflected on the situation. Perhaps he had got a bit carried away. But who wouldn't in his position? It was hard having to stand by and watch while another man stepped into his daughter's life. That was bad enough, but to find out that his daughter's behaviour was being affected really riled him. He hadn't meant to threaten her with custody but the way things were going, if Maddy didn't make some improvements, he might have to think about going down that route.

He tried to calm himself down, knowing that if he was to get to the bottom of things he needed Maddy's cooperation. At the end of the day, his daughter's welfare was his first concern. He didn't like the sound of this Aaron character at all, but he knew that creating a rift with his ex-wife would only make matters worse. So he would have to bide his time and then see if he could find a way to repair the damage that was obviously being done by this negative influence in Maddy's life.

Two days later Andy received another phone call at work but this time he knew who the caller was.

'Clare,' he said, surprised. 'What can I do for you?'

'Hi, Andy. I'm sorry to call you at work,' she said, sounding a bit apprehensive. 'It was the only way I could think of to get hold of you. I didn't know where you'd moved to but I remembered the name of your firm so I rang to see if they would put me through to you.'

Andy became curious. It was clear to him that Clare had put a lot of thought into making this call and he wondered why. 'That's OK,' he said. 'What's the problem?'

'It's a bit too... delicate to discuss on the phone. I think it's best if we arrange to meet so we can discuss it properly,' she said. 'When are you free?'

They arranged a mutually convenient time when they could meet at a coffee shop in the city centre after they had both finished work. But Andy was still curious. Before Clare had chance to hang up, he asked, 'Can you give me a clue what it's about?'

'Yes,' she said. 'It's about Maddy. I don't want to worry you, but I'm really concerned. Like I say, it's best if I tell you when we meet. Then you can decide if I'm overreacting or if there really is a problem.'

Once Clare hung up, Andy was left staring at his phone, his forehead forming deep furrows as he thought about her words. She had said she didn't want to worry him but a part of him still cared about his ex-wife and he needed to protect his daughter and right now he felt powerless.

40

Crystal pulled up outside her parents' home in the battered old Fiesta that she'd recently acquired. She was dressed for work in a short skirt and a see-through top but she'd slung a coat over the top so her parents couldn't see what she was wearing. She didn't want to arouse their suspicion; they still believed her story that she worked in a nightclub, and their reaction to that had been bad enough.

She looked at her daughter, Candice, sitting across from her in her second-hand booster seat. 'Right, sweetheart. Here we are,' she said.

Candice stuck her bottom lip out and Crystal could tell the tears would soon follow. 'Don't wanna go,' she said.

'Come on, Candice, love. Nanny and Grandad will have lots of nice treats for you.'

'Don't care. Want to stay with Mummy.'

As Crystal had predicted, Candice began to cry, her tears accompanied by a loud piercing wail. How she hated having to leave her, especially when they'd had such a lovely day. After picking her up from nursery she'd taken her to the park and then they'd returned home and done some painting, using a set of paints she'd picked up from the pound shop, before Crystal had given Candice her tea.

Crystal got out of the car and went round to the passenger side, undoing Candice's booster seat. It was a tricky operation. The clip on one side didn't work so she'd had to secure it in place with some string, which she'd fed through the buckle and underneath the seat and then tied it at the back. The knot took some undoing and whilst she clawed at it with her nails, the sound of Candice's loud shrieks penetrated her eardrums.

She lifted her daughter out while Candice struggled to break free. Her parents were already at the door before she had chance to knock and she was relieved to part with her screeching daughter.

'Don't worry, we'll soon cheer her up,' said Crystal's father, holding out a bar of chocolate to tempt Candice.

'OK, thanks. I'll see you in the morning,' said Crystal, giving Candice a quick peck on the cheek before she got back inside her car.

Crystal was desperate to escape her daughter's anguished cries. She knew that the longer she prolonged her departure, the more upset Candice would become. It was always awful having to leave her like this. She should be the one to put Candice to bed; to read her a bedtime story and tuck her in before giving her a goodnight kiss.

But she knew she had no choice in the matter. Crystal needed the money and she knew of no other way to get hold of the large amount of cash it took to feed her and

Gilly's drug habit, as well as keeping her and her daughter housed, fed and clothed.

Crystal hated this life and what it had done to her, and the effect it was having on her daughter. She often dreamt of a better life. A life where she didn't have to sell her body to strangers. Where she didn't have to feed the perversions of sick and depraved men. Where she wasn't worried every time she took on a new client in case he abused and beat her. And a life where she could be with her daughter properly, and she, Gilly and Candice could be just like a normal family.

But she knew that was never going to happen, especially with Gilly. She wasn't foolish enough to believe it would ever be more than a dream. She and Gilly would never be equals. She was his property, just like all the other girls who sold their bodies so he could profit, more so, in fact, because she was his first recruit.

There was a time when she had felt special to him. But not any more. Not since he'd set eyes on the journalist. But even though his interest in her as a person was waning, he was still interested in her as a money-making machine. So, for now, her dreams would have to remain as nothing more than that – just dreams.

Andy was sitting in a coffee shop and across from him sat Clare, who was currently taking a gulp of her cappuccino. She put down her cup and looked up, meeting his gaze.

'Thanks for coming, Andy,' she said.

'That's OK,' said Andy, managing a thin smile.

Clare then cleared her throat and began explaining why she had brought him here. 'I don't want to worry you,' she said, 'but I'm a bit concerned about Maddy. Now, before I say anything further, I want you to promise me that this is just between the two of us. I'd hate Maddy to think I'd betrayed her and, well, to be honest, things already aren't too good between us.'

'You as well?' he asked, his eyes narrowing.

Clare sighed. 'Yes. We were due to meet for lunch only Maddy didn't show up. When she was almost an hour late I rang her and, it seems, she'd completely overlooked the fact that she was due to meet me.'

'Strange,' said Andy.

'Oh, it gets worse. Apparently, the reason she'd overlooked meeting me was because she had had to deal with some graffiti on her front door.'

'Really?' asked Andy.

'Yes, somebody had written the word "bitch" and Maddy had got herself worked up over it. Not only that, but she thinks someone has been watching the house; two different cars, apparently.'

Andy looked at her quizzically with creases forming on his forehead. 'Hang on a minute. Did Becky see the graffiti?'

'Maddy thinks she might have done.'

'Shit!' he cursed.

Clare carried on speaking, as though she was keen to get it all out in the open now that she had started. 'But it isn't just that, Andy,' she said. 'Maddy has changed. I rarely see her these days. She seems to spend most of her time with Aaron and, from what I can make out, she doesn't always have a lot of time for Becky either. She's even admitted to being a bit short with her.'

'Really?' Andy asked again, while Clare paused to take another sip of her cappuccino.

'There's more,' said Clare, 'but please don't tell Maddy I told you this.'

'Don't worry. This stays between us,' he said.

Clare continued. 'Well, whatever's going on, it's affecting her work life too. She's missing client appointments and she's even lost work because one of her articles wasn't up to scratch.'

'That doesn't sound like Maddy,' Andy chipped in.

'I know. She's lost the whole of the Sunshine group.'

'Bloody hell! That's a big client.'

'Tell me about it. But, the thing is, she didn't really seem fazed when she told me about it. She sounded more annoyed that they'd stopped working with her on the strength of one article, rather than concerned that her poor standard of work had caused them to do that.'

When Clare finished speaking, Andy stared at her, shaking his head in disbelief. 'Jesus!' he said. 'It's worse than I thought.'

'So, you've got concerns as well?' asked Clare.

'Oh, yes,' he said, but he didn't elaborate.

'You mentioned that things aren't good between you and Maddy either?' she asked.

'No...' said Andy, but he didn't tell Clare about the school ringing him. Even though she was a friend, it was something he didn't really want to share. Instead he said, 'Same sort of thing. She's always running late and seems to be behind with things all the time. I spoke to her about it and, well, things got a bit heated, I'm afraid.'

'Oh dear,' said Clare. 'It's strange that she seems to be alienating everyone round her.'

'Yes,' said Andy, but he didn't continue.

For a few moments they remained silent, the atmosphere between them now a bit awkward. They both sipped at their coffees, each occupied with their own thoughts.

It was Clare who broke the silence. 'Thanks again for sparing the time to meet me,' she said. 'I'm sorry to have had to tell you all those things. I don't really know what you can do about the situation, to be honest, but I just felt that you should know.'

'No, that's fine,' said Andy. 'I appreciate you telling me all this. I mean, obviously I'd rather not have heard it, but I think it's best that I know.'

'OK. Well, I've got to get going now,' said Clare, getting up from her seat, and Andy noticed that her coffee cup was still almost half full.

'No need to rush on my account,' he said.

'No, no, it's fine. I've got things I need to do.' She looked at him with a sympathetic smile on her face before adding, 'I hope that me telling you all this does some good. I'd love to see Maddy back to her old self.'

'Me too,' said Andy. Then he fished inside his jacket pocket and pulled out a business card, quickly scribbling his mobile number on the back of it. 'If you have any other concerns, Clare, please let me know.'

'I will do, and please let me know how things go,' she said. 'I'll text you with my mobile number.'

Once she was gone Andy went over everything in his head. Jesus! It was even worse than he had thought. Why the hell would someone scrawl such an offensive word on

Maddy's front door? He couldn't understand it. And then there was all this carry-on about somebody watching the house. Could that really be true? Or was Maddy jumping to ridiculous conclusions?

The more he thought about everything Clare had told him on top of the concerns he already had, the more he became seriously worried about the environment his daughter was now living in. He wasn't sure what kind of an influence this Aaron person had on Maddy but, whatever it was, it wasn't good.

Just who was he exactly? He recalled Maddy telling him about Aaron a few weeks ago. She had been full of it, all excited about this new businessman she was seeing. He ran an electrical goods wholesale company, apparently, called Lecco. The name had stuck in his mind because he remembered thinking how corny and unoriginal it was.

Maybe he could make a few enquiries and see if he could find out anything more about him. He didn't have a surname for him, but he had the company name and that was a start. Maddy had also told him that Aaron had found a warehouse in Manchester after the first one he was after had fallen through. Andy wished he could recall the name of the industrial estate, but he hadn't really taken much notice at the time. Something beginning with W.

For a few minutes he sat sipping the last dregs of his coffee and trying to bring the name of the industrial estate to mind, but when he couldn't think of it, he decided to finish his coffee and set off for home.

It was while he was leaving the city centre that the name finally came to him. Witney. Yes, that was it. Like the singer, Whitney Houston, except it was spelt differently. He knew this because he was already familiar with that particular industrial estate, having dealt with a few firms located there in the course of his employment.

Witney industrial estate. So now he had the name of the firm and the location for its new warehouse. It was a good starting point. Armed with that information, he intended to find out as much as he could about Aaron before he decided what to do next.

41

It was two weeks since Maddy had found graffiti on her door and since then there had been no further incidents. Neither had she seen any strange cars parked near her home. Time had also passed since her argument with Andy and, although things were still a bit cool between them, at least they were speaking, and she was relieved that he hadn't said anything further about custody of Rebecca. She was trying to put all of it behind her and get on with enjoying life.

Maddy and Aaron arrived back home in the early hours of Saturday morning. They had been seeing each other for three months now, and Aaron had suggested an impromptu celebration to mark the mini-milestone. They'd gone into Manchester, exploring the trendy bars near Deansgate, where they had spent the evening drinking cocktails then dancing till after midnight.

They were both merry when they arrived back at Maddy's house, and were sharing a joke as they walked through the door. Maddy had had another wonderful night with Aaron but, despite feeling elated, she also had something else on her mind. She had wanted to talk to him about it when he'd arrived to pick her up, but he'd been on such a high about celebrating that she hadn't wanted to ruin it.

Now though, given a little courage by the amount she had drunk, she decided to broach the subject. She waited until she had fixed them both a nightcap and they were sitting together on the sofa.

'Aaron, I've been thinking,' she said. She looked across at Aaron, feeling a stab of guilt when she saw his smile replaced by a grave expression. 'Well, remember before when I said we were seeing a bit too much of each other—'

'Why d'you have to fuckin' spoil it?' he snapped, before she had chance to finish what she was saying.

She gasped in shock and stared at him for a few moments. Aaron quickly backtracked when he saw the look on her face.

'Sorry, sorry. I didn't mean to snap,' he said. 'It's just that we've had such a good night. You could have picked a better time to spring that on me.'

His volatile reaction made her choose her words carefully as she responded. 'Well, I was going to mention it before we went out, but you were so happy that I didn't want to spoil it for you. It's not that I don't like being with you, Aaron. I *love* being with you and I'm not trying to cool things between us. It's just that I have so many other things I need to be doing. I'm getting behind with my work again and I'm overdrawn at the bank. I also need to spend more time with Becky.'

'OK, I get it,' he said, his tone still harsh. 'But I don't want to spend less time with you. We can do things together with Becky, like when we went to Blackpool. And you can do your work when I'm not here. I need to go to work too, don't forget.' He didn't mention the fact that she was overdrawn at the bank.

'Well, yes, I know that,' she said. 'But we always stay up so late when you come over. Maybe we should make the effort to go to bed earlier in the week so that I'm still alert when it comes to work. We could still stay out late at weekends.'

'Yeah, whatever,' he said flippantly, and Maddy stared at him again, unable to fathom this change in attitude.

Then he seemed to pick up on her disquiet, and he turned to face her, his expression serious. He took her arms in his, with his hands cradling her elbows so that she was enveloped by his embrace. 'Maddy,' he said, his tone now pleading. 'I'll do anything to make you happy. You know that, don't you?'

Maddy smiled and nodded, so Aaron continued. 'Since I've met you you've made me the happiest man in the world. You're the number one priority in my life and everything else can wait. Work, houses, business, all that shit. It doesn't mean anything without you. We're meant to be together. I love you, and I thought you felt the same.'

'Yes, of course I feel the same about you, Aaron, but—'

'Shush,' he said, placing two fingers over her lips. 'No more of that now. Let's enjoy the rest of the night.'

Then he got up from the sofa and fished inside his pocket, bringing out a small packet. Maddy knew straight away what it was. He unwrapped it and eased it in her direction so she could see the contents.

'After all, this is a celebration,' he said, dipping his finger into the white powder then holding it to his nostril and inhaling. 'Come on, your turn,' he said.

Maddy did as he suggested, not because she didn't want to risk upsetting him further but because, by now, it had become part of their routine. First a few drinks to unwind. Then a snort of cocaine to take them to the next level. And then, a night of passionate lovemaking that would take them higher still and leave them both sated. By the time they woke up Maddy would be so beguiled by him that his moment of moodiness the day before would be completely overlooked.

It was Monday morning and it had been a few days since Andy's meeting with Clare. Despite his determination to find out as much as he could about Aaron, he hadn't done anything up to now. He'd been too busy at work for one thing and, although he knew it would be easy enough to gather the information using his work role as cover, he was a bit apprehensive about doing so.

The main reason why he hadn't done anything, though, was because he'd had a change of heart. After all, he'd always been able to trust Maddy in the past and a part of him felt foolish for doubting her. She was entitled to a personal life just like everybody else and, although it irked him that a man he didn't trust was now playing a big role in Rebecca's life, it was something he had to learn to accept since he and Maddy had split up.

He also knew that Maddy wouldn't be happy that he was interfering, and they were only just getting back on track since he'd tackled her about the call from the head teacher.

But then he'd seen her the previous evening. She was late picking up Rebecca again. He'd looked at her, uttering apology after apology in the hope that it would appease him. Something about her wasn't quite right; it was as though she hadn't taken the usual care and attention before coming out of the house.

Maddy had been wearing her usual messy updo but somehow it had been messier than usual, and it had looked as if it was hiding a bad hair day rather than being casually put together for effect. Despite her make-up Maddy's face had looked gaunt, the dark rings under her eyes still noticeable, and Andy had guessed that she was pale beneath her foundation.

Her lateness coupled with her appearance had been all that it had taken to make him start questioning things again. He'd gone over everything once more in his mind, convincing himself that there was still a problem and that problem wasn't going to go away without some form of intervention. In fact, if he didn't do anything, he felt sure that matters would only get worse.

So, he'd chosen a moment when the office was quiet. He had his own private office anyway, and his staff always knocked on the door before entering. As for senior management, they were usually too busy tending to other matters this early on a Monday morning and he knew it would probably be afternoon before they started doing their rounds.

He started by visiting the Companies House website and doing a search on the name Lecco. He would have expected the company to be limited if it was big enough to have branches in both Yorkshire and Manchester. But there was a chance it wasn't. There was nothing on the website that fitted. All the companies listed with that name were either dormant, different types of industries or had directors' names that didn't fit Aaron's gender or ethnicity.

While Andy was on the Companies House website he did a search for officers of a company. Unfortunately, he didn't know Aaron's surname. He put the name Aaron in anyway, but it was a waste of time. There were pages and pages of Aarons. It would have taken an age to go through them all, and most of them were surnames anyway.

So, it didn't appear that there was a limited company by the name of Lecco that dealt in electrical goods. And he'd found nothing up to now to prove that Aaron was a director.

Andy wasn't finished yet. There was still the industrial estate to try, which would help him to establish whether a company by that name was renting a warehouse. He came out of the Companies House website and did an Internet search for Witney industrial estate. There was a number listed for the admin office so he picked up the phone and rang it.

'Hi,' he said when a cheery female voice came on the line. 'This is Andy Chambers, sales manager for Belper Foods. I wonder if you could help me.'

'Certainly,' said the woman.

'It's a bit of a daft query actually,' he began, feeling himself tense at the prospect of carrying out his subterfuge.

'We've been doing some business with a new company and I can't for the life of me find what I've done with their details. I wonder if you could check if a company called Lecco have rented an office from you?'

'Just a moment, sir,' said the woman. For a few moments he waited, gazing around him to make sure no one was near his office, while he listened to her tapping away on her keyboard. 'No, nothing by that name, I'm afraid,' she said. 'What type of business was it?'

'I'm sorry, I've forgotten that too,' he said, knowing it didn't sound very convincing but also knowing that it was unlikely a food manufacturing company would be dealing with an electrical wholesale company. He didn't want the person at the other end of the phone to make that connection.

'OK. What about new firms in the last few weeks?' he asked. 'Would it be possible for you to let me have a list of them? I may have got the name wrong.'

She hesitated. 'Ooh, I don't think I'm allowed to do that.'

'Are you sure? They'll be listed in the phone directory anyway once they're up and running. Then everyone will have access to that information.'

He sensed her uncertainty as she paused again. 'Very well,' she said, politely, before tapping away at the keyboard again then reeling off a list of three companies.

'Thank you,' said Andy, scribbling down the names on his notepad. 'You've been very helpful.'

He put down the phone and looked at the names he had written down. None of the names were anything like Lecco but he checked them out through Companies House anyway just to be on the safe side. Again, it was a waste of time. None of them were electrical wholesalers or related to electricity in any way, and none of the directors' names were a match either.

He closed down the Companies House website and sat gazing across his office at nothing in particular, reflecting on what he had found out. There was no doubt in his mind that Lecco was a bogus company name that this Aaron had dreamt up to suit his own purposes. He also suspected that Aaron didn't run a company, certainly not a limited company anyway, and he didn't have a warehouse at Witney industrial estate either.

The more Andy thought about what he had found out, the more worried he became. Why would the guy be lying about all this unless he was up to no good? No, there was definitely something shifty going on, and he knew he'd have to face Maddy with it, but he wasn't looking forward to it. No matter how badly he had treated her in the past, he couldn't sit by and let some imposter worm his way into her life, and into his daughter's life, without trying to warn Maddy about it.

He'd ring her tonight after Rebecca's bedtime as he didn't expect Maddy to take it well, and things were bound to get heated. After all, he was about to destroy the happiness she thought she'd found. But Andy just hoped that maybe one day she'd thank him for it.

42

While Maddy was upstairs reading to Rebecca, Aaron poured them both a large glass of wine. It wasn't long before she was back downstairs and he guessed that she must have been as keen to be alone together as he was.

'That's Becky seen to,' she said as she sat down next to him. 'We shouldn't hear anything else from her now.'

'OK,' said Aaron, pleased that the kid was out of the way but trying not to let it show too much.

'Eh, I forgot to ask you, how are things going with the warehouse?' she said, reaching over for her glass of wine.

'Great,' said Aaron. 'The only trouble is that it cost me a lot more than I thought by the time I'd kitted it out and paid the advance rent on it. It's left me short for the house, to be honest. But it's no problem; it just means I'll have to wait a bit longer to get a decent deposit together.'

'How long will it take, do you think?' she asked.

'Maybe a year or more.'

'Really?'

'Oh, yeah, if we're to get the one we want; something like that one I showed you.'

'I wouldn't worry about it,' said Maddy. 'Anything might happen in a year. We might both be living at mine by then.'

Aaron smiled. She was playing right into his hands but he didn't say anything, he just watched the expression on her face.

They hadn't been chatting for long when the phone rang and Maddy got up to answer it. Once the caller had had chance to respond to her cheery greeting she brought the handset over to the sofa with her, mouthing, 'It's Andy,' as she sat back down.

Her cheery tone soon changed as she seemed to be responding to a series of questions put to her by Andy. 'Maybe it's not limited,' she said, followed by, 'Well, you wouldn't find it if you don't know his full name, would you?' and then, 'I don't know. Maybe it has a "trading as" name or something.'

Aaron could tell it was in connection with him and he strained to hear the words at the other end of the line, watching the troubled look that clouded Maddy's attractive features. As he listened to Maddy fending off Andy's questions he found himself becoming annoyed.

'Give it here,' he said, reaching for the phone. 'I'll put him straight.'

But Maddy pulled the handset out of his reach and then held it tightly to her ear. 'Well, like I say,' she continued, 'there's probably a perfectly reasonable explanation. Anyway, I've got to go.'

Aaron watched her quickly drop the phone back onto its cradle as though it were burning her hand. He flashed her an enquiring look, his annoyance evident. Then he noticed the uncomfortable expression on her face.

Maddy wished she hadn't taken the handset over to the sofa. It was bad enough having Andy interrogate her about Aaron, but even worse to have him do it while Aaron was sitting next to her. Damn Andy! she thought, cringing with embarrassment because Aaron might have overheard some of what Andy had said. Thank God she hadn't let Aaron take the phone. She could see by his face that he wasn't very happy, and she had no doubt that she'd just prevented an almighty row between the two men in her life.

'Well?' prompted Aaron when she still hadn't spoken.

'I'm sorry you had to hear that,' she said. 'Andy's been getting on his high horse again. I've already had to put up with him criticising my parenting skills but now he's sniffing around into your business and asking me all sorts of questions.'

Aaron screwed up his face and his nostrils flared as he asked, 'Like what?'

'Oh, he says that there isn't a limited company called Lecco that deals in electricity.'

'The company's new. It won't be listed yet.'

Maddy didn't know how long it took for a company to be listed so she accepted the answer he gave before adding, 'He doesn't think you're a company director either.'

'Where does he get that idea?' asked Aaron.

'Oh, he ran a check, apparently, and nothing came up under your name.'

'Does he even know my surname?'

'No.'

'Well, how the bloody hell would he know, then?'

Maddy shrugged. 'I'm really sorry, Aaron. I know you shouldn't have to put up with this.'

But Aaron didn't seem to accept her apology. Instead, with his expression still stern, he asked, 'What else did he say?'

Maddy cleared her throat. She really didn't want to be having this conversation but, in a way, she thought it was best to face Aaron with Andy's questions. She wanted answers for her own peace of mind. 'He said... well, he's been in contact with Witney industrial estate, apparently, and they say they haven't rented a unit to a company called Lecco.'

'That's because I rented it in the name of the fuckin' holding company! I only set up the new company when I came to Manchester so I could separate it from the Yorkshire-based business. The industrial estate don't even know the name of the new company. We haven't even had a fuckin' sign put up for it yet.'

'OK, calm down,' said Maddy, perturbed at seeing this angry side to Aaron. 'I said it would be something like that.'

'I don't know why you're even trying to explain things to him. It's none of his fuckin' business!'

'OK,' said Maddy. 'There's no need to take it out on me. It's not my fault he's asking questions.'

'What else did he say?' snarled Aaron.

'Nothing.'

'Go on, what else?' he persisted.

Maddy could have kept her mouth shut but she was still curious herself, so she continued. 'He said that there had been no electrical companies renting units from the Witney in the last month. What is the name of the holding company anyway?'

'What the fuck is this?' Aaron bawled. 'Don't you trust me either? Is that it?'

'Aaron, calm down, for God's sake! I never said I don't trust you. I was just curious, that's all. And stop using that bad language; Becky might hear you.'

Aaron bristled and stayed quiet for a few moments but it was obvious to Maddy that he was still riled and it didn't take long for him to carry on ranting. 'I can't believe you're listening to your jealous ex-husband and letting him stir shit up between us. Just cos he can't have you, he's trying to create problems between us.'

'No, it's not like that, Aaron.'

'Well, what is it like, then?'

Maddy didn't say anything. She could see that by now Aaron was really angry and anything she said seemed to be making him worse. Eventually she changed the subject, and asked him if he would like another drink, hoping that if she took his mind off things he would calm down.

It seemed to work and a few minutes later she could see that he was already having regrets about losing his temper. 'I'm sorry,' he said. 'I shouldn't have taken it out on you. But your ex should really keep his nose out of our business.'

'I know,' said Maddy. 'Don't worry, I'll be having words with him.' Then she smiled apologetically. 'Can we please just put it behind us and enjoy the rest of the evening?' she asked.

Aaron responded by lighting a roll-up and smoking it till it calmed him. Maddy didn't really like him smoking cannabis inside her home, knowing that the cloying smell would pollute the air and cling to the furniture, and she worried Rebecca might come downstairs, but, under the circumstances, she decided it was best if she kept quiet. She started a film, snuggled up to Aaron, and tried to forget their cross words. But it was difficult to forget how irate Aaron had become, and she found her mind drifting as she tried to focus on the screen.

Later that night, after they had made love and had a few snorts of coke, Maddy lay in bed, wide awake, her mind going over what had happened that evening. She didn't really think Aaron could be lying. What would be the point of that? And anyway, she'd seen for herself that he was who he said he was. How else could he have afforded to stay in the Midland long-term and drive flash cars? And he *had* taken her to see the first warehouse he was going to rent.

The fact that she hadn't yet met his family in Yorkshire did rankle a bit, but she was sure they existed. After all, she'd spoken to his mother on the phone and she seemed lovely. Aaron had also answered most of the questions that Andy had raised, albeit angrily.

She didn't like to see the angry side of Aaron; he was a bit scary when he lost his temper. But she supposed that she was bound to see the other side of him sooner or later; no relationship could be sweetness and light all the time. And she could understand him being angry in a way; nobody would like to have everything about them called into doubt. She much preferred his softer side and, as she lay there, she went over all his good points.

Aaron was good fun to be with and great at sex, but he was also kind and considerate, always bringing little gifts for her. He was edgy with a hint of danger about him, and she liked that. It made her feel carefree and adventurous, and she loved the excitement of it all.

She gazed across at him; just the sight of his handsome face and lean body gave her a buzz. If she was honest with herself, she liked the fact that he was well off too; it felt good to be taken to all the best restaurants and bars.

He was also very attentive and affectionate, and always paying her compliments. She loved being in his company; no man had ever made her feel as special as Aaron made her feel. And look how he was with Rebecca, taking them all to Blackpool and the zoo just so that she could pay her daughter more attention.

Maddy was still concerned about Andy stirring things up between them though and she was also anxious about the fact that he might yet go for custody of Rebecca. However, he hadn't mentioned it again so perhaps it had been just an empty threat. She hoped so because she had enough to worry about at the moment.

Maybe Aaron was right about Andy. Maybe he was jealous and refusing to fully let go of her, despite the fact that they'd been apart for several years now. Perhaps she should have a word with him when Aaron wasn't around. What she had with Aaron was really good, and she wasn't going to let anybody spoil it just because of petty jealousy.

43

Things were really good between Maddy and Aaron for the next few days. But despite how well things had been going, Aaron was still a bit worried about the ex-husband. Andy was trying to turn Maddy against him and Aaron was bothered about the influence he held over her. Even though he was sure of Maddy's feelings towards him, she might still take notice of the ex. After all, she had been with Andy for a long time, and those sorts of bonds were hard to break.

He knew that the ex was jealous. He was trying to turn Maddy against him by filling her mind with doubts because he wanted her for himself. Well, tough! Andy had had his chance and he'd thrown it away. Now it was Aaron's turn.

Aaron would have felt more secure if Maddy had dismissed all her ex-husband's questions about him. But, instead, she'd responded to her ex-husband's poison by questioning him herself, and he couldn't have that.

He needed a way to convince her of his commitment, and to make her so invested in the relationship that she ignored all her ex-husband's goading. It would also be a way of letting the ex-husband know that he had no chance of winning Maddy back. After thinking about it for the past few days, Aaron had thought of something that might work.

He drew up outside Maddy's home in his smart BMW and sauntered up the drive. He felt self-assured, knowing Maddy couldn't fail to be impressed with what he had lined up, although there was a tiny bit of doubt in his mind. When she answered the door he passed her a bottle of champagne and a box of luxury chocolates.

'Ooh, lovely,' she said. 'What are we celebrating?'

Aaron just smiled enigmatically and stepped inside the house. As he did so, Maddy stood to one side to let him in, then headed towards the kitchen, leaving Aaron to shut the door. He followed her and watched her bend to put the champagne and chocolates in the fridge, admiring the view as the material of her jeans stretched tightly against her firm buttocks.

She turned towards him, smiling at his amused expression. 'What?' she asked, although it was obvious to Aaron that she knew what he had been looking at.

'Stay there,' he said, holding out his hand till Maddy backed away from him.

Then he drew something from his pocket and dropped to his knees. 'Maddy, will you marry me?' he asked, opening a box to reveal an engagement ring.

Maddy gasped, staring in awe at the fabulous ring that he held, which sparkled under the kitchen lights.

'Well, come on. Aren't you going to put me out of my agony?' he asked, attempting a wry smile to mask his uncertainty as Maddy stood there dumbstruck. A tiny quiver of his bottom lip gave his nerves away. 'After all,' he quipped, 'diamonds are supposed to be a girl's best friend, aren't they?'

'Aaron, I… I don't know what to say.'

'*Yes* would be nice.'

Maddy was shocked but delighted. 'Yes, yes,' she said, smiling.

Aaron whipped the ring out of its box and placed it on her finger.

'It fits perfectly,' she said. 'How did you know my size?'

Aaron winked but didn't explain. Instead he said, 'I hope you like it. It's one carat and those two on either side are half a carat each.'

'It's beautiful,' she said. 'It must have cost you a fortune.'

'You're worth it,' he said.

Aaron was relieved. The ring had done the trick as he had hoped it would. He'd chosen it carefully. The stones were mounted on a decorative setting representing one large flower with a smaller one on either side, and the band was white gold, which was polished till it glistened. The whole effect was stunning but, of course, the diamonds weren't real and the gold was only nine carat. Still, there was no way he was going to tell her that. He preferred her to think it cost thousands rather than the couple of hundred quid that it had really cost.

He smiled as Maddy turned her hand this way and that, admiring the ring from different angles, then he hooked his hands under her arms and swirled her round the kitchen floor. She landed with a thud and they both broke into laughter.

'Come on, this is a celebration. Get the glasses,' he said, reaching inside the fridge for the champagne.

Later, when they had almost finished the champagne, Maddy said, 'I really should meet your family now that we're engaged. And you should meet my parents too.'

'Course we should, and we will,' he replied. 'And we'll take Becky to Yorkshire with us too. But, don't worry, we'll have plenty of time before the wedding.'

Once the initial shock of Aaron's proposal was over, Maddy became excited at the prospect of marrying him, and for the last two days she had been on a high. She'd shown the ring to Rebecca that evening when she'd collected her from Andy's but Rebecca hadn't seemed that interested. Still, she was only eight so it probably didn't mean that much to her.

Maddy kept the ring hidden from Andy when she went to collect Rebecca. After spending such a wonderful weekend with Aaron, the last thing she needed was for Andy to spoil it by criticising her decision. But she couldn't wait to share the news with somebody so she waited until Rebecca was tucked up in bed that night, then rang her best friend, Clare.

Since their cross words when Maddy hadn't showed up for lunch, they had made up with each other. And despite the fact that Clare seemed to have a bit of a downer on Aaron, surely she would be pleased for her when she heard the good news.

Clare answered the phone and they chatted a bit before Maddy made her announcement.

'Guess what? Aaron proposed to me on Friday,' she began.

'What? You're joking!'

'Yes,' said Maddy, her voice full of joy. 'So we're now officially engaged.'

'Wow! I don't know what to say, Maddy. I mean, don't you think it's a bit soon?'

'Well, I suppose we've not been seeing each other that long. But sometimes you just know when it's right.'

'As long as you're sure, Maddy.'

'Of course I'm sure. Aaron's wonderful. Honestly, Clare, I can't remember when I last felt this happy.'

'And what does Becky say about it?'

'Not a lot really, but then, she is only eight. But Aaron's wonderful with her. You should have seen him when he took us to Blackpool and Chester Zoo. Becky had a great time.'

'Glad to hear it.'

'Oh, and I'll have to show you the ring, Clare. It's lovely. It's got a full-carat diamond and two half-carat diamonds. I can't stop looking at it.'

'Well, I suppose congratulations are in order,' said Clare. 'When's the wedding?'

'Oh, we haven't really discussed that yet. We've got all that to come.'

'Where will you live?' asked Clare and, to Maddy, this was beginning to sound a bit like an interrogation.

'I don't know yet. Probably here.'

'Really? I thought Aaron was going to buy a house.'

'He is, eventually, but at the moment he's more focused on the business.'

'What about his family? Have you met them yet?'

'For God's sake, Clare. What is this? I know you've got a bit of a downer on Aaron, but do you need to make it so bloody obvious?'

'I'm sorry, Maddy. I'm just looking out for you, that's all. That's what friends do, isn't it?'

'Well, I'm absolutely fine,' snapped Maddy. 'Like I say, I've never been happier, and I'm more than capable of looking after myself.'

'OK. Sorry,' Clare repeated. 'I didn't mean any harm. And if it is truly what you want, then I'm very pleased for you. I wish you all the best, Maddy.'

'Thanks,' said Maddy.

But the conversation remained stilted, Clare's obvious disapproval acting like a wall between them. Although Maddy tried to make polite conversation it was difficult when she knew that Clare would never accept Aaron. But he was her choice and if Clare didn't approve then there was nothing she could do about it. Maddy was determined to spend her future with Aaron regardless of what her friends or family thought.

44

Clare put down the phone and let out a huge gust of air. Maddy's news had completely taken her by surprise. She knew Maddy was smitten by Aaron but hadn't thought she'd be foolish enough to rush into things so soon.

The situation worried Clare. Maddy hardly knew the guy; she hadn't even met his family yet! And Clare had a bad feeling about him. She was convinced he was telling Maddy lies. All the stories about the Porsche and his family in Yorkshire, who Maddy still hadn't met, just didn't seem to add up. Why would he still be living in a hotel? Was it just a front until he'd managed to worm his way into Maddy's home? He already seemed to have delayed his decision to buy a home and Clare wondered why that might be.

Despite her worries, Clare was at a loss as to how she could stop her friend making what could potentially be the biggest mistake of her life. If she passed comment about Aaron, or even asked the questions Maddy should have been asking herself, then Maddy just got defensive. And, as the saying went, you couldn't help those who wouldn't help themselves.

Clare wondered if Andy had heard the news yet and what his reaction would be when he did. It was obvious from their last meeting that he already had concerns and Clare felt compelled to tell him. It might seem disloyal to Maddy, but she knew they had to band together to find a way of rescuing Maddy from this situation. Maybe he could talk Maddy round.

She fished in her purse for Andy's business card, then picked up the phone again and dialled the number he had written on the back last time they had met.

Andy had mixed feelings when he answered the call from Clare. On the one hand, he was pleased she'd rung him. He'd always liked Clare and it meant she was comfortable confiding in him. But, on the other hand, he was apprehensive, recognising that the call was probably in connection with Maddy and, judging by the last conversation he'd had with Clare, it was unlikely to be anything positive.

Clare came straight to the point. 'Have you heard the news?' she asked.

'What news?' asked Andy.

There was a pause before Clare elaborated. 'Maddy's got engaged.'

'No!' said Andy.

'Yes, afraid so.'

'When did this happen?'

'This weekend, I think.'

'Jesus! She never mentioned it when she came to pick Becky up.'

'Sorry,' said Clare.

'No, no, it's not your fault. It's just, well... I thought she would have mentioned it. I can't believe it. She's not been with him five minutes.'

'I know.'

'And she knows nothing about him.'

'I know,' Clare repeated. 'I've said all this to her but she doesn't seem to take much notice. She's overjoyed, like some love-struck teenager, and, no matter what I say to her, it doesn't seem to make any difference. The thing is, she's already letting things slide, like I told you the other day. What will things be like if he moves in with her?'

'It's not only that, Clare, I'm worried about Becky in all of this. Just what effect will it have on her? I mean, I expected Maddy to move on. I knew there would be men in her life, I'm not stupid. But I thought she would take the time to find out more about the man she's seeing before she made him such a big part of Becky's life.'

He didn't voice his added concerns that Aaron might have been lying about his business and the directorship as well, or the call from Rebecca's head teacher. Those were *his* worries and he didn't want to burden Clare with them.

While all these things were going over in his head, Clare asked, 'What will you do?'

'I don't know,' he said. 'But thanks for telling me, Clare. It's best that I know. I need to get my head round it first and then I'll think about how I want to tackle it.'

'OK. Well, I'm sorry to have been the bearer of such bad news,' said Clare.

'It's not your fault, Clare. But, like I say, I'm grateful that you told me.'

'OK, well, you take care,' she said.

'Yes, you too,' said Andy. 'And don't forget to stay in touch.'

'Will do,' said Clare before she finished the call.

Andy sat for a few minutes, incredulous. How could Maddy do such a thing with a man she hardly knew?

Since Aaron had come on the scene Maddy was letting things slide in her work life, becoming snappy with Rebecca, and spending less time with her. The upshot of all that was that Rebecca was becoming so withdrawn at school that the headmistress had felt the need to ring him over her concerns. The thought of having such a man taking over his role as Rebecca's father-figure both angered and unsettled him.

The more he thought, the more worried he became. As Clare had said, if Aaron moved in with Maddy then things were bound to get worse, and they were already bad enough.

He wondered how much Maddy actually knew about Aaron, aside from the things he had told her, which were obvious lies. The man could have been a damn paedophile for all he knew! The thought made him shudder but then he quickly dismissed it; maybe he was getting a bit too carried away. There was probably nothing more sinister than the fact that he occupied too much of Maddy's time, leaving Rebecca feeling pushed out, but that was bad enough.

Andy went over to his drinks cabinet and poured himself a whisky. It was the only way he was going to sleep tonight with all this going over in his head. Several times he was tempted to ring Maddy but he resisted. It was too late, for one thing, and, after his last call when Maddy had hung up, he knew that he probably wouldn't get anywhere. In the end he decided that he would speak to her face to face on Friday evening when he went to collect Rebecca, and he'd make damn sure she listened to all his concerns.

Maddy had only seen Aaron once since he'd left her home on Sunday afternoon and it was now late Friday morning. He'd stayed over on Tuesday but had respected her wishes to have an early night and had left her to get on with her work the following day. Although she missed him when she had to sleep alone, it meant that she was feeling fresher and was making more progress with her work.

This morning she was due to interview a retired police detective who had agreed to dish the dirt on a discredited former colleague. She was looking forward to getting the interview out of the way. Then she would type up her interview notes and catch up with a few bits before collecting Rebecca from school. Later she would cook one of Aaron's favourite dishes ready for him coming round that evening.

As she locked the house and made her way down the drive she was feeling upbeat. But as she got nearer to her car she could see something wasn't right. The side mirror seemed to be twisted. She drew closer and was disturbed to notice that it had been wrenched out of its fixing and the glass was shattered. Somebody must have used something solid like a brick to force it out of position. Not only that, but there was a massive scrape all along the passenger side of the car.

The breath caught in her throat as the shock of this wanton destruction hit her, and she let out an anguished yelp. Thoughts of a connection with the graffiti and the strange cars were spinning around inside her brain, convincing her that somebody with evil intentions had done this.

In her peripheral vision she saw a neighbour approaching. He was an elderly man who lived a few doors down on the other side of the road. Maddy didn't know him well. He was one of those people who said a cheery hello whenever they passed, but now he was striding towards her with purpose. Perhaps he knew something about the damage to her car.

'Is everything all right?' he asked.

'Not really,' said Maddy, her voice a bit shaky. 'Someone's damaged my car.'

The neighbour came round to the passenger side of the car and surveyed the damage.

'I thought it was strange,' he said. 'There was a young woman here last night. Oh, not that I was being nosy. I couldn't sleep, you see. So I went back downstairs for a cup of tea. I often check the windows before I go to bed and I happened to see her after I'd finished my tea. She was there for ages but I couldn't tell what she was doing because she was on the other side of the car. I decided to go outside and see what she was up to but by the time I got to the front door she was gone. Then I forgot about it, to be honest, till I saw you looking at the car.'

'A woman?' asked Maddy, confused as it didn't seem to fit with the man who had been watching the house. 'Are you sure?'

'That's right,' said the man. 'A woman. He'd have been pretty small if it had been a man but, no, I'm sure it was a woman.'

'What did she look like?'

'Well, I couldn't see much of her because, like I say, she was on the other side of the car, and it was dark. But, from what I saw, she had long, bright red hair. It looked dyed, y'know, one of these bright colours that a lot of the youngsters have these days. And I think she was wearing some kind of bomber jacket but, other than that, I couldn't really tell.'

'Right, so you think it was a young woman?' asked Maddy, her heart now beating rapidly.

'Yes, I think so.'

'What time was this?' she asked.

'About half twelve.'

Maddy couldn't think of any more questions to ask so she walked round the car to see if there was any further damage.

'That side's OK,' said the man before Maddy had chance to look.

She came back to the passenger side and stood staring at the broken mirror and huge scratch in the paintwork. 'I can't believe it,' she kept muttering. 'Who would do something like that?'

The man patted her arm, sympathetically. 'I'd get onto the police if I were you, love. They're a bloody disgrace, the youngsters these days, and the girls are getting just as bad. Not that the police will do much, but at least it's a start, isn't it?'

Maddy just looked at him in stunned silence, his words not really registering.

'You can send the police to mine, love. Don't worry, I'll tell 'em what I saw.'

'Thanks,' said Maddy, but she didn't really feel thankful. The aftershock was now beginning to hit her and she could feel her eyes cloud over with tears. Once the neighbour had left her she went back indoors. For a few moments she sat on the sofa going over this and the other incidents in her mind and trying to make sense of it all.

The only person she could think of who might have it in for her was her ex-boyfriend, Rob. But would he really do something as malicious as damaging her property and spying on her? He might have been the jealous type, but she'd never thought of him as malicious. And where did the woman come into it? Unless he had a new girlfriend who was jealous of his past relationships.

But it didn't really stack up. Her relationship with Rob had ended months ago and she hadn't heard from him in ages so why would he start doing spiteful things now? And why would a new girlfriend bother about something that had been over months previously?

Maddy couldn't face her planned interview; her mind was in too much turmoil to focus on work. But she couldn't cope with being alone at the moment either, so she rang Aaron to try to garner some emotional support.

As soon as Maddy heard his familiar voice and began explaining what had happened, she became overwhelmed by emotion and found it difficult to speak.

'Hang on, I've just got a bit of business to attend to, but I'll be round as soon as I can,' he said.

It seemed an age before Aaron arrived and by the time he got there it was early afternoon. In the meantime, Maddy had deliberated over whether to get the police involved then finally decided it was about time she told them everything. When Aaron walked through the door Maddy collapsed, sobbing, into his arms.

'Eh, it's OK,' he said. 'I've seen the damage and we can soon get it fixed. And you should be able to claim it on your insurance.'

'It's not just the damage, Aaron,' she sobbed. 'It's the thought that someone's watching me, someone bad enough to want to destroy my property. I'm worried about what they will do next.'

'All right,' he said, holding her tightly. 'Try not to worry. I'll be with you as much as I can and when I'm not here make sure you keep your doors and windows locked. I think you should phone the police as well and let them handle this now.'

'I already have done,' she said. 'They should be here any minute.'

'Shame,' he said. 'I could have given you something to calm you down, but we don't want them walking in to the smell of dope, do we?'

For precious moments she stayed where she was, with Aaron enveloping her in his strong arms. His presence was soothing; it felt as if a big warm blanket of love and support were wrapped around her. Maddy didn't want him to let go but then the doorbell rang and she felt him pull away.

'It's OK, I'll get it,' said Aaron, and he walked out of the lounge.

Maddy heard him opening the front door, followed by the sound of voices in the hall, and she tried to calm down and mentally prepare herself. The police were here.

Aaron didn't really want the police sniffing around but he had suggested Maddy should ring them because he was doing what would be expected of him. He didn't want to raise Maddy's suspicions but in fact he detested the police and, in the preceding years, he had regarded them very much as the enemy.

He had been on edge as they'd waited for the police to arrive and he had rushed to answer Maddy's front door as there was a chance that one of them might recognise him, and he preferred to face that situation without Maddy watching. Even if the officer didn't say anything, the body language between them might have given him away.

Aaron answered the door to two officers, one male and one female. He was relieved that he didn't know either of them. Thankfully, Flixton was covered by a different police force from the area where he normally operated.

He showed the officers through to the lounge and offered everyone a drink. Meanwhile, the female officer sat on the sofa with Maddy and the male officer sat on the armchair across from them.

By the time Aaron returned to the lounge Maddy was looking more composed as she related her story to the police.

'So, let's look at the incidents one at a time, shall we?' said the female officer. 'Let's start with what happened to your car and then we can discuss the graffiti and the strange cars you've seen outside your house. When did you discover the damage?'

Aaron listened while Maddy answered the officers' questions. He hadn't yet heard all of the details about what had happened to Maddy's car so he was interested in what she had to say, especially the part about the woman her neighbour had seen.

'OK, we'll be speaking to your neighbour separately,' said the female officer, in response to Maddy telling them what her neighbour had said. 'But can you tell me in your own words how your neighbour described the person he saw last night?'

'Yes,' said Maddy. 'He said it was a woman, young, not all that tall, and with long, vivid red hair, dyed, he said. Oh, and he thought she was wearing some kind of bomber jacket.'

'What do you mean by "not all that tall"?' asked the officer.

'He said something about her not being tall enough to be a man.'

'OK. Anything else?'

Maddy shook her head. 'No, that was it. He said it was dark so he couldn't see much.'

'OK, can you think of anyone who might fit that description?' the police officer asked.

'Not really, no,' said Maddy.

But Aaron knew who it was as soon as Maddy described her. And that realisation angered him. He suspected that the same person was probably responsible for the graffiti as well. Aaron felt his muscles tense and outrage showed in his features. He quickly tried to disguise the strained expression on his face.

'Do you have any enemies or can you think of anyone who might have wanted to damage your property?' asked the police.

'No,' said Maddy. 'I deal with a lot of people from different backgrounds because of my work, though, and some of my exposés are hard-hitting. So there's always a chance that somebody connected to an article might be a bit upset. But I make it a rule never to let the interviewees know where I live.'

'OK,' said the police officer while her colleague took notes. 'Is there anyone else you can think of?'

Maddy mentioned her ex-boyfriend, Rob, but then quickly added that she couldn't really see him doing anything like that and he was a man anyway so he couldn't have done the damage to her car.

On and on went the police questions but Aaron had lost interest. Ever since he had realised who the culprit might be, he willed the interview to end. Stuff the useless police with their pathetic questions! He just wanted to get away from here as quickly as possible so he could carry out his own retribution.

Eventually the police interview was at an end and Aaron saw them out before returning to Maddy and giving her another hug.

'You OK?' he asked.

'Suppose so,' she said, pulling away and looking into his eyes. 'I just hope the police find out who did it.'

'Let's hope so. The bastards want punishing!'

'You seem really angry,' said Maddy, and Aaron silently cursed himself for letting it show.

'Well, just hearing you say all that to the coppers, it did annoy me a bit. I just hate to think of what they're putting you through, whoever's doing this.'

'Aw, you're so good to me,' she said, leaning in for another hug.

Aaron stepped back. 'Listen, Maddy. I'm really sorry but I was in the middle of something when you rang and I need to get back to it before they shut for the day.'

'Oh, what was that?' she asked, seeming put out.

'I've been trying to source some materials to kit out the warehouse and I was in the middle of negotiating a good deal with builders' merchants in Hyde when you rang.'

'Oh, I'm sorry.'

'It's OK, no worries. I can go back there, but I don't want to leave it till tomorrow. I can't have him forgetting the deal we've agreed.'

'No, no, you go,' she said, trying to sound unconcerned even though he could hear the fear in her voice at the prospect of being alone again.

He kissed the top of her head. 'You take care,' he said. 'Don't forget: keep your doors and windows locked. And try not to worry. No one will harm you; I'll make sure of that. I'll be back as soon as I can, and I'll stay with you tonight. OK?'

Then he was gone. He regretted having to leave Maddy when it was obvious that she was still in distress but the more he thought about what had been happening, the more annoyed he became. And he knew that he wouldn't settle until he'd punished the person responsible.

46

It was ten to seven in the evening. Maddy had had a strenuous day; first the incident with her car, then having to sit through the police interview, then sorting out the aftermath. She'd rung the insurance company, then rung the retired police detective to apologise and reschedule the magazine interview. Afterwards she had cleared up the smashed glass from the road where her car was parked.

She didn't take the car to school. Instead she made the twenty-minute walk there and then walked back with her daughter. By the time she was home she didn't feel like making Aaron's favourite meal. Besides, she didn't know what time he'd be back. So she made something quick for her and Rebecca instead.

Now she was sitting watching something mundane on the TV while Rebecca played in her room. It was just a way of passing time while she waited for Aaron to arrive and for Andy to come and collect Rebecca, but it was difficult to concentrate on anything as her mind kept drifting to what had happened to her car.

When she heard the doorbell ring she gave a startled jerk, the tinny sound cutting through her worrying thoughts and jangling her frayed nerves. She rushed to answer it, hoping for the comforting sight of Aaron, but it was Andy.

'Hi,' she said, attempting to sound normal. 'She's upstairs. I'll just give her a shout.'

'No, it's OK. Leave her a minute,' he said. 'I need a word.'

Maddy studied his face. He looked serious and she gathered he wasn't very happy. She really could do without this right now.

She sighed. 'All right. You'd better come in.'

Andy didn't take the proffered seat when they walked through to the lounge, telling her he wouldn't be there long. He wasted no time in letting her know what was bothering him.

'I've heard the news,' he said. 'About you getting engaged.'

Maddy was surprised. 'How? Who told you?'

'It doesn't matter. I'm more concerned with the news itself than who told me. Just what the hell's going on, Maddy?'

'I beg your pardon?'

'What's the big rush? You haven't known him five minutes.'

The last thing Maddy felt like was a row but there was no way she was going to put up with another one of Andy's lectures.

'What the hell has it got to do with you?' she yelled.

'It's got a lot to do with me, seeing as how you're letting him into my daughter's life. I mean, what do you even know about this man?'

'His name's Aaron actually, and I know enough to realise that he treats me better than you ever did.'

'That's got fuck all to do with it! I've got serious concerns here, Maddy. Apart from the fact that you've changed so much towards Becky that it's affecting her at school, I'm also worried you're rushing into something with a man you know very little about. I'm not even sure he is who he says he is. From what I can tell, the company he's told you about is bogus. I don't think there's any such company.'

'Are you sure that isn't just jealousy talking, Andy, because he's more successful than you?'

It was a low blow, she knew, but Andy had the ability to anger her more than anyone, which made her say things that she wouldn't normally.

'That's ridiculous and you know it! I've got a really bad feeling about this man, and I can't just stand by and watch you self-destruct, not to mention the damage your relationship is having on my daughter. I'm not happy standing by while this stranger takes over my daughter's life. If you insist on going ahead with this farce, then I will look into getting custody of Becky.'

'You wouldn't! You're too busy concentrating on your career to focus on bringing up our daughter, and you shouldn't have been snooping into Aaron's affairs. Aaron's explained everything to me and I'm happy with that. I don't need to justify my decision to you. I can tell he's a good person by the way he treats me and the way he respects me. He's given me more attention in the few months I've known him than you gave me throughout our entire marriage!'

Maddy saw the change in Andy's facial expression, from anger to hurt, and she knew her words had hit home. For a few moments he stared at her, open-mouthed, before speaking. When he did so his tone was calmer.

'I'm pleading with you, Maddy, not to rush into things until you know more about him. Where is he from? What does he do? What are his family like? Do you even know any of that? He could be a villain or a paedophile or anything for all you know.'

Although Andy was calmer his words were just as inflammatory and Maddy was quick to defend Aaron. 'I know the sort of man I'm dealing with. If he had been a villain then he wouldn't have insisted on calling the police today when my car got vandalised, would he?'

Andy looked stunned. 'Your car got vandalised? When was this?'

'Last night,' said Maddy.

'That's all the more reason you should be cautious. You've already found graffiti on your door, and people watching the house, and all since you met this man. What next, Maddy?'

Maddy was shocked by how much Andy knew. But she didn't have chance to respond to his comments as she heard Rebecca coming through the door, and the words died on her tongue. She wondered how much Rebecca had overheard, and she flashed Andy a warning glare.

Andy turned round and greeted Rebecca, his false jollity sounding obvious to Maddy's ears. 'Hello, sweetheart. I didn't see you there.'

'What were you rowing about?' Rebecca asked.

'Oh, we weren't rowing,' said Andy. 'It was just a bit of a disagreement, that's all, nothing for you to worry about.'

'Have you got everything, Becky?' asked Maddy, helping her ex-husband to extinguish the flames of their row.

Maddy was relieved when they'd gone but also worried. She was alone in the house once more, hyped up after her argument with Andy and nervous of any suspicious sounds. She was also worried about Andy getting custody of Rebecca. Although she hadn't let her anxiety show in front of Andy, she dreaded to think how she would cope if she lost custody of her daughter.

She glanced at the clock. It was now just turned seven and Aaron still hadn't arrived.

With Andy's words echoing in her mind, she couldn't help but have doubts about Aaron. He knew how upset she'd been that day; she would have thought he'd have been here by now. He'd told her he'd be back as soon as possible, and he still hadn't responded to her calls and texts.

But there was something else. His reaction when the police had called didn't seem right somehow. She could understand him being angry at what someone had done but why save that reaction until the police visit? Thinking about it, she realised he had seemed on edge the whole time the police were there, and it felt as if he resented their presence even though he had suggested she rang them.

As she thought about everything Andy had said, as well as Aaron's reaction when the police had called round, she couldn't help but wonder whether there could be a slight chance that Andy might be right about him.

47

Aaron had already been to The Rose and Crown once but there was no sign of the person he was after. So he'd tried phoning and then turning up at their home, but he'd had no luck there either. By the time he walked into The Rose and Crown for the second time that day it was evening and he was feeling agitated. He passed the table where the street girls normally sat but they weren't at that table today. A group of strangers had taken their place, obviously unaware what kind of pub it was.

As Aaron walked to the bar many of the men standing there greeted him effusively. Amongst them was Nick, Aaron's drug dealer, a contrast to the others with his smart designer gear. He flashed his usual dashing smile and broke off from chatting to an attractive blonde while he high-fived Aaron and looked at him expectantly, but Aaron wasn't thinking about getting his supply at the moment. Nor did he want to stand at the bar having a pint and a chat. He was here specifically to see one person and he had just spotted her.

Crystal was sitting at a corner table, deep in conversation with some of the other girls: Ruby, Amber and Angie. One of them made a comment, which caused Crystal and the others to burst into laughter. He looked at her, sitting with her friends, having a drink before work, as though she didn't have a care in the world, and in that moment he despised her, knowing what she had done.

Aaron strode over, his steps fast and furious. 'Crystal, I wanna word!' he ordered.

All of the girls fell silent, picking up on his mood and lowering their heads, except for Ruby, who glared at him. 'Looks like someone's not happy,' she muttered before turning her back to him and carrying on chatting.

Aaron stormed out of the pub, with Crystal following dutifully behind. He passed through the pub's doors, round the corner and down the side street, then turned into a back alleyway.

'Hang on a minute!' shouted Crystal. 'I can't fuckin' keep up.'

He watched as she tottered into the alleyway on her high heels. 'What the fuck have you come down here for?' she asked, her eyes wide with fear despite her brave words.

As soon as she was close enough he pounced on her, pinning her up against a brick wall. 'You fuckin' bitch!' he yelled. 'It was you, wasn't it? Damaging Maddy's car and putting that fuckin' graffiti on her door.'

As he held his fist over her he heard her breath judder in her throat. Her lips drew back and her eyebrows turned in at the corners. It was a look of fear but also a plea for leniency.

'Please, don't hit me,' she begged. Then her body seemed to close in on itself as she prepared for an attack.

Aaron dropped his fist and grabbed her by the shoulders instead, shaking her violently while he shouted. 'Just what the fuck did you think you were playing at? She's fuckin' scared shitless because of you. You stupid bitch!' Then he stopped shaking her but kept a tight grip on her shoulders as he waited for answers.

'All right, let me speak,' said Crystal, growing bolder now the threat of an attack seemed to have abated. 'It was the only way I could get back at you when I found out what you were up to.'

'How long have you known?' he asked. When Crystal didn't answer straight away, he shook her again. 'I said how long have you fuckin' known?'

'Ages. Right from when you first started following her. And then I saw you meeting her, dressed all nice like you are now with your hair all clean and shiny.'

Then Crystal laughed ironically. 'I didn't even fuckin' know your hair was blond till you met her. I thought it was always that manky brown colour. Been to see her again, have you? How the fuck do you think that makes me feel, Gilly? You never dressed like that for me.'

'I'm not fuckin' Gilly, I'm Aaron!' he yelled, his eyes bulging out of their sockets. 'You think I'm just your fuckin' pimp. But I'm not. I could have been someone. I still could. But I'm not having a fuckin' stupid bitch like you spoiling it for me!'

'And how long do you think it will be before she finds out who you really are and how you make your money?' she said, pulling herself free from his grip and stepping away from him. 'And how long before you put her on the game as well? How will it feel having to share your precious Maddy?'

'She'll never fuckin' find out! And I won't be putting her on the game either. She's not just some cheap tart who will shag anyone. She's worth a thousand of you!'

'Oh, you really think she won't find out, do you?' she asked, threateningly. 'If you think I'm gonna carry on taking a back seat while you play Lord Almighty with that fuckin' journalist then you're wrong. You're my man, Gilly, and I'm sick of having to fuckin' share you.'

'No, I'm fuckin' not!' he bawled, slapping her hard across the face. 'I'm Aaron Gill. I don't belong with scum like you and I'm not having you fuckin' spoiling it for me.'

'You wanna bet,' she sneered.

Gilly hadn't expected Crystal to retaliate like this; she was usually so submissive. But, seeing the look of contempt on her face, it was as though someone had flicked a switch, turning him from annoyed to livid. His anger was now so extreme that all he could think about was the need to destroy this thing that stood between him and the bright future he had dreamt about.

He launched a torrent of punches around her head and body, each blow more savage than the last. Her nose broke, the blood splattering onto her face and his fists, and urging him on. He wanted to annihilate this piece of shit!

Crystal screeched in pain but her screams were drowned by the stream of abuse that accompanied his punches. 'Fuckin' bitch! Slag! No good fuckin' whore! Twat! I'll fuckin' teach you! Bitch!'

On and on he went until Crystal dropped to the floor. The only thing that stopped him was the sharp pain of his fist hitting the brick wall as Crystal slumped to the ground.

'Aaaah! Fuckin' bitch!' he yelled, pressing his damaged knuckles up to his mouth.

Then he kicked her viciously. Crystal's body shifted with the impact of his kick but, other than that, she remained still. Suddenly Gilly realised he had gone too far. He bent over to look at her. 'Crystal, Crystal, are you all right?' he asked, praying she was still alive. But there was no response.

Then panic set in and Gilly fled.

Ruby didn't like Gilly. She didn't like most men. They were just a means to an end as far as she was concerned. She'd been thinking of parting company with Gilly for a while. After all, she was as strong as many men and was capable of sorting out most of her troublesome clients. But she'd seen Gilly in action when he was angry and didn't want to risk him turning on her. She wasn't stupid enough to bring problems on herself.

The way Gilly treated Crystal made Ruby like him even less. He was supposed to be Crystal's fella, yet he spoke to her like she was shit and slapped her around whenever he felt like it. She couldn't understand why Crystal put up with it and had told her so many times.

But Crystal was in love with him, so she said, whatever that meant. To Ruby it was a strange kind of love that meant a man could treat you as badly as he wanted, and you'd keep going back for more.

She supposed he was an attractive man, especially lately since he'd been looking after himself and had ditched the tatty cap and hoody most days, replacing them with smart designer gear. But looks weren't everything. She would never let a man treat her the way Gilly treated Crystal, no matter how good-looking he was.

They had been having a good time until Gilly walked into the pub. Ruby could tell he was in a mood straight away. It looked as if Crystal had noticed too as she couldn't get out of the pub quickly enough when he called her over, frightened of disobeying him.

Ruby hissed as they walked away. 'Fuckin' knobhead,' she said. 'I don't know why she puts up with him.'

None of the other girls said anything. They knew Ruby's hackles were up and they were afraid of crossing her. But, despite Ruby's aggressive manner, she cared about her friend Crystal. In fact, it was because she cared that she got so annoyed at the way Gilly treated her.

The mood changed between the girls and for several minutes the conversation felt forced as they sat there downing their drinks. After ten minutes Ruby looked at her watch. Aware that Crystal still wasn't back, she grew concerned and decided to go and see what had happened to her. Even Ruby was a bit wary of Gilly but if he was giving her friend a good going over then she wasn't going to stay here and do nothing.

'She's still not back,' she said to Amber. 'I think we should go and see what's going on.'

'I'm not going,' said Amber. 'I don't want Gilly turning on me.'

Ruby could see the fear in Amber's eyes but she didn't know whether that was fear of crossing her or fear of confronting Gilly. Angie just sat and said nothing. 'Right, fuck the pair of you!' said Ruby. 'I'll go on my fuckin' own.'

When Ruby got outside The Rose and Crown she looked around her but couldn't spot either Gilly or Crystal on the main road. She turned down the side road but couldn't see them there either. Ruby hoped that meant they'd sorted out their differences and that Crystal had gone on to work. She couldn't fathom why Gilly hadn't returned to the pub though. Still, she had to get to work herself so she carried on along the side road in the direction of Piccadilly.

As she passed an alleyway she spotted the vague outline of a person slumped against an industrial-sized bin. Jesus! Manchester is getting worse, she thought. The fuckin' alcys are everywhere. Although Ruby liked a drink and wasn't averse to taking a bit of coke now and then, she didn't have much time for those who abused drugs and alcohol. She'd seen enough of them shouting abuse to passers-by and trying to scare them into giving them cash.

Ruby turned back to face the road ahead but as she turned she saw some spots of blood on the pavement. They snaked a trail that thinned out ahead of her. She looked back and saw that the blood spots grew thicker towards the back alley. Shit, she thought. Maybe this person is in real trouble. That thought had scarcely left her head when another thought occurred to her. *What if it's Crystal?*

Her glance into the alleyway had been so cursory that she hadn't even noticed whether it was a man or woman lying slumped against the bin, or what they were wearing. She turned back and approached the alleyway cautiously until she got to the opening.

Ruby could see the outline of a fake leather bomber jacket, short skirt and skinny white legs. The woman's head was slumped forwards so most of it was hidden behind her body, but Ruby could just about pick out the top of her hair. There was no mistaking that colour.

'Crystal!' Ruby shouted as she ran towards her friend.

Leaning over her, Ruby gently pulled her head back but Crystal didn't move. 'Jesus Christ!' Ruby shrieked, noticing the mass of blood that covered her features. 'Shittin' hell.'

She felt overcome with emotion as she bent further forward and took hold of her friend's wrist. Panic seized her as she struggled to find a pulse. But her own heart was beating so erratically, and her hands were shaking so much, that it was hard to tell. 'Oh, my God!' she cried, thinking that her friend might be dead.

Ruby took a few deep breaths and tried to concentrate. Yes, it was there! She could feel Crystal's pulse, just about. But it was weak and Ruby felt a surge of despair accompanied by anger as she realised her friend was in a bad way.

She took her mobile phone out and rang the emergency services, quickly giving them details. 'Just get here as soon as you can. She's in a fuckin' bad way!' she yelled, trying to bypass the barrage of questions from the operator.

As Ruby took in her friend's injuries while she waited for the ambulance to arrive, her anger intensified. Crystal's face was covered in blood. The flesh surrounding each of her eyes was cut and swollen so much that her eyes were like little slits. Her nose was also swollen and looked as though it was broken.

Ruby sat down beside her friend and rested Crystal's head on her lap. She turned away, finding it difficult to look at Crystal in this state. Her injuries spoke of a level of brutality that shocked even someone as tough as Ruby.

So, instead of looking at Crystal, she kept her eyes fixed on the top of the alleyway, willing the emergency services to get there fast.

She knew who had done this. It was that bastard Gilly! Ruby had no doubt that he was capable of it. She also knew that Crystal would stay loyal to him and not tell anyone what he had done. She never told them anything he got up to. That was the kind of hold he had over her. But Ruby was determined to tell the police. There was no way she was letting him get away with this. Fuck the consequences!

48

Gilly's pace was brisk as he ploughed his way through the streets of Manchester. Intense fury pumped through his body, priming his limbs and forcing all rational thoughts from his brain. Years of drug abuse and abject failure had finally caught up with him.

He turned right into Piccadilly then carried on to Market Street through the swathes of late-night shoppers and shop workers. A multitude of bodies, all shapes, sizes and ages. Teenagers in groups parading the latest fashions and sharing a joke with friends. Families charging through the crowds with their reinforced buggies. And doddery OAPS shuffling along at their own pace.

He passed the homeless with their sad-eyed expressions, forced into begging on the streets. Then the buskers who enticed the crowds, eagerly gathered for a few minutes' diversion from their shopping and their fuckin' perfect lives!

He walked haphazardly, and as he walked he cursed, spat and swore. 'Fuckin' bitch! Whore! Bastard!' On hearing his angry words, passers-by looked at him curiously then recoiled as they spotted the blood spatter on his clothing and fists, and the intense glare of his wild eyes pierced through them.

'What you fuckin' staring at?' he demanded of a man who held his gaze for too long. 'Twats!' he cursed, kicking at an empty can and launching it up the street.

He was demented with rage, desolate and in despair. His life was in ruins. Crystal had spoilt it all. 'BITCH!' Why couldn't she have kept out of it instead of fuckin' interfering? Now it had all gone to shit and he knew Maddy would never want him if she found out who he really was and the things he had done.

Then thoughts of his absent parents flooded his irrational brain. 'Bastards!' It was all their fault. If they hadn't disowned him things would have been so different. He'd have had the life that was due to him instead of having to settle for a cheap slapper like Crystal. He'd have a respectable job and live in a nice house instead of earning a living by taking care of a bunch of tarts and living in a rundown bedsit above a kebab shop.

His mind skipped randomly from thought to thought until finally settling on Maddy. She had been so right, so perfect. He thought back to the first time he had seen her. He'd been drawn to her straight away. She was so attractive with her porcelain skin, gorgeous wavy hair and sexy figure. And so different from the women he had become used to dealing with. She made him think of the life that he'd once had; a life that was probably lost to him now.

He had known straight away that Maddy was special. He loved everything about her: the way she spoke, the way she flicked her hair, the way she was so uninhibited in the bedroom, even the way she was with her daughter. The perfect mother. The perfect woman. Maddy Chambers; perfect in every way.

Memories of his relationship with Maddy now filled his brain. The first time he'd seen her lovely home he'd had a sense of belonging. On their first date she'd looked so sexy in her tight jeans, ankle boots and black silky top. He'd noticed how she had drawn everyone's attention when she'd walked into the bar, and he had been captivated listening to her talking about her life.

Each date after that had been better than the one before. And even after he'd left her he often couldn't resist sitting outside her home, just to catch another glimpse of her. But also to make sure that she hadn't gone rushing off to meet another man or even her stuck-up prick of an ex-husband. He'd spent hours sitting outside in his car, wearing his cap and a hoody so she wouldn't recognise him. He'd been so careful, and now Crystal's petty jealousy could ruin it all. The stupid bitch!

Maddy had soon become an obsession. He had known that he wanted her under his control and he'd used drugs to help him achieve this, but he'd never wanted to destroy her. He just wanted her to give herself wholly to him, to fulfil his vision of them living together as a happy couple in her lovely home. Drugs were a part of his life so it was only right that they became a part of her life too.

And he couldn't bear the possibility of maybe never seeing her again. Even as the thought entered his mind, he shook his head violently, willing it away. It was too painful to contemplate.

As well as being angry, he was jittery. Gilly needed a fix. He also needed to release some of the turmoil that was bubbling away inside him. He picked up a half-brick that was lying in the road and launched it at a shop front. It bounced off the glass leaving a huge crack but he walked on, indifferent.

When he had been walking for more than half an hour his temper began to subside. Thoughts of Maddy were replaced by worry at the situation he now found himself in. He'd acted rashly, leaving Crystal like that. He hadn't meant to hurt her so badly; he'd just lost it. And now, he didn't even know if she was still alive.

What if he had killed her? What if she *was* alive? What if she reported him? He should at least have tried to cover his tracks. But other people would know it was him. They'd all seen him leave the pub with Crystal.

Maybe they wouldn't tell on him. Nobody liked a grass. But, then again, Crystal was well thought of in The Rose and Crown. What if he was arrested? How would he see Maddy then? Somehow he had to find a way to get to her. Maybe he could stay in a different hotel under an alias.

His panicked thoughts swirled round in his brain but he was finding it difficult to come up with answers to his own questions. He needed a fix to calm him down and cursed himself for not getting something from his dealer, Nick, when he had seen him in the pub earlier. Maybe he'd call by his place and get himself sorted out. Or perhaps he could see if Nick was still in the pub. That way would be quicker, but he'd have to see what had happened with Crystal first.

In the end he decided to double back to the alleyway where he had left Crystal. He needed to check she was still alive and, if she was, then he'd make sure she didn't tell anyone that he was responsible for her injuries. Some would guess, but he'd just deny it and invent a cover story about her getting mugged or attacked by a client.

He made his way back to Piccadilly and then through the dingy back streets that led to the rear of The Rose and Crown. He was walking along the side road to the pub when he spotted a heavy police presence further up, near to the alleyway where he had left Crystal.

There were several police cars and an ambulance as well as swarms of police officers. A small crowd had begun to gather and, in the distance, he could just about make out the tall frame of Ruby. Shit, he thought. It's too late now.

He quickly doubled back in the direction of Piccadilly, hoping no one had seen him. He couldn't risk collecting his car, which he had parked close to the pub, and going to the Midland hotel for his hire car would take too long. So he jumped in a taxi in Piccadilly, hoping to make it back to his bedsit before the police came calling.

Ruby stared at her friend, Crystal, who lay propped up in the hospital bed. Her facial injuries looked even worse than last time Ruby had seen her.

The flesh round both of Crystal's eyes was black and blue and her eyelids were angry red and swollen. Her nostrils were packed with gauze and there was a large dressing over her nose. Despite this Ruby could still see bruising on Crystal's cheeks. Her lips were also swollen with a large crack on one side of her bottom lip.

'Fuckin' hell, girl, you gave me a right fright. I thought we'd lost you,' said Ruby, leaning over and giving her friend a hug.

'The doctor said it was my head banging against the brick wall that knocked me unconscious,' said Crystal.

Ruby cringed, both because of Crystal's words and because of the way she struggled to speak through her injuries, her voice sounding distorted.

'Has the bastard broken your nose?' asked Ruby.

Crystal nodded and Ruby noticed the way her brow puckered and her lips thinned with the pain. 'My eye socket as well,' she murmured. 'And two of my ribs are broken.'

'Shit, Crystal! What brought it on?' asked Ruby, outraged. 'I mean, I knew he was a nasty bastard, but I never thought he'd go this far.'

'He found out I'd been following him,' said Crystal, her words slow and muffled. 'He's been seeing someone else. I knew he'd go mad if I faced him with it, so I went for her instead.'

'What? You mean, you attacked her?'

'No. I didn't want her to know it was me. So, I wrote "bitch" on her front door and smashed her car mirror.'

'I don't fuckin' blame you, girl,' said Ruby. 'But why didn't you just call him out on it? That's what I would have done.'

'Because I already knew what he's capable of,' said Crystal, but she didn't elaborate and Ruby didn't ask, thinking that Crystal was referring to the other occasions when he'd slapped her around. She had no idea that Gilly was already a killer.

'Who was she?'

'Remember that journalist?' Crystal said.

'What? The one that interviewed us in the pub?'

Crystal nodded again; this time the movement was slighter.

'What the fuck was she doing with *him*?' demanded Ruby, so loudly that she drew the attention of neighbouring patients, and Crystal flashed her a warning look.

'That's why he started dressing up,' said Crystal. 'At first I saw him watching her outside her house. I wondered if he was planning to rob her or something. But then he turned up all smart and I found out he was taking her out. It turns out he was living a lie.'

She then rested back on her pillows, taking deep breaths through her mouth, her swollen face contorted with pain.

Ruby tapped the back of her hand. 'It's OK. You don't need to say any more,' she said, her voice now lower. 'You try and rest.'

'No!' said Crystal, but then she paused for a few seconds and continued taking deep breaths. Ruby could tell she was preparing herself to say something important, and she waited while Crystal psyched herself up.

'Please, don't tell anyone,' she said, her voice now barely a whisper. 'He'll kill me if he thinks I've dobbed him in. He's completely lost it, Ruby.'

'You're too late,' said Ruby, watching as her friend's face contorted again with the pain. 'I've already told the police. I knew you wouldn't, so I've done it. There's no fuckin' way I'm letting him get away with this. Hopefully they won't take too long to find him.'

'But he'll kill me,' said Crystal.

'No, he fuckin' won't!' said Ruby. 'Because I'll let everyone know that it was me who grassed him up, and I'll let them know what he did to you as well. Don't worry, he doesn't fuckin' scare me. If he goes for me I'll slit his fuckin' throat.'

Ruby's voice had risen again and she meant what she said. She always carried a knife to protect her from troublesome clients and had even used it twice. The clients hadn't reported her; they were too frightened of people finding out how they spent their free time. But a quick nick on the arm or the back of the hand had been enough to let them know that she wouldn't tolerate them getting rough with her.

From now on she'd be wary of Gilly and would make sure she was ready if he decided to attack her. And, if he did, he'd get more than a nick on the hand. She'd do whatever she needed to do in order to defend herself. She felt confident that no jury would find her guilty if it was self-defence.

For a few moments neither of them spoke. Ruby could tell her friend was in a lot of pain so she decided to leave her to rest. 'Listen, I'm gonna go now but I'll be back in a couple of days when you might be in a bit less pain,' she said.

'No,' said Crystal. 'Not yet,' and Ruby could tell there was something else Crystal was determined to say, despite her pain.

'You need to warn the journalist,' she said. 'Gilly's off his head, and she's in danger.'

'Why? You don't owe her fuck all!'

Crystal reached out and covered Ruby's hand with her own, beseeching her. 'It's not her fault. She didn't know. I think she still doesn't know about him. He even stopped using his nickname, Gilly, and used his proper name, Aaron. He's obsessed with her, Ruby. You should have heard how he went on about her. He used to sit outside her house for ages, even after he'd stayed with her. He's fuckin' lost it. He'll be getting desperate now and I'm worried what he'll do. I already feel bad. I've put her through enough, scaring her like that.'

She took a breather again, grimacing with the pain. Then, after a few moments, she said, 'Please.'

'All right,' said Ruby. 'I'll let the police know about her.'

'No,' mumbled Crystal. 'They'll take too long. You need to warn her as soon as possible.'

Ruby looked at her injured friend. Knowing she couldn't risk this happening to anyone else, she sighed resignedly. 'Go on, then. Give me her address.'

49

When Gilly arrived back at his flat, he instructed the taxi driver to park round the corner. After paying the fare, he approached the bedsit stealthily, making sure there were no police around before he went inside. He dashed up the stairs, hoping none of the staff from the kebab shop would spot him.

The smell hit him as soon as he walked through the door. When he'd lived here full-time, he'd become used to it and it hadn't bothered him. But now, as he walked through the door, the combined stench of cannabis, kebab meat and cigarettes assailed his nostrils.

Gilly walked through the lounge, his distaste evident from the pained expression on his face. It was such a contrast to where he'd spent most of his time recently. Maddy's comfortable detached home; the place where he belonged.

He made his way to the cupboards in the small kitchenette where he had secreted his stash of drugs, cash and some stolen credit cards. Gilly always kept these in case of any unforeseen eventualities. His choice of career was a risky one and he'd always anticipated that there might be a time when he would need them. Then he took a quick snort of the coke. He knew he couldn't afford to waste any time, but this couldn't wait.

While he waited for the coke to kick in, he gathered up the drugs, cash and credit cards, pausing at intervals to take several large swigs from a can of beer he'd found in the fridge. As soon as he felt the rush of the coke he left the bedsit, knowing he couldn't afford to go back there.

Gilly had a plan of sorts. He'd go into hiding; rent a room somewhere but not in the city centre. He'd head into the suburbs instead and find a cheap B & B, giving them a false name. Then, once the heat had died down a bit, he'd think about his next move.

It was late Friday evening and Maddy was having a well-needed glass of wine. She hadn't seen Aaron since he'd left her after the police visit and, although she'd rung and texted him several times, she still couldn't get a reply.

She was no longer angry from her earlier row with Andy. Instead she was feeling strung-out after such a stressful day. The fact that she was craving cocaine didn't help but she resisted the temptation, knowing that it would probably make her feel even more anxious in the long run.

Andy's words kept playing over in her head and she wondered whether he might be right about Aaron. Could there perhaps be a connection between Aaron and all the bad things that had been happening recently? The fact that Aaron was being so elusive only made her doubt him more.

But then she told herself she was being foolish to listen to Andy, whose view of Aaron was bound to be biased. Instead she thought about how wonderful Aaron had been to her in so many ways, even today when he'd held her tight and comforted her after she'd found the damage to her car. Some niggling doubts persisted but she would speak to him about them as soon as he showed up, and he would hopefully put her mind at ease.

When she heard the doorbell, Maddy jumped and automatically checked the time on the clock. Twenty past nine. That would be him now. As she went to answer the door she felt a reassuring glow. She should have known he'd be here soon, and he'd probably have a good explanation about where he'd been.

But the person on the other side of the door gave Maddy a start. She had expected Aaron, but instead she was looking at a tall black woman, Amazonian in stature. Her reaction seemed to displease the woman, who glared at her before speaking.

'Crystal sent me to tell you about Gilly,' she said, matter-of-factly.

Maddy stared back, still unnerved, but somewhere in the back of her mind the name Crystal meant something. Then it came back to her. She was one of the prostitutes who she'd interviewed a while ago. The recollection provided a link with the woman standing at her door and she vaguely recognised her. She had been there too; the feisty one. She hadn't spoken much during the interview but when she had, her comments had been barbed. The fact that a woman from such a background had found her way to Maddy's door unsettled her even more.

'What are you talking about?' she asked sharply. 'And how on earth did you know where I live?'

'No need to get funny with me, girl. I'm doing you a favour.'

'What the hell do you mean?' asked Maddy.

'Crystal wants you to know about Gilly and what he did to her.'

'What are you talking about? Who on earth is Gilly?'

The woman tutted then said with attitude, 'Aaron Gill. That guy you've been seeing?'

'Aaron? What about him?'

'He's not who you think he is, girl. He's a bad bastard. He beat my mate Crystal up good and proper. Now she's lying in the hospital, black and blue, and she wants me to warn you. She thinks he's gonna come for you. Crystal says he's obsessed with you – he even used to sit outside your house when he wasn't with you.'

Maddy had now gone from unsettled to terrified. It was bad enough that a virtual stranger had turned up at her door, but what she was saying about Aaron made matters even worse. Maddy couldn't understand what the woman was doing here or why she was telling her all this. Her automatic reaction was to become defensive, her mind loosely connecting this woman with the threatening incidents that had taken place recently.

'I don't know what you're talking about. Aaron isn't a violent man, and he certainly has no connection to prostitutes.'

Maddy went to shut the front door but the woman rammed her foot against it, startling her. Maddy stepped back, and put her arms up to her face in a weak attempt at defending herself.

'Don't worry, I ain't here to harm you, girl, but you gotta hear this for your own good. That Gilly is very fuckin' handy with his fists, and he's put Crystal in hospital cos she didn't like him seeing you. He's her fella, ya see, as well as her pimp.'

'Pimp? What on earth are you talking about?' asked Maddy, the word *pimp* sending a shockwave through her.

'That's right, girl. I don't know what he's told you but that's what he is. He's a bit crazy too. And now he's fuckin' lost it good and proper.'

Maddy's mind was wrestling with the conflicting thoughts that were running through her head. Denial about Aaron's supposed identity battled with recognition of his drug abuse, but both thoughts were sidelined by her overriding confusion and fear.

'Do you know anything about the damage to my car?' asked Maddy, her voice sounding small and shaky.

'Not me, no. I'm your good Samaritan, girl. Not that I'm getting any fuckin' thanks for it. I should have let the police handle it, like I told Crystal.'

'Look, you've said what you came here to say, so could you please go now?'

The woman stepped back from the door. 'Suit yourself,' she said. 'I didn't wanna come in the first place.'

Maddy quickly pushed the door to and as she did so she could hear the woman still talking, her manner now more aggressive. 'Don't say I didn't warn you. When that Gilly comes looking for you, you better be fuckin' ready.'

Then Maddy recoiled as she heard the woman's fist hammer on the door. For a moment she thought she was going to bash the door down but then she realised that it was probably just a parting punch, done in temper. Maddy dashed to the living-room window and peeped through a gap in the curtains, heaving a sigh as she watched the woman walk away.

Maddy was shaking after the encounter but felt relieved that the woman had gone. She'd rarely encountered anybody so intimidating. For a moment she thought about ringing the police and reporting her, but the woman hadn't threatened her. She seemed to think she'd been sent as a warning. But why? Her Amazonian stature, abrasive manner and stern features hadn't filled Maddy with trust, and she wondered what the woman's motive could be.

Maddy knew that Aaron would never hurt anyone in the way the woman had described. He was gentle and caring. And yet, did she really know him? He did get a bit snappy at times. But that was nothing. It was just because of the stress of setting up a branch of his business in Manchester. And it certainly didn't make him a violent man.

She thought about the woman's words. And Andy's words. And the way Clare seemed to have taken against Aaron. No! They couldn't be right. Surely?

She tried Aaron's phone again but once more she was directed straight to voicemail. Maddy cut the call without leaving a message, annoyed. Now more than ever she needed to speak to him. She needed his reassurance and the comfort of his words. She needed him here, holding her tight and telling her it was going to be all right. And, more than anything, she needed him to tell her that everything the woman had said had been a lie.

50

The following morning Maddy wasn't feeling so good after drinking far too much wine the previous night. She had a headache and felt shaky, her hangover helping to fuel the anxiety brought on by yesterday's events. Despite the amount she had drunk, her anguished thoughts had kept her awake for much of the night, meaning she was also overtired.

By the time she'd finally got to sleep she had managed to convince herself that the woman who came to visit her was lying about Aaron. Maddy knew Aaron wasn't capable of the things the woman said, and there was no way she was going to take the word of a malicious, aggressive prostitute about the man she loved and trusted.

When the doorbell rang she half expected it might be Aaron and she automatically checked her appearance in the hall mirror. Despite a swift application of make-up that morning she looked worn out. Her eyes were dull, the pupils mere dots, and the dark circles beneath them were still visible under her foundation.

She swung the front door open to find two uniformed police officers standing on the other side. Straight away something instinctively told her they weren't here in connection with the damage to her car. One of them was an older man who wore a sergeant's stripes, and the other was younger. Both of them bore grave expressions.

The sergeant was the first to speak. 'Madelaine Chambers?'

'Yes,' said Maddy.

'We'd like to speak to you about Aaron Gill. Could we come inside, please?'

'Y-yes,' said Maddy.

A moment of panic gripped her, the breath catching in her throat and her heart racing. She tried to control her shaking limbs as she led the officers through to the lounge and offered them a drink. They both declined; it seemed to Maddy that they were eager to get down to business, so she offered them a seat instead and waited anxiously to find out why they were here.

Again it was the sergeant who spoke while the other officer took out his notepad and pencil. 'Can you tell us what your relationship is to Aaron Gill, please?' asked the sergeant.

'Why? What's he done? Is he OK?' asked Maddy.

'Yes, as far as we know he's OK,' said the officer. 'Could you answer the question, please?'

'Y-yes, he's my boyf… well, fiancé,' she said. 'What's he done?'

'We'll come to that later, if you could just answer a few questions for us first of all, please,' said the sergeant.

It was worded politely but Maddy could tell by the expression on his face that he expected her to cooperate. She nodded and the sergeant carried on.

'How long have you known him?'

'A few months,' said Maddy.

'And how long has he been living at this address?'

'He doesn't live here,' said Maddy. 'He just stays here.'

'Are you sure?' asked the sergeant.

'Yes, why?'

'He gave this address when he hired a car, a BMW.'

'You mean... that wasn't his car?'

'No, it wasn't,' said the sergeant, his tone dismissive, as though it should have been obvious to Maddy. 'Do you have an address for him?'

'Not really, no. He's been staying here a lot but he's originally from Yorkshire.'

The sergeant's eyebrows curled inwards in an expression of scepticism. At this silent prompt, Maddy continued, although her mind was still occupied with thoughts of why Aaron would have lied to her about the car.

'He's opening a branch of his business in Manchester so he's staying at the Midland for now till he sorts everything out.'

Hearing herself saying all this out loud, coupled with the revelation about the BMW, made it all seem implausible even to her, but Aaron had made it sound so convincing.

'OK,' said the sergeant, looking across at the younger officer to make sure he had taken the details down. 'Whereabouts in Yorkshire is he from?' he asked.

'Erm, I don't know exactly,' said Maddy, feeling foolish.

'OK. Do you know his room number at the Midland?'

'Yes,' said Maddy, giving him the number, almost relieved that at least she knew that.

'When did you last see him?' the sergeant asked. His questions were coming more quickly now, which unnerved Maddy.

'Yesterday,' she said.

'What time?'

'Erm, I don't know exactly but it was some time in the afternoon.'

'Could you be more specific?'

'Sorry, no. I was a bit stressed. I erm…'

Maddy was going to mention the damage to her car, thinking that the officers probably already knew anyway, but the sergeant butted in with another question before she had chance.

'Where was he when you last saw him?'

'Here.'

'OK. And you don't know what time it was when he left?'

Maddy thought back to yesterday. A lot had happened since she'd discovered the damage to her car. That was late morning. After that, she hadn't rung Aaron straight away and, when she did ring him, it had been a while until he'd shown up. He'd sat with her throughout the police interview and then he'd gone.

'Erm, I think it was late in the afternoon,' she said. 'Yes, I remember now, it was late because he said he had to go and buy something from builders' merchants in Hyde before they shut for the day.'

'And have you any idea of his whereabouts now?'

'No,' said Maddy. 'He was supposed to come back last night but he didn't show up. I kept ringing and texting him but there was no reply.'

There was now a note of desperation to her voice as the reality of her situation began to hit home. The sergeant looked across to the younger officer, frowning as he did so, and waited while the other officer finished writing in his notepad before he spoke again.

'Can you let us have his phone number, please?' he asked.

'Yes,' said Maddy, and she read the number from her phone's list of contacts while the junior officer wrote it down.

'What's he done?' she asked again, conscious of how high-pitched her voice had become.

'I'm afraid he's wanted in connection with a serious crime but we're not at liberty to give out any details at the moment.'

'Did he beat that prostitute up and put her in hospital?' Maddy dared to ask, dreading the answer.

The sergeant gave her a hard stare, his eyebrows now raised. 'What do you know about that?' he asked, bluntly.

'A woman came to tell me last night. A prostitute. I recognised her from an interview I'd done a few months ago at The Rose and Crown.'

'The Rose and Crown,' repeated the sergeant, checking to make sure his junior officer had written it down.

'Yes, it was for an exposé I was writing about prostitution. She said that Aaron had beaten up one of the other prostitutes, called Crystal, and put her in hospital. She came to warn me... But I didn't believe her...'

Suddenly Maddy felt the impact of her own words. It was as though her brain had flicked the switch from denial to acknowledgement. But the truth was like poison on her tongue. She felt the room sway and her head went woozy.

'I – I don't feel very well,' she said, her voice cracking.

'Take a minute,' said the sergeant. He then turned to address the junior officer. 'Did you get all that down?'

'Yes,' said the officer, who looked sympathetically across at Maddy. 'You might find it better to bend your head forwards,' he said.

Maddy did as he said and waited until the feeling subsided. While she waited, she became aware of the awkward silence in the room, and she willed the faintness to pass so the police could finish their questioning and leave her alone.

She looked up. 'Are you OK?' asked the junior officer.

Maddy nodded and she noticed that the sergeant was still wearing a stern expression. It told her that his patience was wearing thin. He was here to find out as much as he could and then set to work on finding Aaron as quickly as possible. Despite her shock and sorrow she felt guilty at holding him up.

'Just a couple more questions before we go,' he said. 'Are you all right to continue?'

'Yes,' said Maddy, hoping it would soon be over.

'The woman that visited you; do you know her name?'

'No.'

'Can you describe her?'

'Yes. She was a black woman, tall, very tall, almost six foot I think, but slim and quite muscular. She had her hair in cornrows too.'

'Age?'

'Only young. About early twenties probably.'

'Thank you,' said the sergeant. 'You've been very helpful.' Then he turned to his colleague. 'Do you have anything to add?'

The younger officer skimmed through his notes then looked up from his pad. 'No, I think we've covered everything for now, Serg.'

The sergeant stood up. 'Aaron Gill is a very violent man, I'm afraid. You will need to be vigilant. Keep all your doors and windows locked and don't answer the door unless you're sure who the caller is. In the meantime, if he tries to contact you in any way at all, please ring the emergency services immediately and let us know.'

'Y-yes, I will do,' said Maddy. Then she led them to the door without saying anything further, afraid she wouldn't be able to get her words out. She was on the verge of tears and knew that her emotions were threatening to overwhelm her. She quickly shut and locked the door, then dropped to her knees and howled.

51

Maddy was distraught. She couldn't believe it had come to this. Aaron had seemed like the ideal man, and he'd made her feel so happy, and yet he had had these terrible secrets. Her first thought was how she would manage to live without him. All her plans for the future had been extinguished because now she knew exactly who and what he really was. And that deliriously happy feeling of being in love had been wrenched from her.

She couldn't believe that the prostitute had been right about him. And because what she'd told her had been true, it meant that everything else about Aaron was false. He wasn't a businessman at all. He was a violent man, a pimp and a drug addict. Everything about him was a lie. His business. His family. Even his car.

Maddy wondered about the woman who had rung the hotel telling her she was Aaron's mother. Was she really his mother? Did his family perhaps live in Yorkshire but were just not as well off as she had surmised? Or was it somebody else entirely who Aaron had got to pass herself off as his mother?

And it had been Aaron who had sat outside her home watching her, causing her hours of distress. On realising that, she felt as though frozen fingers were drawing a twisted line down her spine, and she shuddered. It was the sickening realisation that she had been targeted by a disturbed and malicious man.

Maddy couldn't believe how she had willingly let Aaron into every part of her life. She had shared so much with him, her dreams and ambitions, and she'd even let him into her daughter's life. She felt so guilty to think that she'd put Rebecca at risk from this lowlife scum.

Then Maddy thought about how intimately he knew her. In some ways he knew her more than anybody ever had. He'd explored every centimetre of her body and, in their mutual quest for the ultimate sexual experience, he had taken her to places nobody had ever taken her.

As she recalled what he had done, she no longer felt a pleasurable thrill. Instead she felt repulsed, defiled and sick to the pit of her stomach. As the physical reaction kicked in, she felt the urge to vomit and she rushed to the bathroom. There she knelt over the toilet bowl and emptied the contents of her stomach, retching violently until she could retch no more.

For several minutes afterwards she remained there, crying pitifully, the tears and mucus dribbling down her face, and the ends of her hair covered in vomit. She tore the engagement ring from her finger and dropped it into the bowl, where it floated amongst the puke before she flushed it away. A fitting end, she thought.

Then something else came to her: the cravings. Because, apart from destroying her life in so many other ways, Aaron had also got her hooked on drugs and she was now in the early stages of addiction. The physical effects of her cravings cut sharply into her sorrow, leaving her bitter and resentful.

It was a while before Maddy got up off the bathroom floor. She had an overwhelming need to feel clean so she took a shower, changed her clothes and reapplied her make-up. Then, determined to pull herself together, she went downstairs and made herself a hot drink.

But the negative thoughts were still invading her brain and she knew she needed someone to confide in. Someone who knew her well and would offer support when she was at her lowest ebb. So she picked up her phone and punched in the number.

'Andy,' she said, trying to keep her voice from shaking. 'Can you come over, please? I need to see you.'

'OK, Mr Faulkner, if you'd just like to sign here, please,' said the hotel's proprietor, smiling at the good-looking young man standing in front of her.

Aaron smiled back then signed the name M. Faulkner on the form that she handed to him.

'I'll show you up to your room now,' she said. 'Do you not have a case with you?'

'No, I prefer to travel light,' he said.

Aaron had settled on the name Malcolm Faulkner as it tallied with one of the stolen credit cards he was carrying. That way it would match up if he paid for anything on the card while he was there. It was a bit of an old-fashioned name and wouldn't have been his first choice, but he wasn't bothered. He just needed an alias.

He had found a cheap hotel a couple of miles from the airport. It was far enough away from the city centre to stop him getting spotted but also near enough to get there quickly if necessary. And, best of all, Flixton was even nearer to him than the city centre.

He knew the police were onto him as he'd stayed with one of his friends from The Rose and Crown on Friday night. After he'd found out what he wanted to know from the friend, he'd decided to get out of there as soon as possible. His friend was asking too many questions about whether he'd really beaten up Crystal and left her for dead, and Aaron was nervous about him giving away his whereabouts.

Once he was inside the hotel room, Aaron lay back on the bed and kicked off his shoes. His mind was still buzzing from everything that had occurred recently. He regretted what had happened between him and Crystal, but he quickly quashed those feelings, telling himself that Crystal had got what she deserved.

The main cause of his sorrow was that he was already missing his precious Maddy. His perfect woman. She had been his. She still was. As he recalled all the good times he had spent with her, a beaming smile lit up his face. He felt a pull towards Maddy that was stronger than anything he had ever felt before. It was like a sense of belonging, because that lifestyle was his due and she was his perfect match.

Their love was powerful and he knew that her love for him was just as strong as his love for her. Surely, then, she would be able to forgive him for what had happened. Maddy would understand why he'd done it. He'd done it for them because they belonged together and he couldn't afford to let Crystal spoil it. And he felt sure that Maddy wouldn't want anything to come between them either.

52

Andy was shocked to receive the call from Maddy. She had sounded upset on the phone but said she preferred to discuss it with him in person, whatever 'it' was. He found it strange that she should be upset after she had just got engaged. He'd have thought she would have been happy.

His mind shot back to last night and their row. He wondered if some of his words had got to her and made her think again. On the other hand, maybe after giving it some thought she had become more annoyed and wanted to have it out with him. He hoped not.

Andy pulled up in his car, across from Maddy's house, and walked to the door with Rebecca. As soon as he saw Maddy he could tell she wasn't herself and he detected a slight tremor in her voice as she said, 'Becky, could you go to your room, please, for a bit? Me and your father need to talk.'

Rebecca tutted. 'Not again,' she said but neither of them reproached her for her attitude. Andy knew she had a point.

He stepped inside and waited till Maddy shut the door, then gazed at her. 'What is it?' he asked.

'Oh, Andy,' she said, the tremor now even more evident. 'It's Aaron.'

Then she dissolved into tears. 'Maddy?' he asked, puzzled, but Maddy was unable to speak so he took her in his arms till her crying abated.

As he held her it was difficult to see her so upset and his heart cried with her. He hadn't seen her this distraught since the day they'd split up four years previously.

Then she looked up at him, her face blotchy, and he could see now that her features were also strained. 'Come through to the lounge,' she said. 'I'll make us a brew.'

Andy was horrified to find out the brutal truth about Aaron. He'd suspected that there was something not right about him, and had been frustrated at his inability to make Maddy see sense, but even he could never have imagined anything as explosive as this.

'Jesus!' he said. 'A bloody pimp and a drug addict, living with my daughter?'

Maddy nodded regretfully and Andy could see the sorrow in her eyes.

'How could you not know?' he asked, outraged.

'He was very convincing,' said Maddy, her voice small and shaky.

He could see that she was struggling with the enormity of what had happened to her and he decided not to press her further, despite his annoyance. It was a big enough shock for him, but he could imagine that the effect on Maddy was much worse. The last thing she needed right now was him saying I told you so.

Andy could tell she was feeling guilty enough as it was. He knew that feeling well. He had carried a feeling of guilt for the last four years, ever since his affair had come to light and he'd seen the effect it had had on Maddy and their daughter.

And in a way he felt partly responsible for Maddy's ill-fated relationship with this imposter as well as those before it. He'd seen how devastated she'd been after the divorce despite her attempts to tough it out and make the break from him. It had left her vulnerable when it came to relationships and he'd had to stand by and watch her make a hash of her life.

'I feel so foolish for not seeing through him,' she said. 'He was just so... so... completely convincing. And... and... I'm so sorry for bringing him into Becky's life. I just hope she'll get...'

Then her voice broke and Andy took her into his arms again and stroked her hair. 'Hey, it wasn't your fault,' he said. 'You weren't to know. Some of these conmen can be very convincing. You hear about it all the time.'

Then he heard footsteps in the hall and the two of them quickly pulled away, Maddy trying to wipe away her tears with the back of her hand.

Rebecca appeared in the doorway. 'Are you crying because of Aaron, Mummy?'

'No... no, darling, it's nothing,' said Maddy, between her tears. 'Nothing for you to worry about. Why don't you go back to your room until me and Daddy have finished talking?'

But Rebecca didn't go back to her room. Instead she crossed the lounge and sat down, looking across at them.

'Mummy, I heard you talking about Aaron. Will he still be coming here?' she asked.

Then she paused and looked guiltily at Maddy, as though unsure whether she was speaking out of turn. She came over to them and snuggled up to her dad as if seeking reassurance from her one sensible parent, and she received it in the form of a strong hand cupped round her shoulder and a knowing smile.

'No, sweetheart,' said Andy. 'He won't be coming here any more.'

'Good, I'm glad,' she said. Then, acting on conscience, she said, 'Sorry, Mummy, but Aaron wasn't a very nice man.'

'Why, darling?' asked Maddy, sitting up straight.

'He used to swear at me when he was angry and sometimes he hurt me to make me go to my room. He did a Chinese burn on my arm and pulled my hair sometimes.'

'Oh, darling, I'm so sorry,' said Maddy, reaching out her arms.

Rebecca went to her and while they hugged Andy looked on, feeling a strange mix of emotions. Anger at Maddy for letting this man into his daughter's life. But also pity for her and what she was going through. And guilt for the part that he had played in leaving Maddy so vulnerable.

Apart from all that, he felt strangely out of place, comforting his ex-wife because of the hurt her lover had caused. Eventually, he announced that it was time for him to get back home.

'I'll take Becky back with me until tomorrow,' he said. 'Are you sure you'll be OK tonight?' he asked for the third time.

Maddy nodded meekly. 'Yes, I need to be alone,' she said. 'And I agree that Becky will be best staying with you tonight.'

'OK, well, you take care,' he said. 'And if you need me, just ring.'

Then he turned to go. His last thought before he left was a desperate hope that both Maddy and Rebecca would come through this all right.

53

It was the following Friday evening and Andy was due to collect Rebecca for the weekend again. During the past few days Maddy had been coming to terms with Aaron's deceit as well as learning to live without him. She felt tired, upset and ashamed of herself for falling for him.

But apart from that she was still experiencing cocaine cravings, even though she hadn't taken it on a daily basis, and they added to her anxiety and tiredness. In fact, Maddy felt so bad that she had to ask the doctor to prescribe her something to calm her down.

Over the past few days she'd berated herself so many times for being foolish enough to succumb to Aaron's charms. It was classic, textbook. Young, good-looking and seemingly successful man meets sad older woman and wins her over by showering her with praise and affection. How could she have been so stupid? She'd heard about these silly old women who'd been ripped off by their toy-boy lovers, and she'd always derided them for being daft enough to fall for it. And now, she was one of them!

As Maddy was finding it difficult to concentrate on work she'd taken a couple of weeks off, but she was determined not to sit at home and mope so she had taken to gym visits and walks whenever she had the energy and they helped to lift her spirits.

Despite how rough she had been feeling, Maddy had rung Clare to smooth things over. She felt that she at least owed her an apology after being so snappy with her when Clare had reacted negatively to news of her engagement. After all, Clare had only been looking out for her, and Maddy now realised how foolish she had been to assume that Clare had been jealous of her relationship with Aaron.

Maddy felt embarrassed to have to admit that her friend had been right about Aaron all along, but Clare had been very understanding. She'd even tried to reassure Maddy with the cliché, 'It can happen to anyone.'

'Yes,' Maddy had said sardonically. 'Anyone who's emotionally vulnerable and desperate to be loved.'

Clare had responded sarcastically to Maddy's self-pity. 'Bloody hell, Maddy. I'll be getting my violin out soon.' It had broken the ice and helped to cheer Maddy up a bit.

Just having Clare back in her life had helped Maddy too. It was good to know she was at the other end of the phone whenever she was feeling particularly down. Andy had also surprised her by how supportive he had been. In fact, Maddy didn't know how she would have got through the past few days without him and she felt reassured knowing she had people round her who cared.

When the doorbell rang at a quarter to seven, Maddy was busy taking the rubbish out. She was expecting Andy so she plonked the bag of rubbish down, quickly washed her hands and dashed to answer the door, forgetting that the back door was still unlocked.

She was pleased that he was early; he'd probably done it intentionally so they could have a chat before he took Rebecca, she thought. So she went to answer the door with a smile on her face, looking forward to seeing him.

She was startled to find Aaron standing in the doorway, and her smile disappeared. He looked different somehow, slightly dishevelled, and he wasn't wearing the smart clothes she was used to seeing him in. Instead he sported a pair of tatty jeans and a hoody; just like he had worn when he had sat in his car outside her house for hours, intimidating her.

He was clutching a bottle of wine, feigning normality, and before she had chance to speak, he stepped into the hall and held the wine out, offering it to her.

'Hi, babe,' he said, planting a kiss on her lips as he walked past her, and she felt herself tense.

Her urge was to run, and to phone the police from a neighbour's house, but she couldn't. Rebecca was upstairs and she needed to protect her. So she took the wine and followed him inside, consumed by a feeling of sheer dread.

'You been OK?' he asked.

Maddy was stumped. She hadn't seen him in a week, a week in which her life had been wrecked, and all he could say was, *'You been OK?'* Even if she hadn't known about the attack on Crystal, his behaviour would have been out of the ordinary. He'd left her, distraught about the damage to her car, promising to return that evening. Since then she'd heard nothing from him, and he hadn't even bothered replying to her calls or texts.

She looked at him intently and immediately sensed a change in him from the last time she'd seen him. Was it because, in light of what she now knew, she saw him differently? No! It was something apart from that. She saw it in his eyes and in his manner too. Maddy recalled the words of the prostitute who had come to warn her, *'He's a bit crazy too. And now he's lost it good and proper.'*

She could now see that, despite Aaron's attempts to act normal, he wasn't quite holding himself together. He was tense, jittery, and had a false bonhomie about him. It seemed to her that he had now stepped over a tenuous line between sanity and insanity. And that thought was terrifying.

She made a quick decision. The best way to play this would be to go along with him. Pretend she hadn't seen a difference in his personality, and wasn't aware of the disturbed individual she was now dealing with.

'I'm not too bad, thanks. Do you want me to get the glasses?' she asked, holding up the wine and pretending to examine it.

'Yeah,' he said, and he plonked himself down on the sofa while he waited for her.

Maddy looked over her shoulder as she walked into the kitchen, relieved that he hadn't followed behind. She cursed the fact that there wasn't a phone in this room so she could ring for help. Her only hope would be to continue playing along with him for now and hope she could come up with some way of enabling her and Rebecca to escape, or at least play for time until Andy arrived.

While she grabbed the glasses she tried to compose herself, taking a few deep breaths and attempting to relax her tense limbs. Then she pulled back her shoulders and pasted on a smile before returning to the living room.

Aaron's eyes followed her as she walked across the room, and she hoped he couldn't see her knees trembling. His intense stare was unnerving, his smile odd. Where she would previously have regarded his expression as the passionate gaze of someone in love, she now saw his eyes as demonic and his smile as a wicked sneer.

Maddy was nervous and agitated, the shock of her recent discovery reflected in her strained features and taut muscles, which she was trying desperately to disguise. She poured the wine into the first glass but couldn't disguise her shaking hands, and the neck of the bottle clanged noisily against the rim.

Her eyes shifted to Aaron, awaiting his reaction. She noticed his face had changed. The smile was gone. He looked grave, questioning.

'You know, don't you?' he asked, his voice monotone, and Maddy felt a rush of fear.

Still hoping to mask her feelings, she continued to pour the wine. Then she responded with a question, trying to sound light-hearted. 'Know what?'

'You know, about Crystal. I know you do,' he said.

She stared at him, dumbstruck, expecting him to lash out, but his reaction shocked her.

'You know why I did it, don't you, Maddy?' he asked, his voice now childlike. 'She was trying to spoil what we've got, wasn't she, Maddy? She was jealous of us, just like your ex-husband. They're all jealous of us, aren't they, Maddy?'

Maddy just stared at him, bewildered as well as alarmed by this strange new change in him. He continued, half protesting, half beseeching; like an affronted five-year-old.

'We won't let them spoil it for us, will we, Maddy? We love each other, don't we, Maddy? Maddy?' he cried, his tone now switching again to a desperate plea. 'Please tell me you love me, Maddy. Tell me I didn't do all that for nothing.'

Maddy continued to stare, her mouth wide open with shock. 'I – I...' she began. Then she hesitated, paralyzed by fear.

'Tell me, Maddy. Go on, fuckin' tell me!' he yelled.

Maddy had never seen Aaron like this before. He was deranged and volatile, his mood switching rapidly from gleeful to upset to angry, like the shifting gears on a car. An indescribable terror took hold of her. Then a look of recognition flashed across his face, as though he had just realised something.

'Where's the kid?' he growled.

'Sh-she's upstairs,' said Maddy. She was tempted to lie to him but knew it would be too easy for him to go and check for himself.

'Fetch her down!' he ordered.

Maddy stepped into the hall, tears in her eyes, feeling as though she was betraying her child. Then she shouted for Rebecca, wishing there was some way of warning her to call for help, some inflection she could add to her voice to tell her daughter of the danger. But there wasn't. And how could she expect an eight-year-old to pick up on the hidden meaning?

Maddy's eyes flashed across to the front door. Would she have time to open it, take Rebecca by the hand and flee to safety? Then she felt Aaron's hot breath on the back of her neck, and tensed as he whispered into her ear, 'Don't even fuckin' think about it!'

Maddy watched her daughter reach the bottom of the stairs, her air of incredulity matched by Maddy's look of apology. Aaron grabbed hold of Maddy, his eyes taking in both her and her daughter as he nodded towards the living room and ordered, 'Get in there!'

54

As Andy arrived to collect Rebecca he was thinking about how the last week had completely changed things between him and Maddy. He was secretly pleased that she'd turned to him when she needed support, but he also felt a twinge of guilt for thinking that way. The circumstances that had brought them closer were horrendous for Maddy.

He parked a short way down the street, which was busy today with more parked cars than usual. He noticed, fleetingly, that there was a silver car outside Maddy's house that he hadn't seen before, but he didn't pay it too much attention. One of the neighbours probably had visitors.

Andy strode up the drive and rang the doorbell, his mood upbeat. He always looked forward to seeing his daughter, but now he had the added pleasure of having a few moments with the new, more receptive Maddy before he set off back home.

There was no reply. Perhaps Maddy was in the bathroom or something, and he knew Rebecca was forbidden from answering the door, especially in light of what had happened. He rang the bell again, and knocked briskly on the door. Then he waited.

They had just sat down in the lounge, Aaron next to Maddy on the sofa and Rebecca on the armchair across from them, when they heard the knock at the door.

'Who's that?' asked Aaron, his eyes wide and flitting about the room, like someone demented, before they settled on Maddy. 'Have you rung the fuckin' cops?' he asked, pushing his face forward, his eyes now fixed on her in a reproachful glare.

Maddy pulled back from him. She noticed Rebecca flinch, then she seemed to close in on herself, her knees pulled up to her chest with her arms wrapped round them. Maddy wanted to go and comfort her, but she couldn't. She was now pinned against the back of the sofa with Aaron's angry body pressed up against her, his face only centimetres away.

'It – it'll be Andy,' she said, 'come to collect Becky.'

'Tosser!' Aaron grumbled, then his gaze shifted again. He looked over to the window where the curtains were still open, and grabbed hold of Maddy's arm as he spoke. 'Quick, get behind there!' he ordered, indicating the narrow stretch of wall next to the window. 'Both of you!'

Rebecca jumped from the armchair and ran to her mother, and Maddy drew her close. She could feel her daughter's trembling body, mirroring her own shaking limbs, as she guided Rebecca slowly across the room. Aaron joined them, taking the space nearest the window so he could peep out of a gap where the curtain almost met the wall.

His head switched from the window to Maddy and Rebecca then back again. 'Don't either of you say a fuckin' word!' he ordered.

Then he pulled something out from inside his hoody. Maddy saw the glint of steel and a rush of fear swept through her. Before she could do anything, he grabbed her, one arm pinning her to him, with his hand over her mouth, and the other hand holding the knife close to her throat.

Rebecca let out a whimper and Aaron aimed the knife at her before swiftly directing it back to Maddy's throat.

'Keep your fuckin' mouth shut, kid!' he hissed. 'Or your mum gets it.'

Andy was beginning to feel uneasy. He'd knocked loudly on the door several times as well as ringing the doorbell, but there was no reply. Maddy's car was on the drive so he assumed she was in. And she wouldn't have gone for a walk with Rebecca when she knew he was due to arrive.

With the familiarity of someone who'd once been a large part of Maddy's life, he walked across to the living-room window. There was no sign of Maddy or Rebecca. How strange! He thought he sensed movement behind the opened curtain but perhaps it was just his imagination.

Andy was just about to go and try the door again when he spotted something. Two full glasses of wine and an opened bottle on the coffee table. He drew in a sharp breath, alarmed. Instinct told him Maddy wasn't with Clare or any of her other friends. If so, they'd have been sitting in the lounge. Besides, Maddy normally waited until after he'd collected Rebecca before socialising.

No, it was definitely Aaron. But why would Maddy be sharing a bottle of wine with him in light of what she now knew?

Unless… Surely, she hadn't let him back into her life? But the man was on the run from the police. No, Maddy wouldn't do that. Which meant that she had probably been coerced. Shit!

He had to get to her, to make sure that Maddy and his daughter were all right. What if that madman had done something to them? Andy quickly reached inside his jacket, grabbed his phone and dialled Maddy's number. No reply. He dialled the landline and heard it from outside, its ominous ringtone piercing the still air of early evening.

'Maddy!' he shouted. 'Are you there? Rebecca, sweetheart. Are you all right?'

Then he heard Rebecca scream, 'Daddy!'

55

Andy was incensed, his instinct to protect his child overriding any fear.

'Becky! Maddy! Are you OK?' he shouted as he punched 999 into his mobile phone.

'Police, please!' he hollered into his phone. 'Can you come quickly, please? My eight-year-old daughter is in danger.'

He quickly gave out Maddy's address, not hearing the operator's words, his mind a frantic maelstrom of panicked thoughts.

'Aaron, I know you're in there!' he shouted. 'Please don't harm them. Come out!'

But there was no reply from any of them, which only made Andy more agitated.

He tried a new tack. 'The police will be here soon, Aaron, so you might as well come out. You're only making matters worse for yourself.'

But there was still no reply. He dashed back to the window but he couldn't see anything. He cast his eyes to the side. Yes, there it was, beyond the curtain. Just the merest hint of something. Or someone. Yes, a person. And as he watched there was movement enabling him to pick out an arm. Maddy's perhaps? But it was swiftly pulled back.

'Maddy!' he shouted.

Then he heard mumbling. It sounded like a man's voice, but Maddy didn't speak.

Andy dashed back to the front door and glanced round the exterior of the house, trying to come up with a plan. He felt so impotent. 'Shit!' he cursed.

But he couldn't afford to feel impotent. He needed to do something. So he ran round to the back of the house and tried the door. It gave. He couldn't believe it! Maddy had left the back door unlocked.

Andy sneaked inside the house, his heart thundering. But, despite his trepidation, he was prepared to do whatever it took. He had to protect Maddy and Rebecca.

He crept across the kitchen and through the archway that led to the dining room. Trying to stay as quiet as possible, he crossed the dining room and reached the door that separated it from the lounge. Then he nudged it open a fraction and peered inside.

They were next to the front window, as he had suspected; Rebecca, Maddy and that bloody madman with a knife to her throat. None of them could see Andy. They were all facing the window, Rebecca on the floor hugging herself.

How the hell was he going to cross the room without being spotted? If Aaron saw him he could slit Maddy's throat and Andy wouldn't be able to stop him in time.

There was too much ground to cover. For a moment he hovered, unsure. But then he saw his daughter's tears and the way she was hugging herself, terrified and helpless, and his mind was made up.

He dropped to the floor and slithered across the ground, like a snake about to attack its prey. It seemed to take forever to cover a couple of metres. He knew he'd have to take his time though. At the moment he was partially hidden by an armchair. But he couldn't risk making any sound that would alert Aaron.

Andy reached the armchair and crouched low behind it. He took a moment to compose himself before moving any further. As he stayed there he became aware of his frantic heartbeat and his sweating palms and face. He pushed a damp lock of hair out of his eyes, then peeped out from behind the armchair.

'Where the fuck is he?' Aaron asked when he could no longer see Andy outside.

Andy could tell he was jittery. As Aaron spoke his arms became tense and he seemed to clench the knife tighter to Maddy's throat. Even from here Andy could see her wince. The bastard must have cut her!

'I don't know,' said Maddy, crying desperately.

Rebecca looked up at her mother, her eyes pleading. On seeing Maddy so distressed, she began to whimper.

'Shut the fuck up!' Aaron ordered and Rebecca jumped in shock then stifled her sobs.

Then she spotted Andy. He was just about to hold his fingers to his lips; a warning to stay quiet. But it was too late.

'Daddy!' shouted Rebecca, running towards him.

Andy sprang out from behind the armchair and pushed Rebecca towards the hallway.

'Run, Becky!' he yelled.

He saw Aaron turn Maddy round till she was facing him, the knife still at her throat, but Andy didn't give him chance to react further. He charged at him, letting out a loud and menacing war cry. The impact of his aggressive charge worked. In the precious few moments while Aaron was in shock, Andy pounced.

As he crashed into them, they all tumbled to the ground, with Andy on top and Maddy sandwiched between Andy and Aaron. The knife flew out of Aaron's hand. He reached out, trying to grasp it, but Andy pulled his arms back and held on tight.

'Quick, Maddy, get the knife!' he yelled.

Maddy struggled to break free of them while Andy was still holding onto Aaron. Then she pulled herself to a crouching position, her knees bent but her right leg still trapped under Andy's body. She pulled her leg out from beneath him. But just as Maddy was about to stand, Aaron reached forward, locking his teeth around her ankle.

The vicious bite felled Maddy to the ground and she let out an agonised shriek. Andy clasped his hand round Aaron's jaw to stop him biting Maddy again. But his savage teeth found Andy's fingers instead and he bit down hard. The pain shot through Andy's hand, making him lose his hold on Aaron, who plunged forward and grasped the knife.

In the midst of the fracas Maddy had managed to break free and she gasped in shock as she saw Aaron gripping the knife. But Andy was still on top of him, the weight of his body pinning Aaron's legs to the ground. Aaron turned the knife round and thrust it backwards repeatedly, aiming blindly towards Andy.

Andy could sense Maddy hovering over them. He tried to dodge the sharp blade and then forced himself to standing. But Aaron's other hand shot out, striking Andy hard on his ankle and unbalancing him. Andy fell to the side of Aaron, who sprang up onto his feet. He swung the knife back, ready to plunge it into Andy while he lay on the ground, stunned.

As Andy put his hands up, in a futile effort to defend himself, Maddy brought the wine bottle swiftly down on top of Aaron's head. He heard Maddy's determined yell then the sound of breaking glass. Aaron stumbled, shocked, and Andy grabbed the knife. The glass shattered around them. Maddy glanced in alarm at the remainder of the broken bottle, which she held between bloody fingers.

Andy stood up, breathless and shaky, and Aaron stared at him, dazed. Shades of red streaked Aaron's face. The molten maroon of the wine flowed freely downwards while the viscous vermillion of his blood oozed through his matted hair, on a slow descent.

Suddenly Andy heard movement behind him. At the same time, Maddy's face showed relief just as Aaron's spelt a fragmented mix of disappointment, anger and resentment.

The police had arrived.

Andy spotted Rebecca hovering close behind. His impulse was to go to her but he left Maddy to comfort their daughter instead. Somebody had to explain to the police what had taken place.

56

A few weeks had passed since the incident with Aaron at Maddy's house. Once Andy had explained to the police what had happened, Aaron had been put in handcuffs and taken down to the station. Maddy and Andy had also been interviewed by the police, which had been exhausting after what they had been through, but Maddy had been relieved when Aaron had finally been charged. Currently he was being held in custody awaiting trial.

The past few weeks hadn't been easy for Maddy as she tried to come to terms with the aftermath of recent events. She was distraught and anxious at times and felt foolish and ashamed of her involvement with Aaron. She also felt guilty because of the emotional trauma that Rebecca and Andy had been through as a result.

Although she'd obtained some tablets from her doctor to help her through, unfortunately there wasn't a prescription that could fix her heartache. But she'd received a lot of emotional support from Andy, Clare and her parents and, if she was honest with herself, she didn't know what she would have done without them. Andy had even lent her some money until she got things sorted out.

Andy's support had helped her, Andy and Rebecca to grow closer as a family again and it felt good to be on friendly terms with him once more. In fact, Andy had hinted at being more than just friends. Up to now, he'd given her space to deal with the fallout of her doomed relationship with Aaron, but she felt it was only a matter of time before they had 'the talk'.

When she heard the doorbell ring, she knew it was him returning with Rebecca after having her for the weekend. She asked him inside for coffee, a habit they'd got into recently. Rebecca, surprisingly perceptive at times for an eight-year-old, left them alone, and when Andy set his coffee cup down and took hold of her hands, she guessed what was coming.

'Maddy, I've been thinking about us,' he began. 'We work well together; you, me and Becky.' She could tell by his face that he was becoming emotional and his voice cracked as he said, 'I was a bloody fool to let you go and I was wondering... well... well, if we could...'

Maddy pulled her hands away from his. 'Andy, stop!' she said.

A puzzled frown clouded his face and his hands dropped to his lap. Maddy felt a sense of inexplicable guilt as she continued. 'I'm sorry, Andy. I can't. I'm really grateful to you for being there for me when I needed you, and for all the support you've given me over the past few weeks. It feels good to be friends again and I'd like to think we'll always support each other in the future, but we just wouldn't work as a couple.'

His jaw dropped; he looked flabbergasted. 'Wh-wh-why? I don't understand. We've been getting on so well. Do you need more time after what's happened, is that it?'

'No, Andy. I'm sorry but I can't do it. What you did would always come between us. I wish I could get past it, but I know I wouldn't be able to.'

'Maddy, I know I hurt you and I'm so sorry for what I did. When we split up I lost one of the two most precious people in my life. You and Becky, you're all that matters to me. You're what makes my life worthwhile. And I swear I would never do anything like that to hurt you again.'

But Maddy had heard the same phrases over and over in the weeks after they'd split, and she didn't view things any differently now than she had then. 'I'm sorry, Andy, but it just wouldn't work. I'd never be able to trust you again. So the answer's no. And I really don't want to have this conversation any more so can we please just stick to being the best parents we can for Becky's sake?'

Andy stood up, his head slumped and his manner despondent as he said, 'OK, if that's how you feel then I won't take up any more of your time.'

Then he bade her a quick goodbye, called Rebecca downstairs for a hug, and went.

Maddy was relieved to have got it over with and she hated herself for feeling guilty. Andy didn't deserve her guilt after what he'd done. It might have been four years ago but it wouldn't just disappear with the passage of time.

Maddy knew that, as bad as the experience with Aaron had been, she would learn from it. But, to do so, she needed to take some time for herself rather than rushing into another disastrous relationship or going back to one that had already failed.

If anything, her troubles with Aaron had given her a new-found determination. In time she would grow stronger and wouldn't need to rely on a man for a confidence boost. She would learn to depend on herself. And Maddy was determined that, if she ever met someone in the future, she would take her time and make sure he was the right one.

Epilogue

Maddy glanced at Rebecca and smiled, pleased that her daughter seemed to be having as good a time as she was.

'Help yourself if you'd like more,' said Rhonda.

Maddy turned to face the elegant middle-aged woman sitting across the table from her. 'I'm fine, thank you,' she said, breaking into another smile.

'Me too, thank you,' echoed Rebecca.

Looking at her daughter again, Maddy swelled with pride. Somehow she'd known she wouldn't let her down, displaying her good manners just as she'd taught her. She was such a good girl, and was growing up quickly. It was hard to believe she was ten already and was turning into a little lady.

She marvelled again at how well Rebecca had come through the events of two years ago. In fact, she'd done well to come through everything she'd been through for the last few years, ever since the divorce.

Maddy was glad things were back on course between her and Andy. She felt sure that their close relationship had a lot to do with the reason Rebecca had remained so well balanced. Eventually he had come to accept that they were friends and nothing more, and he'd moved on with his life. He had now been seeing a lovely lady for almost a year, and his new partner understood his friendly relationship with his ex-wife. It made it so much easier all round, Maddy thought.

She was broken out of her reverie by someone calling her name, and she turned to her left to see Craig with a bottle of wine hovering over her glass.

He laughed in that endearing way of his. 'You were miles away,' he said. 'Do you want a refill?'

'Yes, please,' said Maddy, smiling again.

She'd been seeing Craig for a few months now. Craig, a banker, was two years older than her, and handsome in a mature way. He was also wonderful to be with: kind, considerate, witty and gentle. But, despite all his many attributes, Maddy had been cautious up to now. Her relationship with Aaron had put her on her guard and she was wary of rushing into anything.

Realising she had been hurt in the past, Craig was patient. Nevertheless, she'd agreed to meet his parents. In fact, this was a very important step to Maddy, and even getting as far as meeting them was an achievement as far as she was concerned. At least they were real.

They'd invited her and Rebecca for a meal at their home, a beautiful Victorian semi in Heaton Mersey. Maddy had been a bit nervous about meeting them at first, but any anxiety had melted away as soon as she'd walked through the door.

Rhonda and Ged couldn't have been lovelier. They were everything she would have expected of Craig's parents, and did everything they could to make her and Rebecca welcome. It was easy to see where Craig got his humour and his affable charm from. Nothing was forced with them; it was all completely natural.

Maddy felt more than relief. She was happier than she had been for a long time. Looking round the table at them all, Craig and his father sharing light-hearted banter and Rhonda making a fuss of Rebecca, she felt sure that her future with Craig would be everything she could have wished for. At last she had found a genuine guy. And next week she was going to a works do with him to meet his friends and colleagues. Because, despite her happiness, she knew she wouldn't settle until she felt absolutely sure that he was 100 per cent genuine.

Acknowledgements

I am so excited to have started work on my new series of books, The Working Girls, and would like to thank my editor Sarah Ritherdon for welcoming my ideas for the series with such enthusiasm. As always, Sarah has been a joy to work with and I appreciate her backing and support.

Big thanks go to all the other staff at Aria who are a dedicated and hardworking team. I'd particularly like to mention Hannah Smith, Victoria Joss, Nikky Ward, Laura Palmer and Sue Lamprell. It is a privilege to work with all of you.

I would also like to give special thanks to Caroline Ridding. It is down to Caroline that my career with Aria began and although Caroline has moved on to pastures new, I would like to acknowledge the part she has played in my writing career and wish her well with her future.

Special thanks go to the Writers Bureau where my writing career started twenty years ago when I took a creative writing diploma with them. This year I have had the privilege of being featured in the Writers Bureau advertising campaign as one of their success stories. I feel both grateful and humbled to have been chosen to appear in their ads. The Writers Bureau is an excellent writing school which has helped to launch the writing careers of many successful authors and writers, and I wouldn't hesitate in recommending their creative writing course.

As always I would like to thank all my readers for continuing to buy and review my books. Thanks also to the book blogging community who perform a very valuable role in bringing authors' work to the attention of readers. I hope that you will all enjoy this new series as much as I am enjoying writing it.

Last but not least I would like to thank all my family and friends for their ongoing support.

About the Author

HEATHER BURNSIDE spent her teenage years on one of the toughest estates in Manchester and she draws heavily on this background as the setting for many of her novels. After taking a career break to raise two children Heather enrolled on a creative writing course. Heather now works full-time on her novels from her home in Manchester, which she shares with her two grown-up children.